F
OCE Ocean, T. Lynn
      Southern Fatality

DATE DUE

OCT 2 6 2007			
NOV 0 8 2007			
NOV 2 4 2007			
DEC 1 3 2007			
DEC 2 7 2007			
1·10·08			
FEB 1 2 2008			
APR 0 7 2008			

SOUTHERN FATALITY

PREVIOUS WORKS BY T. LYNN OCEAN

Fool Me Once

Sweet Home Carolina

T34883

SOUTHERN FATALITY

A Jersey Barnes Mystery

T. LYNN OCEAN

THOMAS DUNNE BOOKS
ST. MARTIN'S MINOTAUR ⚜ NEW YORK

This is a work of fiction. All of the characters, organizations, and events portrayed in this novel are either products of the author's imagination or are used fictitiously.

THOMAS DUNNE BOOKS.
An imprint of St. Martin's Press.

SOUTHERN FATALITY. Copyright © 2007 by T. Lynn Ocean. All rights reserved. Printed in the United States of America. No part of this book may be used or reproduced in any manner whatsoever without written permission except in the case of brief quotations embodied in critical articles or reviews. For information, address St. Martin's Press, 175 Fifth Avenue, New York, N.Y. 10010.

www.thomasdunnebooks.com
www.minotaurbooks.com

Design by Maggie Goodman

Library of Congress Cataloging-in-Publication Data
Ocean, T. Lynn.
    Southern fatality : a Jersey Barnes mystery / T. Lynn Ocean. —1st ed.
        p. cm.
    ISBN-13: 978-0-312-37367-2
    ISBN-10: 0-312-37367-8
    1. Women private investigators—North Carolina—Fiction. 2. Swindlers and swindling—Fiction. 3. Bank fraud—Fiction. 4. Kidnapping—Fiction. 5. North Carolina—Fiction. I. Title.
PS3615.C43S68 2007
813'.6—dc22

                                                                    2007019021

First Edition: September 2007

10   9   8   7   6   5   4   3   2   1

ACKNOWLEDGMENTS

To all the folks who happily answered hypothetical questions, including Steve Lawson, professional SUTS, and Tamie Nixon, a commercial boat captain who served in the Marine Corps.

To manuscript readers Dave Barnes, Nancy Lawson, and Ted Theocles for their time and honest input.

To my author friend Delano Cummings, who gave me the inspiration for a Lumbee character.

To all the people lucky enough to call Wilmington home and who make the vibrant port city what it is today—a wonderful setting for *Southern Fatality*.

To Katie, a terrific editor, and all the savvy people at SMP and Holtzbrinck.

To all the fiction-loving folks who read *Sweet Home Carolina* and sent e-mails to say they were eagerly awaiting my next novel (your feedback is my fuel).

And to all the fabulous booksellers who make the publishing world go 'round by putting books in the hands of readers.

Many thanks!

SOUTHERN FATALITY

ONE

The custom-made brace strapped to my left leg made it difficult to navigate the mountain of steps that stretched up to the South Carolina state supreme courthouse, and as I neared the main doors, it occurred to me that I could have taken the zigzagging wheelchair ramp. I was not thinking like a handicapped person. Breathing deeply, I reminded myself to get into character.

Well concealed inside the brace, two pieces of a .410 derringer snugly taped to opposite sides of my knee were only slightly irritating. The barrel easily separated from the action and I'd timed myself reassembling it, in the dark. Three seconds. Five, if I also loaded the buckshot shotgun shells.

Hurried people glided around me as I paused at the top of the courthouse steps to admire the historic building. It was magnificent, really, from the engraved granite beneath my feet to the stately columns at my sides. I resituated my crutches and adjusted the shoulder strap of my leather attaché, deciding that the weather was perfect. It was a beautiful day to shoot somebody.

Smiling, I found the handicap-friendly door that opened automatically with the push of a lever and entered the huge, air-conditioned lobby. Directly in front of me, a wall was laden with framed portraits: a male-saturated time line of those chosen to judge the rest of us and decide our fates. To my left stood a well-groomed security guard wearing an expensive dark suit, his look screaming retired Secret Service. To my right were three state-employed security screeners. Two of them processed the flow of visitors through metal detectors while the third monitored an X-ray machine. A bored cop leaned against the wall, watching the activity around him, perhaps wondering what his wife would be cooking for dinner.

Struggling to stay upright while using the awkward crutches, I concentrated on walking toward the group. Plant the rubber tips of the supports, swing the bulky brace. Plant, swing. By the time I reached the screeners, I had a steady rhythm going and swayed when I stopped to hold up the press pass I'd made earlier that morning. I'd hung it around my neck and just for good measure, attached a few pins to the lanyard: a blue rotary club, a pink breast cancer awareness, and a yellow smiley face. The ID declared that I wrote for *Business Track* magazine.

"Good afternoon," I said to a screener with a deep breath that made my size D implants arch out. "I've got a deadline to meet, but unfortunately, I've also got stainless steel pins in my leg. I'm pretty sure they'll set off the metal detector."

He gave me the once-over and grinned. "Heck of a getup you've got there."

Smiling through a grimace, I noted that the other screener was paying zero attention to us. The private security guard, on the other hand, was covertly following our conversation. With a slight grunt, I shifted my weight on the crutches. "You got that right. Tore my knee up pretty good water-skiing. From now on, I think I'll stay *inside* the boat." I shook my head, as if remembering the incident. "Should I go around the tunnel?"

"I'll have to use the handheld wand on you. Move over here, please, Miss . . ." He leaned in much closer than necessary to read the name on my press pass. "Miss Lawson. And put your bag on the table for X ray."

When I removed the strap of my attaché, the tip of a crutch caught on the edge of the table leg. I rocked back and forth for a split second, trying to catch my balance, and fell hard onto the floor with a yelp. The attaché dropped from my grip and landed safely beyond the entrance to the tunnel.

Several men jumped to my assistance.

"Are you okay?" It was the Secret Service–looking guy. "Can you get up?"

I stayed on the ground, clutching the leg brace and biting my lower lip. "I think so. That was really stupid. I've got to learn how to use these damn crutches."

He offered an arm, allowing me to hoist myself up at my own pace. With some effort, I managed to get back on my feet. Seeing that everything was under control, the crowd around me dispersed and the security screener handed over my crutches. Feeling foolish, I apologized.

"No problem," he said, laughing in response to the awkward moment. He was just glad that I hadn't hurt myself worse, he told me. He ran the handheld metal detector around my waist, beneath my arms, and up and down the outside of the leg that wasn't encumbered by a brace. The private guy held the sign-in clipboard while I scribbled a signature, after which he retrieved my attaché and returned to his post near the front doors.

After thanking everyone and apologizing a second time, I hobbled around the metal detector and made my way into the handicapped stall of the first restroom I came to.

I quickly stripped down. The brace came off. A small tool kit was transferred from the hollow handle of a crutch to my handbag. The derringer was assembled and placed into an ankle holster beneath tan slacks. The white athletic shoes were exchanged for black leather flats. The bright red blouse came off to reveal a solid black silk T-shirt and a lightweight cropped white blazer. The bobby pins came out of my reddish brunette hair, allowing it to fall loosely around my shoulders. I removed the brown contacts to reveal my God-given hazel-green irises, and flushed the lenses down the toilet, using my foot to depress the handle. Last, I wiped away my fingerprints, including those on the stall's doorknob, the crutches, and the brace.

As soon as the restroom was empty, I shimmied beneath the stall door, leaving it locked from the inside. I taped a note to the outside, declaring the toilet out of order. Maintenance probably wouldn't get around to investigating until later that evening, after the courthouse had closed. Even then, they wouldn't know what to make of the bulky leg brace and crutches that rested in one corner, or the bright red sweater that hung from them.

Entering the bathroom, I'd been a reporter with a knee injury. Leaving it, I looked like any other professional. A casually dressed attorney, businesswoman, or a paralegal, perhaps.

Getting into the courthouse had been surprisingly easy. Getting into the judge's chamber was even easier. I'd correctly guessed that her entry code would be the same as her home security alarm code and I didn't have to use my tool kit. Six-two-eight-seven. Oats. Short for Oatmeal, the name of her Yorkshire terrier.

There were two entry doors into the judge's chamber and I had to wait only forty minutes before I heard the electronic beeping of a code being punched into one of them.

I stood and aimed the gun. "Bang. You're a dead woman."

She let out a shriek and spun around to face me. When she realized who I was, the look of fear on her face morphed into a mixture of relief and anger.

"Good Lord, Jersey," she said, holding a hand over her heart. "You scared me to death."

I dropped my stance, letting the gun point to the floor, and smiled. "That was the idea, Judge. You need to be a little scared. Your security around this joint sucks."

She looked at the gun with a raised eyebrow and loosened the collar on her black robe. "Tell me that thing isn't real. Surely you didn't get a real gun through security."

"Of course it's real. And very effective at close range, especially when loaded with shotgun ammo instead of .45 longs. A staggering drunk could hit you with this. Not to mention the escaped animal who has methodically murdered five women."

She paled beneath cocoa-colored skin and took another look at my gun.

"It's not loaded, Judge. I got the ammo through security, too. But I'd never point a loaded weapon at you."

She sat down heavily. "That's good to know."

"Ordinarily, I wouldn't aim a weapon at anyone unless I fully intended to shoot them," I said with a shrug. "But I needed to make a point."

"You've made it." Studying me, she frowned. "How did you get in here?"

"Piece of cake."

"Good Lord," she said again. "You're a harmless-looking petite thing. You can't weigh much more than a hundred pounds."

6 / T. LYNN OCEAN

"One twenty-nine," I corrected. "And five feet, eight inches tall isn't petite. Sometimes, if I wear heels, I actually tower over most people."

"Well, you look like a damn Barbie doll. And you just waltz into a state supreme courthouse, right through top-notch security, with a deadly weapon. And then you mosey on into my chambers, where incidentally, I just had new electronic locks installed."

"That's why I earn the big bucks," I told her, twirling a chunk of my hair and shooting her a dumb-blonde look, even though my hair was currently a mahogany red. I actually had been a blonde on many occasions with the government.

She smirked at me. "You do the bimbette look well, Jersey. But seriously, isn't there anything you're afraid of?"

"Chickens. Put me in a yard full of clucking chickens and I'm totally freaked out."

"That's funny."

"I'm serious. Can't stand to even look at a picture of one." I had a vague childhood recollection of my father making me watch my grandfather slaughter a chicken for dinner. After he chopped the head off using a hatchet and a tree stump, he threw the bird to the ground and laughed as its decapitated body continued running. In the nightmares I had afterward, a headless chicken chased me incessantly around the house.

The judge frowned, determining if I was trying to be funny or not.

"Oh, yeah," I said, "and dead people. I'm terrified of dead people. It's irrational, obviously, since a dead person can't hurt you. But I've never been to a funeral. I can't even stand to be at a crime scene before the bodies are carried off." I shrugged. "So there you have it, the dirt on Jersey Barnes' phobias."

"You'll take on terrorists, but you're afraid of live chickens and dead people."

I smiled but my mood turned serious. "This security breach was a freebie for a good friend. You saved my ass once, Judge. And now I'm trying to save yours, by giving you a wake-up call. He is a ruthless killer who hates women and you are the female who put him behind bars for life. It could have been him standing in your chambers instead of me. Or someone he hired."

She nodded, but was still not accepting reality. "My private guard is quite good. He used to be—"

"Let me guess. Secret Service? Tall dude in the navy suit, stationed in the lobby?"

She nodded.

"Nice guy," I said. "He's the one who helped me up after I fell, and handed me my attaché. Which, by the way, holds a package of what looks very much like plastic explosives along with a motion-activated timing device. It was never X-rayed."

The judge sat down, stood up, paced, sat back down.

"See, Judge, if I was the bad guy and was worried about not being able to get away after shooting you, I'd blow you up instead." I pointed to the case. "I could stash it beneath your chair one night and be slurping an icy margarita in Cancún by the time you sat down to read the day's docket and activated the motion sensor."

"Unlikely anyone besides you could get in here. Especially not that monster. Everyone's on the lookout for him."

I took a deep breath and studied the ceiling. It was a shade of drab beige.

"The man has money. Why chance getting caught when he can hire someone to kill you?"

A translucent tear slid down her cheek as she stared at the top of her desk. I'd finally gotten through to her. She knew that to him, it was all a game. There was no telling when, how, or where he would strike. If I could get to her so easily, so could someone else. And I'd been welcomed like a buyer on a car lot. They all but fawned over me.

After checking her appearance in a compact mirror, the judge called her private guard. Seconds later he entered her chambers and stood at attention while she cut into him. He launched into an explanation of how he was on the lookout for the escapee, not a female.

"And you were Secret Service?" I said.

His face colored.

I explained how I'd gotten in with a simple diversion, one of the oldest tricks in the book. The judge's humbled daytime guard listened with half-shaded eyes as I rattled off a rundown of precautions they needed to implement. I relayed that, before I flew home, I would meet with Axis Security to discuss the judge's overall protection plan, including her private residence in Columbia.

"Thank you, Jersey," the judge said when her retired Secret Service fellow left the chambers. "I protected your cover when you were involved with busting that warden who was on the take, sure. But you really may have saved my ass today with your . . . 'wake-up call,' as you put it."

"You put yourself in danger to keep my cover that night, Judge," I countered. "You could have been killed, were I found out."

Transitioning back to her normal tough demeanor, the judge dismissed my comment with a wave of her hand. "I'd do it again to help put that loser on the right side of the prison bars."

$\mathcal{I}$ sat across the desk from Pete Hammons, owner of Axis Security. Axis was a small but prestigious security contractor that specialized in personal protection for high-profile clients, and they were the folks who provided the judge's private bodyguards. After landing in Atlanta, I'd headed straight to his office, hoping we

could get the meeting over with quickly. I wanted to catch a five
o'clock return flight to Wilmington, North Carolina, to make my
dinner date with Bill.

Pete and I made small talk until another man joined us. After
introductions, I learned that he was Pete's new man in charge of
recruiting and training. He was ex-military and had an impressive
pedigree. He was also the person who hand-selected the private
guard who had ushered me through courthouse security.

"So as not to waste your time, gentlemen, I'll make it short.
Earlier today, I entered the judge's private office with a .410 derringer, a handful of shells, and an attaché packed with what looks
very much like plastic explosives and a detonation device." I
smiled at their reactions. "You can imagine the judge's surprise
when she came in to find me waiting on her."

I laid a few Polaroid photos on his desk. One was a shot of me
relaxing in the judge's chair, aiming the gun; I'd used the camera's
timer. The second shot was of my attaché, opened and resting beneath her desk. Just to be cute, I'd written *BOOM!* on a Post-it
note and stuck it to the base of her desk chair.

"Well, I'll be a son of a bitch," Pete said, shaking his head.

The other man paled but remained silent.

"How do you do it, Jersey? I'll be a son of a bitch," he repeated.

He did a mental fast-forward of what would happen were the
judge to be murdered. The repercussions would be ugly. A few
minutes passed before he slowly shook his head at me. I gave him
my smug smile. After a successful security breach, I always felt a
little cocky, like an athlete who had just completed a marathon in
the front of the pack. Dinner with Bill later would be great, and
the sex after that would be even better. I glanced at my watch. I
had only half an hour before I needed to be back at the airport to
make my Wilmington flight.

"The courthouse screeners need to be much better trained in

hand-checking items like crutches and walking aids," I told them. "For example, had they handled my set of crutches, they would have noticed that one was much heavier than the other. Also, they need to pay more attention to people in wheelchairs who don't go through the tunnel."

Just last month, my associate, Rita, posed as a disabled retiree in a wheelchair and wore a silver wig, old-age makeup, and a colostomy bag complete with a faint fecal odor. Since the chair's frame would have set off the metal detector, she was pushed around it. She was asked to lean forward in the chair and after receiving a hasty scan with the handheld wand, a helpful guard escorted her right into the courtroom. Problem was, Rita had a Colt 9 millimeter tucked into the waistband of a girdle. It wasn't loaded because the thought of ammunition that close to her reproductive parts made her nervous, but it very well could have been.

I explained to Pete how Rita got through last month and how I'd done it today. Axis's head of recruiting and training melted into his chair. He studied something, invisible to me, on the carpeted office floor.

"They weren't on the lookout for a grandmother in a wheelchair or a female reporter on crutches," Pete's associate finally said.

"Don't you think an assassin might be a little sneaky?"

Pete sighed. "Don't have to be a smart-ass."

"Can't help it," I said. "Sarcasm runs in my family."

He handed me a plain envelope. This job was a freebie, but I knew without looking that the envelope held a several-thousand-dollar check for a previous job. I almost regretted my decision to retire.

"I'll FedEx the full report with recommendations to you tomorrow and, as always, yours is the only copy," I told him. My clients always got the originals and I always got a paycheck. With the type of jobs I did, trust was priceless.

Pete studied me briefly then burst into laughter.

"It's a good thing you're straight, Jersey. I wouldn't want you working for the enemy."

"Actually, I won't be working much for anyone anymore. Didn't you get the word? I'm retiring."

His head jerked as though I'd sucker punched him. "What?"

"You know, retiring. Not working anymore. I'm gonna tinker on my boat, maybe do some fishing, and spend more time with Bill. He keeps pestering me to settle down and marry him."

"Retiring to get married? No way, not you, Jersey Barnes. You're the only person I know who enjoys this business more than I do."

"It's true, Pete. The letter already went out to my clients. I want to travel and relax and live a normal life. Might even decide to adopt a kid and do the mom thing."

"But . . ."

"My partner, Rita, is taking over for me, and she'll bring someone else on board as soon as we find the right woman. I'll still be around to put in a word or two when needed."

I really didn't plan to be around much at all but it sounded reassuring, especially to clients who hadn't yet established a relationship with Rita. Besides, I would be available by telephone. Sometimes.

"Rita isn't as good as you," he complained.

"Yes, she is," I said without hesitation.

"Ah, well," Pete said, rebounding in the quick manner of a successful businessman. "Gotta do what you gotta do. But don't rush into the marriage thing. It's not all it's cracked up to be."

TWO

The Barter's Block was in full swing when I arrived home from the airport. The Block, as everyone calls it, is a grill and pub that serves huge deli sandwiches, sweet potato fries, locally caught seafood, and iced-down bottled beer. Its name comes from the fact that it had been a trading center in the early eighteen hundreds, when the town of Wilmington first began. Because it borders the Cape Fear River, the Block was a perfect location for manufactured goods coming in by riverboat to be traded for locally made wares. The historic building had been witness to Civil War struggles and during World War II it housed families of workers who built ships. Eventually, the Barter's Block became a shoe shop and later a brothel, where casual entertaining was done on the lower level and the real entertainment took place in the upstairs bedrooms. Finally, it was renovated and leased to retail merchants and, like a hound on a scent, the name Barter's Block had stuck with the building through its eventful past.

When I bought it four years ago with plans to put in a pub downstairs and live upstairs, changing the name was not an option. It didn't occur to me until after I'd signed the closing papers that I had absolutely no idea how to run a bar. Not to mention the fact that I was running my own security agency and had no time to run another business. But I'd always wanted to own a pub and when I stumbled upon the building with a breathtaking view of the river that could double as my home, I put in an offer the next day. The Block became a mostly peaceful, occasionally boisterous joint that attracted longtime locals like an old oak tree's shade on a sweltering summer day.

Sandwiched between the Atlantic Ocean and Cape Fear River, the city of Wilmington is basically a peninsula with a magnetic atmosphere. I first visited during my stint with the government and knew immediately that I'd make it my home someday. While the action and danger that came with my government job was addictive, I'd decided to fold my hand and get out of the game while I still had a big pile of chips on the table. I relocated to North Carolina and used some of those chips to open the Barnes Agency, a private security firm specializing in all security issues that affect public safety. What I never imagined is that I'd end up with two men I thought I'd lost forever: my father and my best friend from high school. Duke Oxendine appeared first and, after I talked him into becoming my partner in the Block, I knew I'd made the right decision in buying the property.

It is always fun to travel for an exciting job and it is always wonderful to be back home afterward, I thought, strolling through the Block and smiling at the regulars.

Ox grinned at me from behind the bar, where he poured draught beers from a tap, holding four mugs in one large hand. "I think your father is trying to cook again. Smells like burning peanuts up there."

A Lumbee Indian from Robeson County, North Carolina, Ox had traditional Native American features such as high cheekbones, deep-set eyes, and thick, dark hair. But he also had some other interesting features mixed in, including a square chin with a dimple smack in the center of it. My friends thought he was a stud and couldn't understand why I didn't have a steamy romantic relationship with him. Or at least sleep with the man once in a while. I'd thought about it on several occasions, but the idea of sex with Ox scared the hell out of me. With him, there would be no turning back, and I liked to keep my options open.

"Maybe he's trying to roast peanuts or something." I sighed, hoping my father hadn't done any major damage to the kitchen. "I'll go check on him."

"Things go as planned with the judge?"

"Of course."

"So your retirement from active participation in your agency is official, then?"

"Sure."

"How does it feel?"

"Good, I think. Pretty darn good."

"Hope it sticks."

"Me, too." I headed up the stairs to see what trouble my father had managed to stir up, once again reminded how sweet it was to be reunited with my best friend. Like the intertwined roots of adjacent trees, our high school years together had fashioned a permanent bond of sharp memories, lively debates, and youthful dreams. Now that I had gotten used to sharing days with him once again, I wasn't sure I'd be able to manage my life without Ox in it, should he ever decide to move on.

We were both sixteen when his family relocated to my home-town of Lexington, Kentucky. I first spotted him in the school's hallway, angry about being uprooted from the Lumber River that he loved and glowering at everything around him. I taught him the eleventh-grade ropes and he taught me how to box. For the nearly two years that followed, we were inseparable. A day after high school graduation, under the influence of youthful ignorance, we talked each other into joining the marines, specifying to the recruiter that we wanted only the "most dangerous shit."

The recruiter took us at our word. The fact that I had the bad taste to have been born female meant that Ox and I were abruptly split up two weeks later. The screaming hit my ears before I'd even stepped off the bus at Parris Island and I immediately real-ized two things: that being separated from Ox had pierced a hole through my young heart and that it was going to be a very long six years.

They'd purposely scheduled the busloads of new female re-cruits to arrive in the middle of the night so we were disoriented and couldn't bolt from the island with a sudden spurt of remorse. Sheer anger gave me the will to survive basic training, and I dis-covered that I enjoyed fighting, was pretty good with an M-16, and excelled at the physical challenges. I became an MP working for a brigadier general. Three years later, I was relieved of com-pleting my tour by the government, which had hand-picked me and a few other female marines for a "privileged" assignment. I found myself employed by a branch of the government I'd never heard of, learning how to do things I'd seen only in action movies. Meanwhile, Ox completed his tour and, surprising me and every-one who knew him, opted for a military career. He went through OCS and continued playing marine games until he earned the rank of major.

If you've never seen a six-foot-tall, two-hundred-and-twenty-pound Lumbee in full dress blues, you ought to. Even civilians were tempted to salute the man during the weekend I surprised him by flying to Camp Pendleton, California, for a birthday party planned by his master gunnery sergeant. Although we had stayed in touch with brief e-mails and generic Christmas cards, Ox and I hadn't seen each other since our teenage years. We hugged so tight and for so long that the embrace drew a nasty glance from his wife. He'd decided to retire from the service after one more year, Ox told so me later that night, which would be his twenty-year mark and the point at which he'd receive a half-pay pension. He wanted to head back to the East Coast and explore new career options.

I decided to do the same thing, and twenty years after Ox and I had first stepped into the recruiter's office, I left the government with little fanfare to start my own business. Ox's retirement from the military was coupled with divorce papers. His wife dumped him the day he retired, announcing that she was in love with someone else. She waited until then, he realized later, so that she could get her share of his monthly retirement check.

When he visited Wilmington, still dazed by the turn of events in his life, I needed a pub manager and he needed a change of pace. It only took four or five tequila shots chased by a few beers before we reached an agreement on the Block and another several swigs of tequila straight from the bottle before we almost went to bed together.

"Your body is still amazing," I'd said, running my hands over his shoulders and down his chest. I wasn't sure if he'd unbuttoned his shirt or I did, but the feel of his smooth skin beneath my palms electrified something buried deep in my brain and I suddenly realized that I yearned to fulfill a twenty-year-old fantasy.

"As is yours, my spirited soul mate," he'd said, outlining my silhouette with strong hands while capturing my mouth with his. Like an anchored boat rocking gently from side to side, the kiss stretched on and on, tantalizing and comforting, seeking, yet ending way too soon and leaving an untouched ocean to explore.

His hands found mine and held them tight. "But let's wait until you're sober and my heart has healed. Right now, I need a place to hang my feathers and you need someone to manage this dump of a bar on the river."

That was five years ago and Ox still runs the Block. We never did fall into bed together, but oddly, I was closer to him than anyone else in my life. Semper fidelis, as the marines like to say. Always faithful.

As I climbed the stairs in search of my father, the weird odor grew stronger and snapped my attention back to the present. "Spud? Are you home? What's that smell?"

Wearing an apron and looking like a shrunken, much older version of Wolfgang Puck, Dad stood in the kitchen scraping blackened plops from a cookie sheet with a putty knife. "It's the delicious aroma of cookies baking. Women like men who can cook home-baked stuff. I saw that on *Oprah*." He pounded one of the plops a few times to loosen it up. It cracked into several coal-like pieces. "So I'm making peanut butter cookies for Sara Jane."

I leaned in for a closer look and crinkled my nose at the sight. "Spud, why don't you just buy cookies at a bakery and *tell* her you made them?"

"Well, for crying out loud. Why didn't I think of that?"

"Besides, we promised the fire chief that you wouldn't use the stove anymore."

He removed the apron and a tuft of flour billowed around him. "Wasn't my fault this place had bad wiring," he grumbled. "Those Spam and cheese sandwiches were delicious, by the way.

And anyway, I'm not using the *stove,* kid. You make cookies in an *oven.*"

My father had materialized a few months after Ox showed up. A career cop, Dad missed my ninth birthday and never returned. Through the years, with the assistance of a private investigator, he'd kept track of what I was doing and where I was living. But we'd had no contact until, without warning, he checked up on me in person. Traveling through North Carolina on his way to move in with a Florida girlfriend, he stopped by the Block to say hello. It was the first time I'd seen him since grade school and my reflexes argued whether to hug him or slug him. I did both, in that order, and pulled the punch so as not to break anything because he seemed frail. And then—I don't cry, mind you—I cried. Inexplicable tears that erupted on and off for two days, until Ox wrapped his thick arms around me and whispered, "The spirits brought him here for a reason, Jersey. Look forward."

Spud never did make it to the Sunshine State and moved into the efficiency apartment adjacent to my upstairs condo. His place had a private entrance with a stairway that connected to the Block's parking lot. But he usually came and went through my place, since our kitchens were connected by French doors that always remained open.

Soon after buying the Block, I'd employed a designer to completely renovate the living quarters, and either kitchen could have competed with those seen in *Architectural Digest* magazine. But in our case, outfitting the place with Thermador stainless steel appliances was like buying lace stockings for a nun. Spud promised not to cook anymore after he'd almost burned the structure down and I rarely used anything except the microwave. We preferred to eat out and most often quenched our appetites with cuisine from the Block. It was much safer. We don't have a traditional father/daughter relationship by any means, but we do have some sort of a blood bond that may be love. Or perhaps we just put up with each other out of curiosity, to learn more about the other. Whatever it is, it works for us.

Spud sneezed, and the motion caused another stray patch of flour to drift down from the top of his head. "Or maybe you should get that microwavable cookie dough," I told him. "You just slice it and nuke it."

"These are better than some stupid microwave cookies." He scraped a hardened piece from the pan and offered it to me. I shook my head. He waved an indignant hand at his ungrateful daughter. After making sure the oven was turned off and nothing was on fire inside it, I changed into running gear and returned to the kitchen to down some water before hitting my favorite path along the river.

Bent over the kitchen sink with his tongue stuck out, Spud frantically wiped pieces of a partially chewed cookie from his tongue. He turned on the faucet and, using his hand, scooped water to rinse out the remaining crumbs.

Arms locked behind my head, I twisted from side to side a few times to loosen up my torso. "I hope your peanut butter cookies don't get the same reaction from Sara Jane."

Eyeing me with a peculiar expression, Spud turned off the water and spit a final time. "These cookies would gag a moose. I think I'll just buy some from a bakery and tell her I made them."

Spud often regurgitated my advice as his own idea. "Good thinking," I said and picked up a knee to stretch my thigh muscles. "See you in a bit. I'm off for a run."

"Hey, uh, before you go, I'm just wondering something," Spud said, studying me with a cocked head. "I know I wasn't around during your formative years and all that, but I sure don't remember any photos of you looking that big-titted . . . ah . . . uh, I

mean, big-breasted. And your mother wasn't large in the rack department, either."

Looking down, it occurred to me that my new sports bra didn't
flatten me out like my old one did. This one was more like a push-
up bra and it accentuated my shape. I stuck out my chest. "So you
don't think these are genetic?"

Spud shook his head.

I showed him my breezy smile. "Government enhancements.
My bosses decided that some cosmetic procedures would improve
my undercover abilities, so your tax dollars paid for a breast aug-
mentation. They also lifted my eyebrows and injected my lips
every six months."

Staring at my boobs, Spud frowned. "Well for crying out loud.
I never would have agreed to my tax dollars going for a pair of implants on my daughter."

"Yeah, well, you never would have agreed to spend money on
sponsoring a NASCAR team or producing a video game, either, if
Uncle Sam had bothered to ask."

Spud, licking the air like a dog who'd just chewed a dropped
aspirin, reached in the refrigerator for a bottle of beer. He probably figured it would wash away the burnt peanut taste. "I might
have given the go-ahead for the NASCAR, but a video game?"

"Back in 1999, the Army had missed its recruitment goals for so
many years that the Department of Defense decided to spend more
than two billion dollars on marketing and PR. A big chunk of that
was used to develop a video game. It took three years and several
million dollars but was finally released as a free game in a big debut.
Supposedly, playing the game would encourage teenagers to get off
the sofa and go join the military." I bent over to touch my toes and
held the stretch for several seconds, enjoying the feel of the pull in
my calves. "You'd be amazed at the things our government spends
your money on."

"But video games and boobs? That's just crazy."

Agreeing with him, I finished stretching and headed for the stairs. "At least my boobs only cost taxpayers ten grand."

"You and the twins have a nice run," Spud called.

I always run between four and five miles—enough distance to clear my head and release endorphins—and today's run was ideal. I jogged the riverwalk for the first mile, easily moving through walkers and sightseers, the captivating Cape Fear on one side and an eclectic mix of shops, town houses, restaurants, and hotels on the other. Outside decks and verandas, built to take advantage of the water view, were speckled with cheerful people.

After a cool shower and spritz of my favorite perfume, I applied lipstick, layered on black mascara, and shimmied into a sensual skin-colored La Perla bra and silky panties. I have a weakness for quality lingerie and never pass up an opportunity to shop for my favorite labels. Chemises and camisoles alone fill three of my dresser drawers. After stepping into a short and clingy dress, I made a conscious decision not to strap on my shoulder holster. In addition to drawerloads of beautiful lingerie, I have an amazing collection of blazers that are the perfect length and cut to conceal a handgun. But if I was going to be retired, I would have to learn to relax and leave home without a weapon.

Indecisive, I plopped on the bed and reconsidered donning a blazer so I could carry my everyday piece, a Glock 21. I felt strangely naked without the security of a .45 strapped to my body. In the past, its thirteen-round capacity had proved enough to get me out of most sticky situations, especially since I always carried an extra magazine and kept more in my vehicle.

Shaken at the thought of going anywhere without a weapon, I compromised by carrying the piece I usually wore in an ankle or thigh holster, my Sig Sauer P232. I toted the Sig in a belt holster and concealed it with a denim blazer, which buttoned at the waist and revealed plenty of cleavage.

In the kitchen, I downed two glasses of water, explained to a perplexed Spud that he'd have to soak the scorched cookie dough from the pan, and headed for El Vaquero. Retirement felt good and my body was ripe with anticipation. For both the Mexican food and a night with Bill.

Hello, darling," I drawled in my sexy voice. "You look yummy." As always, the sight of Bill sent a shiver of appreciation through my body. A model and actor who scored roles in made-for-TV movies, he was comfortable in any setting and turned heads in a classy five-star restaurant just as easily as he did while perched on a bar stool at a local dive. Tonight, he wore crumpled jeans and made them look fabulous with a tight silk T-shirt and expensive Ralph Lauren blazer. I was happily retired and ready to enjoy some spicy food with an adventurous male. Life was good, until I noticed the woman cozied up to him. A gorgeous blonde who appeared to be on familiar terms with my man.

"Jersey." Bill flashed me an apologetic smile. "This is my friend Lisa, but everyone calls her Lolly. We went to the same college to study acting and helped each other get modeling jobs," he explained. "She called me out of the blue a few hours ago, so I invited her to join us for a drink."

Lolly stuck out a manicured hand. "So nice to meet you, Jersey. Billy has said so many great things about you."

I flinched at the bastardization of Bill's name, but was in too good a mood to let a curveball ruin my night. I shook her hand. "Hello, Lolly. Love your dress." Although she was far beyond the typical modeling age, there were no ugly DNA globules floating around in Lolly's gene pool and I wondered if she'd made the run-way or the catalogs. Regardless, she struck me as the type of woman who could control people with a flutter of her eyelashes.

"Thank you," she replied. "And I love the way you combined a jean jacket with a little black dress. Very few women can pull off that shabby-chic look."

I could appreciate a compliment just as much as the next per-son, even if it was stuffed inside an insult. My confidence comes from the fact that if anybody really pisses me off, I can kick their ass. Or in lieu of that, shoot them. Subconsciously, I pressed the inside of my elbow against the reassuring Sig. Like an alcoholic who relaxes at the mere sight of their first vodka of the day, I was immediately comforted by the hardness of the steel. I joined Bill and his friend, positioning myself so that my back was to the wall and I had an unobstructed view of the restaurant's entrance. Old habits die hard.

"What brings you to Wilmington?" I asked Lolly.

"Oh, I just moved here with my husband and stepson," she said, fluffing the short white-blond curls. "I'd heard that Bill was living in Wilmington and had to look him up. We were the *best* of friends back then, in school. This is just such a trip, running into him after all these years!" she squealed.

Bill's eyebrows went up, as though it was news to him that they'd been best friends. "Well, it was certainly a surprise to hear from you, Lolly. What have you been up to?"

Flashing back, the two of them gossiped like girls at a slumber party, but I didn't mind being left out. I've never been much for gossiping, talking on the phone, or shopping—but Bill could hang with the best of them. If I didn't know better, I'd think he was gay.

When a server appeared, Lolly ordered a glass of sangria and decided to skip the food. Bill and I chose nachos with extra jalapeños, chicken and shrimp enchiladas, and a pitcher of beer. I drink beer like other Southerners drink sweet tea, and, soaking up the ambiance while Bill and Lolly continued chatting, I resolved to make some changes in honor of my retirement. Studying a neon Corona beer light, I began a mental to-do list and put two items on it: leave home without a weapon and cut down on the beer.

As if to test my new resolution, the pitcher of frothy beer was served instantaneously and the nachos arrived shortly after, radiating mouthwatering steam that rose from tons of melted cheese. Downing almost half a mug of beer with one tilt of my head—to wash down a loaded nacho, of course—I deleted the cut-down-on-beer goal from my mental list. After a few seconds of thought, I replaced it with: be more ladylike while drinking beer. I would much rather have focused my attention on Bill, but Lolly's presence made that difficult to do. Slightly annoyed and attempting to be patient, I refilled my beer mug.

"Gosh, Jersey," Lolly said as if suddenly remembering I was there. "Bill and I are so busy catching up, we're just totally ignoring you! Sorry to homestead on your boyfriend." She blinked my way in slow motion and thick black lashes seemed to flirt with me. I think she flirted with everyone, both males and females, out of habit.

Chewing on a nacho, I told her not to worry, that Bill and I would have plenty of time together later. Sweet, celebratory time, I thought. Because Bill modeled and went on casting calls, his schedule was as unpredictable as mine and it had been three weeks since we'd spent a night together. We were way overdue. To celebrate, we'd start by opening some bubbly. He always kept a bottle of Moët & Chandon champagne in his refrigerator for special occasions and I figured that my official retirement qualified. Then, we'd jump naked into his outdoor hot tub for a few minutes of steamy, frothy foreplay, I thought, my mind racing forward in anticipation. . . .

"Oh, it's horrible, just horrible!" Lolly cried, interrupting my fantasy.

"What's horrible?" I involuntarily asked, wiping a spot of cheese off my chin. I think her outburst made me jump.

"Sam. He's cheating on me. My husband is having an affair!" she wailed, going from a confident knockout to sniveling damsel in distress in record time.

I looked to Bill for direction. He always knew the proper thing to say or do in situations like these. A few diners glanced our way and I shrugged my shoulders in helpless apology.

"Oh, honey," Bill told Lolly, "just because y'all are having problems doesn't mean he's got another woman! It could be any number of things." He toed my leg under the table, encouraging me to back him up.

"Well, uh, yeah . . . Bill is right," I said stupidly. I hate it when women cry. For that matter, I hate it when anybody cries for no good reason, except babies and toddlers. They can't express themselves by talking yet, so they are entitled to a good wail now and then.

Bill gave me another toe nudge, urging me to offer something more substantial. He figured a woman ought to know what to say to another woman, as though sporting a set of breasts gave me unobstructed access to Lolly's psyche.

"Men sometimes have a lot of pressures at work," was what came out of my mouth. "What does Sam do?"

"He's a stockbroker, one of those financial guys. He says he's working late, but then when I call his direct line at the office, he's not there. He doesn't answer his cell phone. When he comes home, he just showers, drinks a few bourbons, and passes out like he's exhausted. A few times I've heard him whispering on the telephone in the den when he thought I was asleep."

Our enchiladas arrived and we paused conversation to rearrange the table. Sniffling, Lolly pierced a bite of my food with a fork and slowly chewed. I asked the server to bring another plate, as Lolly's appetite had apparently kicked in.

"Bill said you just moved here. How could Sam be having an affair so quickly?" Logic told me that it would take at least a few months of knowing someone before you jumped into an illicit affair with them. A one-nighter, maybe, but not an ongoing fling.

"I don't know," Lolly said in a tiny voice. "We've only been married a year. And we did just get to town. Sam is opening another branch office and he's doing this one in person so he can train his son, who just graduated from the Citadel. Sam wants Jared to become a broker and work with him in the business." She dabbed a napkin beneath a set of very blue eyes. "But maybe it's somebody in his company. Some secretary who's also here to open the new branch . . ." Her voice trailed off and ended in another bawl.

"Open a new branch of what?" I asked, shooting a mind-your-own-business look at a nearby couple who was openly staring and obviously eavesdropping.

"Chesterfield Financial."

A piece of shrimp stuck in my throat and I had to chug some beer to keep from choking. Chesterfield Financial was one of the biggest brokerage firms in the country, whose founder could affect the price of a blue-chip stock with an offhand comment during a press interview.

Lolly raised a hand to wipe her runny nose, and suddenly it hit me. The rock on her ring finger had to be a full four carats' worth and it was accented by a solid emerald-and-diamond tennis bracelet. The outfit she wore was of the designer variety and her appearance reeked of pampered wealth, from the fashionable hair color to the professionally done acrylic nails. She was both beautiful and well kept.

"Lolly, what is your last name?" I asked just to be sure.

"Chesterfield."

"Is your husband, uh, *the* Samuel Chesterfield?"

"Yeah. But he goes by Sam. I call him Sammy when I'm not mad at him."

I could only shake my head and even Bill seemed astounded when the realization clicked in his socially calculating mind. Apparently, he and his college gal pal hadn't stayed in close touch. Although he knew she'd gotten married, he hadn't made the connection. Lolly had snagged *the* Samuel Chesterfield, catapulting her into a position of obscene wealth and notoriety. She didn't need to work any longer, that was for sure.

Bill's perfectly shaped jaw dropped half an inch and he remained speechless, a rare condition for him. The president of the United States could have walked through the doors of El Vaquero and Bill would have waltzed up to say hello. But Lolly's disclosure had awed him into silence. Either that, or he was practicing for an upcoming movie scene that called for some major astonishment.

Lolly explained that Chesterfield's son was being groomed to take over the conglomerate Sam founded. The family planned to live in Wilmington for several months, giving Chesterfield time to oversee the opening of the new branch office while teaching his kid the ropes in the process.

I took her hand. "Lolly, I don't know what's going on. But Samuel Chesterfield would not cheat on his new bride. He's a financial shark, but a shark with integrity. The American public loves him. That's why they keep sending him their money." Thinking my mini speech sounded pretty good, I tipped my head back to finish another beer. Bill regained his senses, closed his mouth, and refilled our mugs, emptying the pitcher.

Racking my memory banks, I recalled that Chesterfield had openly shared his professional and private life with the media, but that was when he'd been married to the same woman for some thirty years, raised two handsome children, and was friends with all the influential Hollywood types. The nation wept with him when his wife died in a boating accident, after which Chesterfield reverted to a very private, very dateless life. I'd read something about him remarrying, but had no idea that the new missus was twenty years his junior, not to mention an acquaintance of my boyfriend.

Lolly made a show of carefully dabbing a napkin beneath teary eyes in what looked like a scene from a soap opera. "But he must be having an affair! That's all it could be." Delicate sniffles escaped her throat and threatened to become hiccups.

Questioning me with his eyes, Bill raised his eyebrows and waited for an answer. It took me a few seconds to realize what he wanted. I was already shaking my head in the negative when Lolly brought up the "D" word.

"Hey, aren't you some kind of a detective, Jersey?"

"Something like that," I answered. If you could call breaking into top-security buildings, penetrating foreign safe houses, and stealing back stolen government electronics being a detective.

"So, then I could hire—"

"The thing is, Lolly, I just retired. I'm not working anymore. I didn't do domestic cases anyway."

"How old are you?"

"I don't keep track. What's your point?"

"Well, whatever your age, it's certainly too young to retire," she surmised.

"You're never too young to retire," I countered. Especially when you had been doing the kind of work I had been doing. The last time I was shot at, even though the lead missed my head by several inches, it made me wonder what I was working for. I had enough money and investments to live comfortably. I loved my work, but I also loved my life and decided to start living it in a more stress-free, normal manner. Thankfully, our next pitcher of beer arrived, and pouring the liquid into empty mugs gave me a minute to formulate my turndown. Unfortunately, all I could come up with was a simple "no." It would have to do.

"Oh, couldn't you please help? You're the only detective I know in Wilmington."

She'd known me for exactly half an hour. "Sorry, but no."

"Pulleeeze?"

I started to put her off again when Bill spoke up. He didn't know exactly what Rita and I did—only that my clients were all good guys and that I occasionally did some dangerous stuff. But he did know that I was not your average street dick and he was starting to irritate me by pushing the issue.

"Honey, couldn't you just look into things for Lolly? Find out for sure if the bastard's cheating on her, before she divorces him?"

I had no desire to take on some two-bit domestic squabble case. "I don't think so, Bill, but I'll recommend a good local private investigator."

Both of them frowned at me and suddenly I was the bad guy.

"It would just take you a day or two, Jersey Barnes." Bill used both my names only when he really wanted something. I sighed, silently cursing my lack of willpower when it came to that pleading puppy-dog look he could produce at will. It was especially effective when he aimed it my way after I'd had a few beers. Sighing, I returned the cut-down-on-beer goal back to my mental to-do list and, knowing it probably wouldn't happen, downed another tasty swig.

"Okay, okay. I'll just tail Samuel for a day or two and check into some things." Surely it wouldn't take too long. I'd get some photographs, maybe a recording of a phone conversation. Lolly would cry, get really mad, get an incredibly lucrative divorce settlement, and get on with her life. Another cheating hubby caught in the act. I still found it hard to digest the thought of Samuel Chesterfield screwing around on his new wife, especially one who looked like Lolly. On the other hand, a lot of smart men have made a lot of bad decisions, thanks to the ability of testosterone to turn even the sanest person into a blithering idiot. I could always begin my retirement next week.

Lolly clapped her hands in thanks and Bill gave me a quick but succulent kiss, the depths of which reached every nerve ending in my body. Even though I'd just agreed to take a job against my better judgment and I wanted to be mad at my boyfriend, the only thing occupying my mind at the moment was the thought of my hands running the entire length of his lovely body. And, of course, how he would reciprocate.

THREE

It took only two days of tailing Samuel Chesterfield to realize he was involved in some funny business and it didn't appear to be with another woman.

Tailing people is not one of my favorite chores. It's a boring task, but relatively easy to do in my Mercedes-Benz AMG S-series. Its jet-black finish makes it inconspicuous and a hopped up V-12 engine makes it brutally fast. Uncle Sam confiscated it from a Colombian drug dealer who had the bad taste to dip his fingers into the terrorism pot, and my handlers gave the sedan to me when they discovered that it had a Hess & Eisenhart armor job with bulletproof everything. I was jazzed about the deal, especially when I learned the car was armored by the same folks who made all the presidential limousines. Driving it, I felt like a diplomat, until the first time bad guys were after me and Secret

Service agents didn't swarm in to help. Still, the car had some major cool factor and, to my delight, it became my personal property when the government decided to pull it from service. Surprisingly, my lowball offer was the winning auction bid. It probably helped that the man running the auction owed me a favor.

Chesterfield's vehicles, on the other hand, were difficult to miss. Both of them. He owned a chauffeured Lincoln stretch limo, but while I'd been tailing him, he'd been driving himself in a white Lexus sport utility vehicle. Yesterday, he had two different lunch appointments, both less than half an hour. Even for a guy of his stature, two lunch appointments in one day, in one hour, was a bit much. Especially since he only drank coffee during both of them.

Earlier today, he paid a visit to a dry cleaner but instead of retrieving laundry, he spoke briefly to another customer at the counter. I attempted to follow his friend, but the fellow exited the rear of the building and vanished.

I figured the quickest way to get some answers would be to bug Chesterfield's home phone lines. It would be an illegal tap, but I usually didn't let a little thing like the law stand in my way. Not being one to work any harder than necessary, I called my partner and asked her to do it.

Rita laughed into the phone, but it wasn't a ha-ha humorous laugh. More like disbelieving. "Are you nuts, Jersey? The phone is going crazy with people calling to ask if it's true that you retired. I'm handling my jobs plus your leftovers. My knee is still killing me from that little brawl I got in last week and Suzie started having labor pains, so now we've got no secretary." She paused, laughed again. "Sure, I'll just drop everything to go and install a little wiretap for your lazy, thoughtless fat ass. Besides," she continued, "what do you need a tap for? I thought you retired."

"I am retired, and I take offense to you calling me fat. But you're better at tapping than I am."

"Maybe you need a little practice," she complained. "Who you listening in on, anyway?"

"Samuel Chesterfield."

"*The* Samuel Chesterfield? He's in town?"

"Yes, and yes."

"I don't *even* want to know why you're interested in Chesterfield."

"No, you probably don't. It's not real exciting. But my evening with Bill made it all worthwhile. We went through an entire can of whipped cream, and it wasn't on top of the pie."

Rita snorted. She had laughed at a typical request and hadn't laughed at my normal humor. She *was* stressed out.

"Okay," I said, "hire a temp to help you out until Suzie pops out the kid and comes back to work. Just keep the temp out of the files and out of the blue room." The blue room housed lots of nifty gadgets including several illegal ones. We certainly didn't need a nosy temporary employee rummaging around in there.

"In other words, you're telling me to hire a warm body to sit here and take messages that I'll have to return anyway?"

"Sure. In fact, tell the temp service you want a hunky guy—he'll make for nice scenery. If nothing else, he can type some correspondence and keep the coffee brewing. Oh, and have him send something to Suzie. Flowers, or diapers, or whatever it is you're supposed to send a new mom."

"First of all, go do your own tap. Second of all, hunky guys don't know how to draft business correspondence. Forget the temp agency. I'm going to hire a sexy masseur who can operate a coffeemaker." Rita hung up without saying good-bye. I climbed in my car and headed to the office for the equipment I'd need to tap the Chesterfield's home phone line.

———

Because most of its occupants were at work, the residential building was relatively quiet when I arrived. Luckily, Chesterfield's alarm system was not set and it only took a few minutes to break in. It would have been easier to ask Lolly for a key, but I didn't want her to know that I planned to rummage through her belongings.

The first thing I noticed about Chesterfield's place was that it seemed pretty nice for a short-term rental. Then I remembered that, according to courthouse records, he'd just bought the building. The outside wasn't much, but the interior oozed taste with designer furniture, carpeting thick enough to envelop bare feet, and randomly placed original artwork that could have been painted by any five-year-old, but was probably insured for hundreds of thousands of dollars.

I decided that if I was going to tap the phone, I might as well drop an earpiece or two at the same time. Lolly was out shopping with Bill, and Chesterfield and Jared were doing the male bonding thing at the newest Chesterfield Financial branch office, so I had plenty of time. I placed a mike in the bedroom and another in the bar and lounge area, which separated the kitchen from the living room. I probably wouldn't have a need for them, but at least they were in place if I wanted to become a fly on the wall.

I briefly wondered where I'd be had my retirement plans gone as expected. Probably lounging on *Incognito,* my forty-eight-foot boat that was a gift from a very appreciative past client. My one extravagance, I kept it docked at the Point Cape Fear Marina and hired a dockhand who made sure the refrigerator was well stocked and that the boat was always clean and ready to go. *Incognito* was an upscale sport-fishing boat, but like my kitchen at home, the outriggers were never used. She cruised at thirty knots, and Bill and I enjoyed taking her out for promiscuous weekend trips. Had we been on the boat right now, we'd probably be drifting just off the coast, making good use of the master stateroom. . . .

Shaking my head to clear distracting thoughts, I got down to business. I took care of both phone lines. An answering machine was plugged into the main number and the other line had only one outlet in the son's room, next to a computer desk loaded with various hardware. When I first met her, Lolly mentioned that Chesterfield was training Jared, and that Jared had just graduated from the Citadel in Charleston.

With that in mind, it wasn't unusual for a twenty-one or twenty-two-year-old to live with his parents temporarily, but studying the son's room, I had to wonder if Jared had decorated it himself. It had a decidedly feminine touch: everything in perfect order, light pastel wall colors, and no dirty clothes lying around. Aside from the cluttered desk, nothing personal was in sight. A single framed photograph of his mother, Lolly's predecessor, and a current copy of *GQ* magazine lay on the night table beside a low-profile platform bed that was piled high with striped pillows. I'd have to run a full background check on the kid to see if anything interesting turned up.

On the other side of the roomy condo, the master bedroom reeked of opulence and came complete with its own flat-screen television, wet bar, and leather sofa. Without leaving signs of intrusion, I did a cursory search through Chesterfield's dresser, paying careful attention to the sock drawer. I once found a government handheld satellite tracking device nestled between two pairs of white athletic socks. Like digging a hole on the beach just for the hell of it, I theorized that concealing goods in a sock drawer was a genetic thing for males. Women were much more creative. Much to my disappointment though, Chesterfield's sock drawer revealed only clean socks, neatly folded into matching pairs.

Moving on, I tossed his study, the wet bar, and the entire kitchen. I didn't know what I was looking for, and as if to meet my expectations, I found exactly nothing. I suddenly wished that Ox were by my side, along with one of his brilliant suggestions. His input was always laced with striking clarity and he often helped with challenging cases when I asked—and sometimes when I didn't. Occasionally, he'd have an epiphany that was preceded by a vision, which I found both disconcerting and intriguing. But the man's suggestions were always legitimate, albeit borderline psychic. And in addition to his connection with protective spirits, he could kick some major ass when the situation called for it. Not to mention the fact that ever since he played the starring role in a vivid dream I had last week, the mere sight of him made me tingle in all the right places. Thoughts of quitting work and entering a new phase in life may have nudged my subconscious to consider Ox as more than a best friend and business partner. Or maybe I'd wanted to explore the possibility of sex and romance all along, but the timing hadn't been right.

My hands started to sweat beneath the latex gloves I wore. Medical-quality gloves are the perfect choice to work quickly without leaving prints, but they do not breathe. I continued poring through Chesterfield's personal life and, after twenty minutes, found a curiously placed flash drive stored inside a leather case. About the size of a wand-shaped key chain, the data storage device had a USB interface on one end. A lot of computer users prefer flash drives in lieu of floppy disks or compact disks, but it was odd that I found the thing concealed in a gym bag, in the coat closet by the front door. I'd have to find out which health club the Chesterfields belonged to.

Immediately, I called my friend Soup—who happens to be one of the best computer guys in the country. He answered on the first ring. The good thing about computer junkies is that they're always home, in front of a flickering monitor, hacking into prohibited cyber-territories.

"Talk to me." Soup was an ex-Fed, and acquired his name because he always ate soup right out of the can when he was on a surveillance assignment. Everyone else would scarf down candy bars, doughnuts, or pastrami sandwiches but Soup was more inclined to drink his meal. He was a soup connoisseur, and could discuss the subtle flavor nuances of dill tomato bisque or asparagus crème the way other men analyzed football.

"Soup, it's Jersey," I responded, as if he didn't already know. With the gadgetry he had, Soup would know if the queen of England was calling before she uttered her first royal word. "I need you here yesterday, and bring something that will copy the files from a USB flash drive. I want to know what's on it, but leave the original. And, of course, it might be copy protected. Can you do it?"

"Damn, Jersey," he complained. "I'm in the middle of lunch. And, I'm condom-close to breaking in to my favorite airline's reservation system. I'm working on a few first-class tickets to Cozumel."

"Lunch can wait. You owe me," I said. "Not that I'm keeping count, or anything, but I believe that last time we tallied, you were in the hole by quite a wide margin. Real wide."

"Crap," he said.

"You have to be quick about it. No stopping at the deli on your way over for a cup of minestrone." I heard the rapid click of his computer keys in the background and knew he was closing whatever files he had open.

"I'm on the way. Give me the small print from the memory stick."

I read the product information from the flash drive including something that ended in gigabytes.

"With that much memory, it's a relatively new one. It'll hold way more data than a DVD, believe it or not."

I told him I did believe it, gave him the address, and hung up to wait.

FOUR

"*Where the heck* have you been, for crying out loud?" Spud said in greeting when I walked through the door. "I need to get to the drugstore before they close. I'm all out of heartburn pills."

It was a Sunday afternoon in the middle of June and the day called for enjoyable outdoor activities. I was supposed to be re-tired and frolicking on my boat, Bill had just told me that Lolly was planning to go public with her cheating-hubby accusations, and to top it all off, I'd received an offer for a Medicare-paid scooter along with free coupons for adult diapers and fiber supple-ments. Rita probably put my name on their mailing list just for laughs, but I figured I ought to at least have been slurping a ba-nana drink with a little umbrella in it, enjoying a water view from somewhere, before opening such insulting mail.

Filling my lungs and holding the breath for a long beat, I willed myself to take Spud and his attitude in stride. *Incognito* wasn't going anywhere. She would still be in her dock next week, patiently awaiting my arrival. Or next month, the way the Chesterfield thing was panning out. It had been days since I'd bugged the family's high-rise condo and so far, nothing had jumped out and announced itself as a clue.

I let the breath slowly out and displayed my benevolent smile. "Hiya, Spud. I thought it was cholesterol pills you were out of." Even though my father collected prescription drugs like an investor collects portfolios, he was in good health. Although arthritis caused a stiff walk and knobby knuckles, he got around just fine, especially when using one of his hand-carved wooden walking canes. The one he sported today was adorned with a mermaid in lieu of a handle. Her curvaceous nippled breasts were the finger grips.

"Yeah, well," he said. "I won some cholesterol pills from Trip last week during our poker game. But now I need heartburn pills. I'm starting to belch, and you can't attract babes sounding like a frog, for crying out loud." Spud's idea of a babe was any woman who could walk faster than he could, regardless of any healthcare aids in use.

"Okay, I'll drive you to the pharmacy before they close," I agreed. "Let me get something to drink first." Spud's eyesight had deteriorated to the point that North Carolina deemed him unable to safely operate a vehicle and took away his license.

Seeing me tote him around, people assumed Spud was my grandfather. They didn't factor in that he'd impregnated my mother when he was twice her age. If I thought too long about the injustice of regaining a father just in time to play chauffeur for his aging body, I felt cheated. But as Ox pointed out, the spirits had a purpose when they deposited Spud on my doorstep.

"I was going to drive myself but Ox busted me just when I

cranked the ignition." The mermaid's tail swished with annoyance. "He threatened to call Dirk and have me arrested."

A smile tugged at my mouth, as I knew it to be an empty threat. Ox was a direct approach type of guy. If forced, he'd have gently removed Spud from the car and deposited him in a booth at the Block.

A month ago I had received a call from a highway patrolman at the Department of Motor Vehicles, where Spud had failed the eyesight test and thrown such a tantrum that only the mention of arrest quieted him down. When I arrived to collect Spud and his vehicle, I paid an off-duty cop to follow us home in Spud's car. Dirk Thompson ended up joining us for dinner and swapped insults with Spud right up to the point of cheesecake with fresh blueberries. By the time we sipped after-dinner drinks of Baileys Irish cream on ice, Spud admitted that maybe it was best if he didn't drive. Later, Dirk told me he hadn't enjoyed a night out so much in a long time and that, if I ever needed anything out of the department, I should give him a call. He'd since become my main source for running quick vehicle registrations and license checks.

"Any response on your classified ad yet?" I asked Spud, opening the refrigerator with a Coke in mind.

"Hell, no!"

When the interior light popped on, a Bass ale screamed my name but I grabbed a can of Coke instead.

"Not a single response!" Spud raved.

He had tried to sell his car to Dirk, then to the neighbors, and then to the world via the Internet before succumbing to the high classified rates of the local daily newspaper. Selling the car had become his sole mission in life. He was obsessed with getting rid of it since North Carolina revoked his driving privileges.

His cane stabbed the air. "Our newspaper is supposed to have a circulation of sixty thousand readers. You'd think that just one of them would decide my Chrysler is the best deal going, for crying out loud."

Spud's car is a bright red Chrysler LHS. I'm still not sure what the LHS stands for, but the car looks exactly like the old New Yorker. Spud's has tan leather seats, power everything, and a sunroof. Immediately after he'd lost his license, we tried to sell it to a dealership, but they weren't too impressed with the fantastic deal we offered. Spud claimed that the car had been pampered and was worth at least fifteen thousand dollars. The eager kid who'd mistakenly thought Spud was there to trade it in on a brand-new car explained that the sales manager could buy a similar LHS off the auction block for five thousand dollars. Spud told the kid exactly where his sales manager could put the five thousand bills.

"No big deal on the newspaper ad, anyway," Spud said, "because we've got another plan to get rid of the car."

"We who?" I questioned.

"My poker buddies. Bobby, Hal, and Trip. They know how to solve a problem. Four heads are much better than one." I wasn't so sure, considering it was Spud's poker buddies that we were talking about. In their case, four heads probably equaled one and a half. Maybe two.

"Okay." I had to spur him on. "Tell me about it."

"Insurance. I'm going to just collect the average retail value of the car from the insurance company."

"I don't think they'll go for that," I told him. "They probably don't need a used Chrysler."

"I'm not going to *sell* it to them. They're going to pay a claim. The car will be sunk, you know, horrible accident and all that." I didn't know whether to laugh or scold him so I just waited for the rest.

"Next time it rains real heavy, Bobby is going to accidentally drive it into that retention pond in the middle of the parking lot at the shopping center where our barber is."

"I think that's called insurance fraud," I said, "and that would be illegal. Not to mention dangerous."

Spud's cane dismissed my concern with a wave. "It's no more dangerous than driving on these roads every day. Besides, Bobby's gonna drop us all off at the barber, *then* go drive into the lake. He'll have his window rolled down, so he can climb out before the thing sinks. We'll act shocked, dry his wrinkled ass off, then call the coppers. And, it ain't illegal if it's an accident."

My father's logic never ceased to amaze me. Especially considering the fact that he used to be a cop. Enforcer of the law and keeper of the peace.

"Sounds like you've given this some thought," I said.

"Of course we have. Got it all planned out. Bobby's the best swimmer, plus he volunteered to do the deed." Bobby was well over eighty and probably hadn't seen the inside of a swimming pool in more than twenty years.

"Spud, tell me this is all a joke."

"Okay. It's all a joke," he agreed much too quickly. "All I want is a decent price for the damn car. It's useless to me," he said in a rising voice, the mermaid's breasts almost touching the ceiling. "The damn state of North Carolina ought to buy it after what they did! Taking away an innocent man's license to drive. What's next, they gonna tell me I can't take out your boat?"

Spud had never captained *Incognito,* at least not to my knowledge. I'd have to remember to hide the keys, just to be sure. I downed the rest of my Coke, Spud propped a bright yellow beret on top of his obstinate head, and we journeyed to the pharmacy.

———

A red blinking light on the answering machine caught our attention when we returned. It was Soup instructing me to call him.

"Soup here," he answered on the first ring.

"Whatcha got on the flash drive?"

"Very interesting. *Very* interesting. I got a clean copy, but it's completely encoded."

"So?" Encoded data was a speed bump to Soup. He could navigate over or around anything.

"No, I mean really encoded. Some unusual shit; I haven't been able to break it yet. I think it could be government stuff, though." Government? What was Chesterfield doing with government data on a flash drive hidden in a gym bag?

"Keep trying. I'm good for your time." He knew that we would settle up eventually—whether via money, trade, or otherwise.

"I'm on it," he agreed and disconnected.

Whatever Chesterfield was involved in, it certainly wasn't a case of infidelity. I should just explain to Lolly that her hubby wasn't cheating and get on with my life after retirement. But it was against my nature to walk away from unanswered questions. I was cursed with a noble—or possibly stupid—desire to unravel mysteries and plow my way directly to the motivating core of a person's actions.

On the other hand, I had only agreed to tail Chesterfield as a favor to Bill. Lolly wasn't paying me a dime for this assignment. In fact, I didn't have an assignment. I had stumbled upon something that, on the surface, appeared illegitimate. I could dig deeper or I could forget about it, and I really had no reason to get involved. Not sure what to do next, I headed downstairs to enjoy a cold drink and mull it all over.

Cracker greeted me with a wet-nosed nuzzle when I reached the bar.

"Did you have a good time studding yourself out at the breeder's?" I asked, scratching the dog's neck.

"Trip reported that your dog performed beautifully," Ox answered through a grin, "especially considering it was his first time."

A white Labrador retriever, Cracker was won in a poker game the night I sat in for Bobby during Spud's weekly card night. The pup was being trained to retrieve birds by Trip's grandson, a local breeder who thought the animal was a light-colored yellow Lab. But, when he approached a year of age and his fur hadn't darkened from its snowy-white color, he became useless as a hunting dog since—according to the grandson—he would stick out like a redneck at a wine tasting. Spotting him from the air, ducks would bolt before entering shotgun range. So the grandson gave the pup to Trip.

I learned that purebred solid-white Lab puppies were rare and easily sold for five hundred dollars apiece. A halfway trained white Lab would sell for a thousand, or so Trip claimed when he put the dog up against my royal flush. The pot was only worth one hundred and eight dollars, but I told Trip that he wasn't getting back any change. Not only that, but he should pay me to take a worthless mutt off his hands. The royal flush beat his four deuces and I acquired a dog, with the condition that his grandson could borrow the pedigreed Lab on occasion for breeding purposes.

Spud called the puppy Cracker, since it was "too white," and the name stuck. The lucky Lab's days were spent lounging around the Block and he frequently jumped in the river to take a swim just because he could. The Block's regulars always had a treat for Cracker when they arrived and, if I were a dog, I couldn't imagine a better life.

"You look perplexed," Ox said after I'd situated myself on a bar stool. His deep voice resonated in a surprisingly neutral accent when you considered that he grew up in North Carolina and Kentucky. He served me a Guinness draught without being asked and our fingers touched momentarily when I reached for the glass. I caught his glance and for a flicker of a second, wondered if he somehow knew about the sensual dream I'd had about him. I wondered if I fell asleep thinking of Ox, I could enjoy the same dream again.

"Jersey?" he said, snapping me out of my reverie.

"Took on a job as a little favor to Bill," I explained, forcing myself not to wonder about what Ox would be like in bed. Sex with the man would be indescribable, until it happened, and maybe not even then.

"What's the job?"

"An old friend of his thinks that her hubby is the cheating sort, but it turns out the guy isn't being unfaithful. Thing is, I found a computer storage device and Soup thinks it could be encoded government data."

"Who's the husband?" It was a bright afternoon and a marshy gust blew across the water, Gulf Stream and sea breezes playfully mating. All four of the Block's industrial-sized garage doors were wide open, welcoming Mother Nature's late-afternoon gift, and the place had begun to fill with happy-hour regulars.

"Samuel Chesterfield."

"Of Chesterfield Financial?"

"Yep."

"Damn, Jersey. You really know how to get yourself tangled in some deep river weed." He laughed. "And you're supposed to be retired, relaxing on *Incognito,* going where the tide takes you." Ox wore a pair of jeans and a plain black T-shirt with the sleeves rolled up. His olive-brown skin reflected the reds and blues of neon beer lights that were suspended on chains around the bar. I paused to admire my best friend's build before focusing my concentration on the matter at hand.

"Tell me about it," I complained, seeking sympathy. "I should be sipping a bottle of bubbly right now, somewhere with a fabulous view."

"You've got a fabulous view right now, so quit bitching and tell me what you're going to do," Ox said, ignoring my quest for pity. "I have customers to serve."

"I don't know. Something deep under the table is going on, but is it my business? I'm not getting paid to figure it out. Should I just walk away?"

"If Chesterfield is involved, you may be talking high stakes. It could get dark." Describing a situation as "dark" was Ox's way of saying hazardous to my health. I had come to rely on his instincts because they were always correct. Some people would say it was mere gut instinct, but I knew that Ox had access to something more.

"I already thought of that. But I've got to at least figure out how high the stakes are before I decide whether or not to bail out."

Ox nodded while I spoke, as though he knew what I was going to say before I said it. "If you need me, you let me know."

That went without saying. He always appeared when I needed him and covered my ass even when I thought I didn't. He'd saved my life last year during a bloody shootout in Raleigh, and as he was driving me home, said only, "You want to stop for burgers or pizza?" Unusually shaken, I'd answered that I wanted a cheeseburger and promptly had a meltdown. Ox stopped and we walked into the woods, where we leaned against a huge oak tree and he held me tight until I was cried out, at which point we went for cheeseburgers.

It was the second time I'd ever cried as an adult, the first being when my father reappeared. In both instances, I didn't feel foolish around Ox for dropping tears. To him, a situation simply was what it was.

The sudden realization that my bar manager could comfort just as effectively as he could kill made something elemental move inside me. What could be more sexy than a man who was both wise and lethal? I'd bet money that his performance in bed would be just as perfect as his performance in combat.

Pleasantly aware of the boats gliding steadily by the Block, I watched my beer disappear and threw a tennis ball for Cracker. It occurred to me to wait until I knew what the flash drive contained before I decided whether or not to drop the Chesterfield case. Meanwhile, something told me that it would be a good idea to get a tracker on Chesterfield's digital phone. Smaller than a dime, the trackers I use provide an avenue to listen in *and* track the location of the individual carrying the phone. They are basically a miniature GPS device, with the added benefit of a nifty chip that allows me—or Trish—to listen in by dialing a preprogrammed phone number.

Trish is a local street dick who does occasional contract jobs for me. I'd have her accidentally bump into Chesterfield, ask to use his phone, and insert the tracker inside the battery compartment. As long as he didn't change the rechargeable battery, the tracker would go unnoticed. It was an expensive gamble that would cost the Barnes Agency several thousand dollars if we didn't recover the device. With electronics, the smaller, the more expensive, and most everything was available in a miniature version if you were willing to pay for it.

Feeling good about having a plan of action, blind though it was, I celebrated with another draught and a dozen hot wings. Maybe I'd call Bill and cajole him into joining me for an evening of total-body massage therapy. Maybe spending the night with him would take my mind off of Ox. Or maybe not. Either way, I'd worry about Lolly, Samuel Chesterfield, and their problems tomorrow.

FIVE

A steady drizzle fell outside my window and an empty bed greeted me when I awoke Monday morning. Bill had left me a handwritten note, propped against the bathroom mirror and held in place by a foil-wrapped protein bar: "Enjoy your breakfast, and see you Wednesday. Luv U."

He'd mentioned something about doing a photo shoot for a new casino opening in Vegas. Wondering what type of costume they'd make him wear, I unwrapped the granola bar and headed for the Mister Coffee machine. Spud sat at the kitchen table, reading the newspaper and drinking a bottle of chocolate Yoo-hoo. An empty plate with remnants of what resembled scrambled eggs rested on the table in front of him. Cracker had wedged himself between the legs of Spud's chair, hoping for a fallen morsel.

"The damn dealerships are advertising two-percent financing on selected new vehicles, for crying out loud," he grumbled.

"Morning, Spud."

"Who's gonna buy my Chrysler, when they can keep their money in the bank to earn interest and get a new car at two percent?" he demanded.

I eyed the empty plate in front of him and decided that he'd had grits, too. "Good breakfast?" I asked, munching on a bar of what tasted like toasted dirt with dry leaves mixed in.

"Bill cooked for me. Two scrambled, cheese grits, bacon, and toast. He even shook my Yoo-hoo." Spud traded the classifieds for the metro section and made a show of wadding up the former.

"So glad my boyfriend thinks more of my father than me," I muttered, stomach growling.

"Some cantaloupe left. Eat a piece of that with your horse food."

My brain was still foggy with sleep and I couldn't grasp a snappy retort to throw back at Spud. The phone rang as I poured a much-needed cup of coffee. "This is Jersey."

"It's Soup. I've been up all night." He sounded wired. "You're not going to believe what was on that flash drive."

My brain perked up in an instant. "Lay it on me."

"Social Security."

"Come again?"

"Remember the Social Security Reform and Privatization Act that went into effect in January?" he asked.

"Of course." Everyone remembered the Social Security Reform Act. It was one of the most hotly debated political issues that had come along since cloning.

The SSRP Act said that Americans, beginning at age thirty, could elect to leave their Social Security benefits in the hands of Uncle Sam or choose to manage their own retirement money. The idea was that by age thirty, an adult knew enough about investing to make a wise decision. If one wanted to control their own Social Security funds, they could transfer their entire balance from Uncle Sam into a Social Security investment privatized account, or SIPA. Future Social Security taxes withheld would be transferred from the government's account to the individual's account four times a year, on the first day of each quarter. And it was all going to take place electronically.

Some people claimed the new program could only result in tax increases, while others believed it was time to make a change because the Social Security retirement program originally enacted by President Franklin Roosevelt in 1935 had grown into an unmanageable monster.

Regardless of the continuing debate, the act passed last year and took effect in January. So far, only four national firms had been given Uncle Sam's blessing to handle SIPAs and I recalled reading something about Chesterfield Financial joining the SIPA-approved list.

"Well, I've got what appears to be Big Brother's list of taxpayers who turned thirty last year and elected a SIPA," he explained. "Or, at least a piece of the list. From two states. In the file for each individual, there's a little chunk of data inside another encoded field. I haven't gotten into it yet. The code is different."

"Different how? Somebody accessed a federal database of names, then added their own stuff to each name?"

"Something like that." Soup sighed, not wanting to waste time explaining technical details. "Basically, somebody is using these names for another purpose, other than what the original database was set up for. I just don't know what yet."

It was not unfeasible that Chesterfield Financial would have a list of taxpayer's names, especially if they had just made the approved list of SIPA brokerage firms. But, what was the additional data that had been tagged on to the database? And, back to my original question, why was the flash drive hidden inside a gym bag in Chesterfield's home?

"How long before you break it?"

"Damn, Jersey, you don't ask for much," Soup complained. "I do have other jobs on my schedule, you know."

"A week's vacation on *Incognito*. With Captain Pete. Fueled up, fully stocked with food and booze, anywhere you want to go." Pete transported yachts for a living and he owed me a favor. I'd probably owe him after he had to put up with Soup and his techie pals for a week, but that was the nature of my business. Give and take. Keeping tabs on who owed whom.

"Deal," Soup said immediately, envisioning the party he would throw on my boat. "I'm on it." The line went dead while I still had the phone pressed to my ear.

Energized, I called Trish and explained how I wanted her to tag Chesterfield's wireless phone. She agreed that it would be done within a day. My kind of private investigator.

When I hung up the phone, Cracker licked my bare feet in approval but Spud wasn't as enthusiastic. "I thought you retired."

"I did. I am. This is just a little job I'm doing as a favor."

"Uh-huh." Looking above the reading glasses that were perched low on his nose, he studied me from across the top of the newspaper. "Don't go an' let your guard down, now, kid. Be careful."

"I always am, Spud."

SIX

"*Jersey, you've got* to tell Lolly what you know," Bill told me over the telephone from Las Vegas, after interrogating me as to the status of my investigation. He had never before been concerned with any case I was working, and even though Lolly was an old friend of his, I didn't appreciate Bill trying to micromanage how I dealt with her. Unaccustomed to discussing my work with anyone other than Rita and Ox and sometimes Spud, I asked why he was so anxious about Lolly and her situation.

"Because I'm the one who got you into this thing to begin with," he said.

"True," I agreed.

Changing the subject, I asked about his Vegas photo shoot. He confessed that they made him wear Roman warrior headgear and carry a long-handled spear, adding that the only other part of the costume was a thong fashioned from real copper. Ouch.

"Did the metal thong, uh, damage anything down there?"

"No, it was only metal in the front. The rest of it was made from cloth. And before you start giving me a hard time, you should know the job paid six grand, even though I'm worth much, much more."

"Can you keep the costume? I'd like to see it."

He ignored me. "At least tell Lolly that Sam isn't cheating on her. If you don't, she might go public and the tabloids would go nuts. She already told that dumb social columnist that her marriage might be in trouble. Now the lady's hounding her for the rest of the story."

I asked myself again: why did he care so much? "How well do you really know Lolly, Bill?" I asked. "It's been, what, fifteen years since you've spent any time with her?"

"Well, yeah. That's about right. Even though we stayed in touch for a few years after graduation, I don't know what she's been up to. But what difference does that make?"

"If I talk to her now, Lolly might be so relieved, she'll confess to Chesterfield that she hired me to tail him. Then my cover's blown for whatever *is* going on."

"So, what's going on?" he prodded.

"That's the problem. I don't know. But it's looking real interesting."

"Do you really need to be involved anymore, Jersey? I thought you were retired," he said. "When I get back tomorrow, I've got a whole week with nothing to do but pamper you. Please, just talk to Lolly and walk away."

It sounded decadent. Once again I was tempted to drop everything and escape with Bill on the boat. But not tempted enough to do it. Like a swamp gator with her teeth sunk into something that tasted sweet, I wasn't going to let go until I found out exactly what it was.

"I *am* retired," I said for what seemed like the fiftieth time in the past week. "But I'm involved with this now, and I have to get to the bottom of it. You shouldn't complain since, as you just said, you are the reason I'm involved to begin with."

"Okay," he relented. "Just tell Lolly that Sam is involved with something but he is not seeing another woman. So she should just go about her normal routine."

"Right." To say I was skeptical was saying that the pope attended church.

"Please? That magazine lady is going to wear her down."

"All right." I gave in. "I'll talk to Lolly today."

"Thanks, hon. I'm having a ball in Vegas, but I miss you. Let's do something fun when I get back. You game?"

"Absolutely," I said. "See if you can smuggle out the Roman warrior helmet. I've never had sex with anyone from the B.C. years before."

The costume attendant had already taken the helmet, he informed me. But he might be able to sneak the metal thong out, he said, and added something about loving me bunches.

"Same here," I said and hung up. One of these days I'd work up to telling Bill that I loved him, too. One thing at a time.

I called Trish and asked her to keep tabs on Chesterfield's place. I'd already done the hard part. All she had to do was plug in, turn on the recorder, and wait for something worthwhile. She would also keep an eye on who was coming and going from the building and monitor the tracker she'd placed on Chesterfield's phone. I only wanted her for two or three days and luckily, her schedule was open.

Next, I called Lolly and arranged a lunch meeting for one o'clock. Finally, I jogged to the gym, which was only half a mile from the Block. I did the free weights for forty-five minutes, then put on some boxing gloves and rendezvoused with the heavy bag. I finished with a sauna and a shower. I didn't feel retired but overall, I felt pretty darn good.

Lolly wore a revealing silk tank top and a pair of tight button-down jeans that tapered to hug each ankle. She sat at the bar of Paddy's Hollow Restaurant & Pub with an untouched glass of wine in front of her and had attracted two horny businessmen in the short time she waited for me. Ignoring the ridiculously large rock on her finger, they stood in stereo on either side of her and boyishly argued about who had cheated on his golf score last weekend. Too polite to tell them to get lost, Lolly pretended to listen. I verbally elbowed my way in.

"Lolly," I said. "Great to see you. Is that hunky cowboy husband of yours coming tonight? I'd love to see another bone-crunching brawl, like the one that happened the last time a couple of schmucks couldn't take a hint."

Lolly smiled.

The two suits took a look at me and wordlessly disappeared. I watched closely, thinking they might be more than a couple of corporate suits trying to flirt during a business lunch. They weren't.

Lolly and I moved to a table and ordered drinks. She asked for an iced tea and I requested ice water and a Bass ale. I'd drink them in that order. When the server returned with glasses in hand, we ordered two Caesar salads topped with grilled shrimp and a basket of garlic rolls.

Lolly sat with a leg tucked beneath her in the chair, giving me a look that was half victimized wife and half seductress. Her elbows were on the table and a pinkie finger, in a nervous but guy-catching gesture, played with her bottom lip as though her mouth was a toy. A nearby patron stopped eating his hamburger to openly stare at her.

"He's not cheating on you, Lolly," I said.

"He's not?" She looked genuinely surprised.

"No. There may be something going on at his firm that could be troublesome, but there is definitely not another woman. Feel better?"

She looked at the ceiling and breathed a deep sigh of relief. Her breasts swelled momentarily with the effort, causing our neighboring diner's eyes to nearly bulge. Just for kicks, I mimicked Lolly and stuck out the twins, as Spud had aptly named my government-paid implants. The fellow's eyes moved from Lolly's chest to mine and when I winked at him, he nearly choked on a mouthful of food. It was good to know that my semiretired self still had it.

After a beat, Lolly's forehead wrinkled in confusion. "I don't understand. What's happening at Chesterfield Financial?"

"I don't know," I told her. "But Bill thought you needed to know that Samuel isn't seeing someone else."

"I guess. It was dumb to have even confided in that woman to begin with." Lolly turned the full force of her crystal blue eyes on me. "She was just so . . . sympathetic."

"Nosy would be more like it. She's a social columnist. She's a piranha."

Reprimanded, Lolly remained silent.

"Look, Lolly, I don't know you. But I do know Bill, and since you're his friend, you're my friend." There was no gentle way to put it. "Being married to someone like Chesterfield is going to present challenges and people may try to take advantage of you. They'll want your story, your money, and yes, at some point you may encounter a woman who wants your husband. But for now, just focus on your marriage and be happy with your good fortune."

"You're right," she said. "My mother told me the same thing. When I was little, I mean. She used to tell me to plan my strategy, like you do in a game of chess, before I acted on a thought. To know how it would turn out." Lolly's eyes were focused on a distant spot over my shoulder, as though her mind was far away. Suddenly, the pupils shrunk and she focused her gaze on me. "I never could figure out how to play chess. I'm not real smart, like Bill, or you. But I love Samuel so much. He's the best thing that ever happened to me. The thought of him with somebody else made me crazy. And, contrary to what people think, I didn't marry him for—"

"The money." I finished the thought for her, thinking she was trying hard to convince me that she was a good person. I finished my water and started on the ale.

"Yes," she agreed. "I really didn't marry him for the money. I don't want to have all that money. There are other things much more important than money."

I wondered if she was telling the truth. If given the opportunity, what person wouldn't want to have millions upon millions of dollars at their disposal? Nobody that I knew.

"Well, you are where you are, in a new town with a new husband. If you love Chesterfield, you'll deal with being his wife in a responsible manner. Running to the tabloids with accusations that he was cheating on you would not have been good."

She looked ready to cry, and for a moment, I felt bad. Like I had just punished an innocent child. Or, like the time I popped Cracker on the snout hard enough to make him yelp because he'd snatched a peeled shrimp off of a customer's plate at the Block. In both cases, they may have just been following instinct.

"I see your point. I just don't know if I've got what it takes," she confessed.

"Of course you do. Modeling isn't an easy thing, and if you can learn the ropes enough to stick with that for ten years, then you can learn how to deal with being the wife of Samuel Chesterfield."

Our salads arrived. Lolly asked for fresh ground pepper and grated Parmesan. "Now I can see why Bill loves you," Lolly said after a miniature bite of romaine lettuce.

"Hmm?" I was here to talk about Chesterfield and Lolly, not my love life.

"Well, you're pretty. But you're also smart and you understand things, you know? Even if you do guzzle beer and follow people around and stuff."

I squeezed my eyes shut for a second to keep from rolling them upward. "Let's get back to why we're here."

"Is Sammy in trouble?"

"I don't know. But I am going to try to find out. And if it turns out that he is, well, we'll just deal with it then. All right?"

She took a deep breath. "Okay."

"You trust me?"

"Yes."

"You're not going to go run off and chat with the media?"

"No."

"You understand that he's not cheating on you?"

"Yes."

"Good girl," I said and purposely changed tack to catch her reaction. "By the way, where are your parents now? Are they still together?"

She looked startled. "Uh, they're in Europe. Traveling."

We finished our lunches and I wasn't sure whether Lolly was better off after our little meeting or not. I hoped that I had helped her somehow, regardless of the outcome.

I walked Lolly to her car, a blue BMW, before climbing into my own vehicle. Feeling bad about dumping everything in her lap, I decided to stop by the agency to see how Rita was holding up.

What was wrong with me? First I felt bad about scolding Lolly and then I'm suddenly feeling guilty about bailing out on my partner? I, Jersey Barnes, was developing a conscience? This was a first. As I navigated the roads, I wondered if I was approaching a midlife crisis. I hadn't experienced the urge to run out and buy a red convertible sports car, get my eyelids done, or have an affair with a young college football hero. Although Bill was younger, I didn't purposely date him because of his looks. Not entirely, anyway. I'd have to ask Ox about my new conscience sometime, get his take on things.

The Barnes Agency is located in what was previously a two-story residential home in the heart of Wilmington. If traffic was moving, it was only a ten-minute drive from the Block and would take just slightly longer to get there from Paddy's Hollow. The agency's central location also put it near the airport, which came in handy since Rita and I frequently traveled by air. Although the Wilmington airport was small and had very few direct flights to anywhere, the benefits of living in Wilmington more than made up for minor inconveniences.

I had just pulled into the flow of traffic when my cell rang. Few people had the number, so it was usually something important. Or Spud, needing a ride somewhere. Or Bill, just to say hello. Since I'd announced my retirement, he'd been keeping closer-than-usual tabs on me.

"You might want to check this out," Trish told me when I answered. She was sitting inside the agency's mobile surveillance unit, an old Chevy van with a variety of magnetic door signs and license tags. It was currently a TOOL-TEK HOME REPAIR van.

"Chesterfield just got a call on his wireless. It was his assistant,

Darlene, telling him that Eddie Flowers was found dead. Apparently, Flowers was one of Chesterfield's top people. The vice president of accounting. He flew into Wilmington for some reason and got himself shot."

I aimed the Benz in the direction of Chesterfield Financial and, during the drive, called Dirk at the police station to fish for information. He didn't know anything, but made a few calls and dialed me back within minutes.

Flowers had been found dead inside his car. Apparently the man had gone to Taco Bell for a fast-food lunch. He purchased two burritos inside the store and returned to his car, where somebody put a bullet in his head at point-blank range. Either he'd rolled down the window to speak with the shooter or he'd been driving with it down to begin with. The deed was done in broad daylight. No witnesses came forward.

I don't much believe in coincidences. I had no way to be sure, but my gut told me that the accountant's murder was related to the flash drive I'd found. It was time to have a talk directly with Chesterfield.

SEVEN

The next morning when I approached Chesterfield at his company's Wilmington office, I posed as an investigator hired by Flowers' family to help find the murderer. I wore a cheap navy suit with plain leather heels and carried a nondescript briefcase. I was Josephine Bell.

A distinguished man in his late fifties, Chesterfield was even more handsome up close and in person, with dark hair that had grayed at the temples and warm brown eyes covered by nearly invisible wire-framed glasses. An aura of energy surrounded him, radiating success.

"Thanks for seeing me without an appointment," I began. "It's so important to get on something like this immediately."

"Well, Miss Bell—"

"Please, call me Josephine," I interrupted with a smile.

"Josephine, I'll help however I can. But I am curious about something."

"What's that?" I gave him my most friendly, trustworthy smile.

"The family has never heard of you."

I'd underestimated him. He must've called to verify my alias during the ten minutes I'd been kept waiting in the lobby. In the immediate wake following a tragedy, most people didn't take the time to *think* about anything. It usually hadn't yet occurred to them to be suspicious; they just complied and did what they were told to do. But Samuel Chesterfield was not most people.

I decided to come clean. Sort of.

"I've obviously misjudged you," I said frankly, "and for that I apologize." Taking a chance on angering Lolly, I explained to Chesterfield how I'd come in contact with his wife and how she'd been suspicious of him having an affair.

"She's been told that you are not seeing another woman," I finished.

A surprised laugh escaped from his mouth. "My goodness, I can't believe she suspected me of infidelity. Poor thing. Lolly is such a sweet one and I love her dearly, but she's a bit . . . naïve sometimes."

"Yes."

"And, you are here now for what purpose?" he asked straightforwardly. I had given him my real name and the real story, but left out the fact that I'd rummaged through his home and found a mysterious data storage device. I also hadn't questioned him about the odd lunch meetings I'd witnessed.

"It seems coincidental that Lolly said you've been acting strange and days later one of your vice presidents is murdered."

"The police say it appears to be a failed carjacking and I'm sure their judgment is sound." He leaned forward, elbows on the desk, and touched his fingertips together. "You still haven't told me why you're here. Who's paying you to continue with your little investigation? Surely not Lolly."

"No, she never paid me to begin with," was all I said.

He leaned back in his chair. "Look, I'm a busy man. I don't know what you're after and I don't have a good reason to cooperate with you. Yes, there's been a tragic murder. Eddie was not only an officer of the company, he was a close friend. But none of this has anything to do with you."

He had a good point. It wasn't my business. Before leaving, I wrote my home phone number on a Barnes Agency business card and offered my hand. Surprising me, he shook it.

On my way out, I heard a secretary buzz Chesterfield on the intercom to say the maid needed him and it was an emergency. He picked up and listened briefly before letting the handset clatter to the floor. His face turned ashen and he looked as though he might get sick. I'd seen the same look on men before and it usually meant that something terribly bad had happened to someone they loved. I immediately thought of Lolly.

"Your wife?" I said.

He moved his head side to side in shocked, slow motion. "No, not Lolly. Jared. My son," he said, not caring that I was a stranger. "He's gone. There's a note."

I didn't know if he meant gone as in suicide or gone as in missing.

"Kidnapped?"

"Maybe."

I waited for him to ask for my help, but he didn't. He was a cautious man. He had no idea who I was and, for all he knew, I could have been the kidnapper.

"Please leave," he said and it was not a request. "I can assume that what you've just heard will be held in confidence?"

I nodded, noting that he slipped my business card into his pocket.

My cell phone rang an hour later, while I was at the Block seeking companionship from Cracker.

"It's Samuel Chesterfield," he said.

"I thought you might call."

"You're not a licensed private investigator."

"No, I'm not. Nobody in my agency is, and we do not advertise that we are," I said. "Actually, we don't advertise at all. A majority of our clients are carryovers from a previous career of mine."

"With the government."

"Your resourcefulness surprises me."

"I was unable to ascertain what exactly it is that you did for the government. But you do have a most impressive background, Miss Barnes. At least what I could find of it. Quite a bit seems to be missing." He had done his homework and he was quick. With the resources he had at his disposal, he could probably find out anything about anyone more quickly than I could. The difference was that I called in favors, while he simply put out the cash.

"Please, call me Jersey."

"My son is missing, Jersey. It appears to be a kidnapping. Nobody has been notified because the note instructed that Jared would be shot if police were called."

There was nothing for me to say, so I waited.

"I'm, ah, a little out of my league here," he said and I heard a hint of desperation creep into an otherwise calm voice. "I can pay any amount to hire anyone for anything. But I have no idea who to hire or what to do. With your background, I figure you ought to at least be able to tell me who to call."

This was a tough situation. Since it involved Samuel Chester-field, the Feebies should be called, but as much as they tried, they couldn't be invisible. A professional would spot FBI boys in a second, and might just carry out the death threat that was in the note. Although any kidnapper who killed their captive would lose their bargaining chip, so it was probably an empty threat. On the other hand, it may not have been an ordinary kid-napping. The murder, and now the missing son, were most likely tied to the computer data that Soup was working to de-code. People, even billionaire financiers, just didn't keep a data-base of United States residents' Social Security information in a gym bag lying around on the floor of their penthouse condo-minium.

"I can't give a recommendation until you level with me."

"There's nothing to level with you about. My son is missing. He's a good boy and he wouldn't just disappear like this."

"Flowers?"

"I don't know who killed him, or why. It had to have been a random thing."

"Lolly's suspicions?" I didn't want to let on that I was formu-lating several of my own suspicions.

"Groundless. She may think I've been acting odd, but she doesn't know me well. We've only been married less than a year."

"You have several options," I said carefully. "The local police, the sheriff's office, the SBI—State Bureau of Investigation, private investigators . . . or all of the above. I can't really say until I see the note, talk to some people, and get a line on who may have taken him. If, in fact, it really was a kidnapping. But generally speaking, you must notify the law in a situation like this. And since it's you we're talking about, I can pretty much guarantee the Feds will jump in. It's very simple to make a case that the kidnapping of your son could have national consequences, especially since he's also an employee of your firm."

"Whatever your rate is, I'll pay it. I'm a smart enough man to know when I need outside help, and this is one of those times."

"Problem is," I said, "I only work for the good guys. And, while I am sorry that your son appears to be missing, I'm not so sure that you're the good guy in this scenario. I think you're giving me a *Reader's Digest* condensed version of the story."

He slammed something down, a closed fist perhaps, and the hollow thud carried through the phone line. "Look, damn it! There is no story!"

I didn't reply.

He blew out an agitated sigh. "What if I just hire you to get my son back? Everything else is inconsequential at this point. Whatever it takes. Just get him back."

"My rate is probably much more than you suspect, but I imagine that you probably don't care."

"I don't."

I thought about it briefly, and decided that helping the man I was investigating could work to my advantage. Plus, it never hurt to get paid for what you were already doing anyway.

"Okay. I will try to help you get your son back and I'll take your money for doing so. But you need to understand that just because you're paying my salary for the time being doesn't mean that I'll ignore whatever I uncover. Aside from that, if you truly want Jared back, alive, it would further your cause to tell me everything you know."

"I'll come to your place," he said quickly. "The Block, is it?"

"Yes. Who else knows about this?"

"The housekeeper, my secretary who took the call, me, you. Lolly doesn't know. She's out of town at a health spa and we're playing telephone tag. I don't want to leave it on a message."

"Right, better to wait until she comes home. Meanwhile, call the secretary and tell her it was all a mistake, that Jared's fine. We don't want her gossiping."

"Good point. I'll do it now," he agreed.

"The housekeeper," I said. "Tell her not to answer the phones, keep the doors locked. Don't talk to anyone."

"Already did that."

"Good. See you shortly," I told him. "And bring the note."

Chesterfield disconnected.

Cracker nuzzled my legs, wanting attention. I scratched the back of his neck and looked at Ox, who had heard my end of the conversation.

He grinned. "Some retirement. You take another job?"

"Affirmative. I'm officially employed again."

"Are you working for Bill's friend, the one that thought Chesterfield was double-dipping?"

"No," I told him. "I'm working for Chesterfield."

Now I had Ox's full attention. He motioned for me to tell him the rest.

"His son is missing, and Chesterfield thinks the boy has been kidnapped. Chesterfield's accountant was murdered yesterday, but local police theorize that it was a simple carjacking gone bad. And Soup is still trying to decode the rest of the data on that flash drive I told you about."

"Getting in deeper and deeper, Barnes." Ox displayed a row of perfectly straight, white teeth. "And I thought you retired people just played shuffleboard all day."

"I may need you," I said, ignoring his sarcasm.

"Yeah, I think you may," he agreed and moved down the bar to collect money from a couple who were standing and ready to leave.

When Chesterfield arrived, I was still at the bar keeping company with Cracker. The dog sniffed the tassels on his leather loafers and waited for a return greeting. After receiving an absent-minded pat on the head, he sighed loudly and lay down by my bar stool. Chesterfield asked Ox for a glass of ice water.

"Interesting place you've got here," he observed. "Nice view."

"Thanks."

He laid the note on the bar. It was a basic one-paragraph note, printed in black ink on a plain white piece of paper. It was probably done with a computer and some type of ink-jet printer. It read: "We've got your son. If you want to see him ever again, do not contact any authorities. If you do, he will be shot. You will receive further instructions in a day or two."

The term "we" indicated there was more than one person involved. But it was not much to go on and didn't say what the kidnappers wanted in exchange for the boy. Without being asked, Ox handed me a plastic Ziploc freezer bag. Using a paper napkin, I picked the page up and slid it into the Baggie before sealing the top. There probably weren't any usable prints or fibers, but it was best to be sure. If we did bring in the local or state cops, they'd be a little miffed at me for tampering with evidence. But Chesterfield, the distraught father, would take the rap and nobody would think twice about it.

"Any contact from them yet?" I asked.

"No. Nothing."

"You tell anyone?"

"No." His features were tight, drawn. He was well composed, but it was obvious that he hadn't gotten any sleep since the news about Flowers.

"Any idea what it's about? Or who took him?"

"None. I've thought about it and I'm drawing an absolute blank."

We were rapidly approaching an impasse. He wasn't being helpful, but he appeared to be telling the truth. So far.

"Let's talk about Flowers."

He took a deep breath before answering. "He called me from the main office in New York about a week ago. Said that he'd found some problems with a certain category of new accounts and that he needed to talk with me immediately. In person." Chesterfield's hands rested on the bar and he stared at the river as he spoke. His hands were wide and capable, the nails clean and perfectly trimmed. The humidity caused a heavy layer of condensation to form on both of our mugs, but a steady breeze circulated the air enough to keep us comfortable.

From where we sat, we had a view of the Cape Fear Memorial Bridge. Although most vessels easily cleared the arch, it was a drawbridge and opened when needed. As though stretching after a nap, the metal giant slowly rose into the sky to let a cargo ship sail through. I always enjoy driving over the drawbridge in my sedan. Whenever I return from an out-of-town trip and hear the bridge's segments whine and clack beneath my tires in greeting, it's like being welcomed home.

"Eddie said not to mention anything to anybody, because someone inside the company could be involved. He was most certain of that. He didn't go into details over the phone and after he flew in from New York, we didn't have a chance to talk before he was killed. He came straight to the new branch office from the airport, but I was in a meeting so he went to pick up lunch and didn't come back. That's it. That's all I know." His head shook from side to side, disbelieving the reality that he'd found himself faced with.

"You have no idea what type of problem he found?"

"None," Chesterfield said, focusing his gaze on me. "I just know it was something terribly serious and it involved my firm.

Eddie wouldn't make a big deal over nothing. For him to want to speak to me in person, well, I can't even imagine what the problem was."

"Did you tell this to the cops?"

"Of course not. I don't want a bunch of investigators pushing their noses around in Chesterfield Financial's business. I can launch an internal audit, quietly. If and when I find anything out that could be relevant to Flowers' death, I'll pass it on." He reminded me of me. He preferred to do things his own way.

"Did he say which category of new accounts was involved?"

"The SIPAs. We just recently got on the list of brokerage firms approved to handle them."

Bingo! I thought silently.

"The SIPAs are not moneymakers for the firm," he continued. "But the idea is young people will put their Social Security accounts with us and then use us for their traditional brokerage needs as well. To us, the SIPA business is really just a source for obtaining new clients."

"Did Flowers leave you with a computer printout or a report of some type? A computer disk or USB memory stick, perhaps?"

"No, nothing. He brought something with him because the secretary remembers seeing him carrying his briefcase when he left to pick up lunch. But the police said there was nothing found in the rental car. And his briefcase was not at the office."

"Who found him?"

"A fellow on a Harley pulled into the parking space next to Eddie's car, saw him slumped over the wheel, and dialed nine-one-one."

I thought a little bit, swallowed some beer, then thought a little bit more.

"Do you work out?"

The question took him by surprise. "Come again?"

"You look like you're in pretty good shape," I said. "I was just wondering if you work out at a gym somewhere. Play tennis or racquetball, maybe?" I remembered the aerobics class schedule that was in the gym bag and wondered whose it was.

"Not lately. We've got a family membership at the Kingsport Health Club, but I haven't even been once, I've been so busy with Jared and the new branch office. I think Lolly goes a few times a week. And Jared plays some racquetball."

"Hmm," I said. Was he purposely not telling me about the flash drive, or did he really not know about it? I wondered if the original was still resting in the gym bag in Chesterfield's coat closet. And if not, who had it? Perhaps I should have just taken the original when I first found it.

"When I was tailing you last week, I noticed that you had some interesting lunch meetings." I changed tacks again, wanting to keep him slightly off balance. Maybe he'd let something slip.

"You were tailing me? I never noticed anyone following me," he said, tilting his head to examine me a bit more closely.

"Yeah, well. That's sort of the idea," I told him. "The meetings? The restaurants where you didn't eat? The dry cleaner where you didn't pick up laundry? Who were you meeting and what was it about?"

"That's a personal matter, Jersey."

"And retrieving your son isn't? If I'm going to work for you, there are no boundaries between personal and business. I'm not a nosy person. If I ask something, it's because I need to know."

"Who I met at the restaurants and the dry cleaner has no relevance to my son. That is what we're talking about, right? Getting my son back?"

I remained silent. If I was going to work when I was supposed to be retired, I was going to do it my own way. Come to think of it, before retirement I'd always done things my own way.

Chesterfield fidgeted with his water glass, spinning it in tiny circles on the counter. Ox respectfully kept his distance while he followed our conversation. We caught each other's eye, and he discreetly shrugged a shoulder. He couldn't tell if Chesterfield was leveling with me or not.

"Your choice," I said. "You want my help, you talk to me."

"All right, Jersey, I'll tell you, even though it's nothing to do with Jared." Chesterfield calmly drank water. "The building that Lolly and I are living in until we return to New York?" he began with the explaining type of question that wasn't really a question.

"The Bellington Complex, I believe it's called," I said. "Eight stories of luxury apartments, six units per floor. Two penthouse suites on the top floor—one of which you are occupying. Grossed a lease income of just slightly over one-point-four million last year."

His eyebrows rose in surprise for a moment and then he nodded his head in affirmation. He'd underestimated me, just as I'd originally underestimated him.

"I, or rather the company bought it just over a year ago, because I knew we'd be opening a branch office to serve the Carolinas. Buying it solved the problem of where we'd live while I trained Jared, plus offer a bit of a tax shelter," he explained.

I nodded.

"There's a married couple, on-site property managers. Came with the building and live on the first floor. They get a modest salary, a free apartment, and came with a strong recommendation. I kept them on when we bought." He drank some more water and asked Ox for a refill. "Anyway, a few weeks back, I was teaching Jared how to read operating financials and profit-and-loss statements. I pulled copies from the manager's files—there's an office on the first floor, just off the lobby—and figured it would make a good learning lesson for Jared. We were sitting at the kitchen table, plowing through the numbers when he found a problem."

"Jared found it?"

"Yes," Chesterfield said with obvious pride. "The student found something the teacher overlooked."

Ox set a fresh glass of ice water in front of Chesterfield and a Guinness draught in front of me and moved silently away. We both drank. Below me, Cracker yawned, rolled over on his back, and stayed that way. Spread-eagle, with all four limbs sticking out, and the flap of his snout hanging away from his teeth, he resembled fresh roadkill. Although it didn't look comfortable, it worked for Cracker because it was one of his favorite sleeping positions. If it weren't for the snoring that immediately began filtering through his nose, arriving patrons probably would have thought the dog was dead, which wouldn't have been good for business.

"Bottom line is that this couple embezzled nearly fifty thousand dollars from me during the year I've owned the building. They did it by deducting for maintenance and repairs that were never done. They also recorded rental income on two units as less than they actually collected. Both tenants always paid in cash. They were told, if they paid in cash, they'd get discounted rent."

"And you think this is totally irrelevant to the kidnapping?" I asked. "How do you know they're not behind it?"

"Couple's name is Hertz. Melinda and Gary Hertz. They found out I was on to them and guessed correctly that I'd press charges. They skipped town, and after I did a thorough check on them, I found out that they had a past record. But it was all small-time stuff. She was busted for credit-card theft in 'eighty-four and they were both implicated in embezzlement charges, another residential complex, in 'ninety-eight. They're not kidnappers. They're small-time screwups whom I hope to locate and put in jail."

"Back to my original question," I said. "What about the lunch meetings? The dry cleaner?"

"I was doing some legwork. The owner of one of the restaurants is a tenant at the tower. He's one that has been paying two hundred and twenty dollars a month more than what was reflected in the books. In cash. The other restaurant you saw me enter was another tenant. He never had any water problems from a busted water heater in the unit above him. But the financials reflected forty-four hundred dollars worth of drywall repair and carpet cleaning."

"And the dry cleaner?"

"Same thing. Fellow I met with there is also a tenant. He owns three dry cleaning stores and two liquor stores. Stays busy and often spends the night with his ex-wife, who got the house but still loves him. He's not home much, but he definitely did not need a refrigerator and microwave replaced due to a supposed power surge. Said his appliances work just fine."

"Why'd he leave out the back door?"

"Back door?"

"The two of you chatted, you left, he disappeared out the rear of the store."

"I don't know. He said he had to collect deposits from the liquor stores. I guess he parks behind the building and he happened to leave the same time I did."

It made sense and would be easy to verify. I had no reason, at least for the time being, not to believe him.

"I'm curious as to why you didn't just hire a private investigator to do the legwork for you. You're a pretty busy man, I'd imagine. Why bother wasting your time tracking down amateur thieves?"

"If it got out that someone embezzled from Samuel Chesterfield . . . well, it would be bad PR. We manage a lot of people's money. How would it look if those people find out that we can't even manage our own money?"

"You're not invincible. Nobody is. Investors would understand."

"I have written four books, all bestsellers," he said. "The most recent, due to hit the shelves next month, is about real estate investment. How to find the best deals, create tax advantages. How to implement a system of checks and balances so you don't get ripped off by management companies."

"Oh." I swapped my beer for a glass of water and drank. That wouldn't have looked very good. Chesterfield's new financial advice bestseller on the shelves at the same time the media reports that he'd had fifty grand embezzled on an apartment building deal.

Cracker woke himself up with a particularly loud snore. Startled, he flipped to his belly and jumped clumsily to his feet. He surveyed his surroundings and then shook himself off. Acting like scaring yourself awake was no big deal, he ambled off in search of a treat from a customer. If he didn't get one, Ox would probably give him a Milk-Bone from a jar stashed behind the bar.

"Tell me," I said to Chesterfield, "why are you so sure that your managers, the Hertzes, don't know anything about your missing boy?"

"Because they're just petty thieves. They aren't smart enough to pull something like this off. Plus, whatever Flowers found got him killed. I don't really believe it was a random carjacking gone bad. The Hertzes couldn't be involved with an internal problem at my company. Jared disappearing the day after Flowers was murdered is not a coincidence."

"I agree," I told him. "I understand you have a daughter, too? She still living in Fort Worth?"

"Yes, married and still in Fort Worth. I told her I'd received some threats and was putting a bodyguard on her just to be on the safe side. I hired two, actually, to shadow her until I tell them to quit."

"Good thinking," I said. "What's the husband do?"

"He's a cop, believe it or not. I guess you can't control who your kids fall in love with."

"Nope."

"I just want you to find my son, Jersey," he said, looking into my face. "Please help me find him."

He handed me a retainer check in the amount of twenty thousand dollars and laid a one-dollar bill on the counter as a tip. Ox looked from my check to his dollar bill with a raised eyebrow. I shrugged my shoulders at the injustice and the corners of his mouth twitched with amusement. He knew that it always evened out in the end between us.

"You'll want to come to the penthouse, then?" Chesterfield asked.

"Yes."

He drove the Lexus as I followed him to the Bellington Complex.

EIGHT

My second search of the condo, the one with Chesterfield there, didn't reveal anything more than I found the first time. The gym bag and USB flash drive were gone, though. They seemed to have disappeared along with Jared.

According to Chesterfield, the note had been left on the kitchen counter and nothing was missing. Jared hadn't taken a suitcase or any of his personal belongings, and there were no signs of struggle. It looked as though Jared left either of his own volition, or at gunpoint. If he left preceding the barrel of a gun, it made sense that he probably knew his assailants since there was no forced entry.

Background checks on Eddie Flowers, Gary and Melinda Hertz, Jared, and his sister and her husband didn't tell me much more than I already knew. I also ran checks on Lolly and Samuel Chesterfield, and again, didn't find anything useful.

It wasn't too surprising that, according to tax records, Chesterfield owned real estate worth a combined thirty-six million dollars. His personal net worth was estimated to be somewhere in the neighborhood of seven hundred and fifty million. There were several buildings purchased in the name of his company, including the Bellington Complex, and I hadn't bothered to look up the estimated value of Chesterfield Financial.

The thought of having so much money boggled my brain. I couldn't even imagine possessing that kind of wealth. How much of it were the kidnappers going to ask for, or was it something other than money that they wanted? For that matter, did the kidnappers exist? It was entirely possible that Jared staged his own disappearance.

Although the note instructed not to bring in any uniforms, it was time to do so and I explained why to Chesterfield. Ninety-five-plus percent of the time, ransom notes instructing not to bring in the authorities were an empty threat. Obviously, if the kidnappers murdered Jared, they'd lose their bargaining power. Chesterfield agreed.

I began by notifying Dirk, who had been promoted to lieutenant in charge of investigative services. The title sounded nice, but he was simply one of the Wilmington Police Department's high-paid detectives. Within hours, the New Hanover County Sheriff's Department and the State Bureau of Investigation were involved. This type of news traveled fast and it was just a matter of time before the Feds were notified. Everyone in law enforcement would want a piece of the action and a piece of the potential glory. A power struggle was already brewing between the local and the state boys, and when the Feds appeared, it could very well turn into a circus.

The ransom note I'd collected had already passed through several pairs of hands and been examined by two different crime labs. Chesterfield's penthouse suite had been thoroughly swept for prints and hair and fiber samples. Unmatched hair and fiber samples would be held as evidence to match with the felons', if they were ever caught. Residents of the building, delivery people, maintenance workers, and surrounding area neighbors were being questioned. A list of anyone who had anything to do with Jared, from his barber to his physician, was being compiled for scrutiny and questioning. It was the typical information-gathering effort that would fuel the upcoming plan of action.

My plan of action was to stay out of everyone's way and pursue my own leads. Unfortunately, I didn't have any at the moment.

It was a sun-drenched Wednesday afternoon and the Fahrenheit reading threatened to move uncomfortably high. I was on my way to pick up groceries and the chilled air pumping through my car's vents felt delightfully good on my skin. Later, after I reloaded my and Spud's refrigerators, I would spend the rest of the afternoon digging. But my plan for the evening entailed a bottle of creamy chardonnay and a bag of Chinese takeout. Bill was back from Vegas and would meet me at the marina, along with the copper thong he'd managed to appropriate. We'd go for a sunset cruise before anchoring in the secluded cove I'd discovered months earlier, and we'd spend the night on the gently rolling boat, doing our own rocking above deck.

NINE

I'd showered and changed after jogging six, maybe seven miles. It was more than I usually ran, and the last mile had tested my willpower. Running was cleansing, though, and erased the clutter from my mind. Ox called on the spirits to meditate; I ran.

Attempts to keep news of the Chesterfield kidnapping from the media were futile, and once a whiff got out, the story spread like raging wildfires. It was the lead story on the three major networks. It hit the Associated Press wire, and was the front-page centerpiece for most dailies. Lolly had resurfaced after spending a few days at a health spa and handled all the media attention like a seasoned pro, with just the right mix of vulnerability and determination to help her husband. Under different circumstances, she would have enjoyed the incessant cameras pointed in her direction. Either she was maturing into the enviable position of Chesterfield's new wife, or the years of modeling had paid off. Maybe both.

The emerging investigation, which to be politically correct was a coordinated effort between all the authorities, was getting nowhere fast. To be truthful, it resembled a Ringling Bros. and Barnum & Bailey circus troupe in training for a new season. Everyone knew what their individual job was and they could do it well. But as a group they were clumsy, bumped into each other, and hadn't yet slipped into a comfortable rhythm or chain of command.

I poured milk into a bowl of Frosted Flakes and joined Spud at the kitchen table. He slurped a bottle of chocolate Yoo-hoo between bites of cold leftover Domino's pizza. Cracker had positioned himself under the table and utilized Spud's slippered feet as a pillow. Without bothering to lift his head, he sniffed the air, eternally hopeful for a fallen crumb.

"Anything new with the missing boy?" Spud said over the top of the sports section.

"No, but something should be happening soon."

Although the kidnapping had just occurred yesterday morning, a lack of communication from the perpetrators had me puzzled. It certainly had to be wearing on Samuel Chesterfield. His condominium was outfitted with an incoming-call tracing device, as well as a recorder and two round-the-clock suits, not to mention twenty-four-hour perimeter security. The tracing and recording equipment was carried in a package about the size of a large suitcase and had been spread out in Chesterfield's living room. The Feds discovered the earpieces I'd planted, as well as my phone tap on the main line. I claimed to know nothing about either one, even though I would have liked to get the equipment back. It was an oversight on my part to have not retrieved them sooner. Actually, it was plain stupid of me. I prayed that retirement hadn't already soothed my brain in to a state of lethargy.

"Well, I gotta run," Spud said, standing up and drawing an annoyed look from Cracker, who'd lost his human pillow. "Bobby's picking me up downstairs. We're headed to the barber for a trim."

It had rained overnight, heavily, reminding me of Spud's car insurance plan. "Whose car are you taking?"

"His. Unless we take mine," Spud said. After I shot him a questioning look, he added, "For crying out loud. That sinking the car thing was all just a joke."

I didn't have time to quiz him further because Soup paged me. While I returned the page, Spud traded his bedroom shoes for sandals, put on a NOT OVER THE HILL JUST ENJOYING THE TOP baseball cap, and ambled out with a redwood walking cane leading the way. Shaped like an upside-down female leg, its handle was a slender arched foot.

Soup answered on the first ring without his traditional greeting. "Jersey, you've got some serious shit here."

I forgot about Spud and his quest to sink the Chrysler. "Go on."

"The additional data tagged to each taxpayer field? It's part of a virus. Code diverting exactly one thousand dollars of the initial SIPA deposits from Uncle Sam into another pocket. Probably an account established out of the country, Swiss maybe."

"Wow." The spoonful of cereal stopped midway to my mouth as my mind processed that tidbit of information. Since Americans choosing SIPAs could open their account only at the beginning of each quarter, the sum of three months' worth of initial deposits could amount to a lot of money.

Talking fast, Soup agreed with my assessment. "Exactly. At first I thought it might have been done by a blue hat. You know, someone hired to bug and test a new system before its launch? But this thing is for real. It has an outrageously elaborate packet sniffer—"

"Soup, please." I'd never comprehend all the technical jargon if I waited for an explanation of how he did it. "Just give me the bottom line."

"Overnight, the bad guys will skim a big chunk of change from new SIPAs coming into Chesterfield Financial," Soup said. "My guess is they'll skip town before the individual statements arrive by mail, so nobody will even realize that their balance is off, unless the SIPAs are Internet-enabled."

"They're not," I told him. I'd done some research and quizzed Chesterfield on the entire process. "Not at first anyway. SIPA applications are processed as they come in, but the money isn't transferred from Uncle Sam to the individual brokerage accounts until the first day of each quarter. Then, all verifications of transactions are by mail. The government bean counters decided that SIPAs can't be accessed via the Internet until next year. That's to ensure the program is operating smoothly before they add a new element."

"Deposits are only made once a quarter?"

"To cut administrative costs," I said. "Same with the paper statements." That meant three months' worth of new account applications, multiplied by a thousand dollars each, stolen in one night.

"This is bad freakin' news, isn't it?"

"Worse," I said. "I'm on my way over to your place."

I fed Cracker a breakfast of dry food and threw in a remnant of leftover pizza crust from Spud's plate. He gobbled the crust first, as though it were a morsel of prime rib.

I wanted Ox to hear everything firsthand from Soup because I could use the insight, so I called and told him I'd be by to pick him up in ten minutes. Being his good-natured self, he didn't ask why and cheerfully agreed to go. After pouring my coffee into a travel mug, I pointed the Benz toward Ox's house, leaving my uneaten cereal behind.

Ox and I sat in Soup's efficiency apartment, on opposite ends of a white leather sofa. The place was sparsely furnished, except for an overwhelmingly large flat-screen plasma television, an entertainment center loaded with stereo components that were probably worth more than Soup's vehicle, and loads of computer equipment and electronics that were alien to me.

Like a veteran pilot in a familiar cockpit, Soup sat at a U-shaped table, simultaneously operating the controls of what appeared to be three separate computers. He did so in the well-orchestrated and effortless manner of a concert pianist. The lettered keyboards were his grand piano and the tiny apartment was his Carnegie Hall. Grinning at each other, Ox and I had the same thought: we were the audience witnessing a master at work.

"Only accounts processed through the new Wilmington branch office will be affected," Soup told us, then dropped a bombshell. "Unfortunately, Chesterfield has designated Wilmington to handle all their SIPAs for the eastern half of the country. Say for instance, a SIPA customer walks into a branch office in Pittsburgh, their account is still earmarked for Wilmington processing."

"Even though the Wilmington branch is brand new?"

Soup nodded.

It was astonishing to contemplate a thief stealing so much money from the helm of a computer. Robbing a bank at gunpoint was physical and real. Burglarizing a jewelry store was tangible. Operating a telemarketing scam was comprehensible. But a computer virus that stole money in cyberspace opened the door to limitless possibilities.

"So you've just been waltzing around in Chesterfield Financial's system without so much as a hall pass?" Ox asked.

"Yeah," Soup answered, slurping what appeared to be tomato-with-rice soup from a coffee cup. "You need to tell your Samuel chap that his company has the security of a corner hot dog stand," he said, not taking his eyes from a printed readout that was being sporadically spitted out from the bowels of a computer table. "And that he's got a major problem with the Chesterfield Innovative Technology no-load fund. The manager for that fund is funneling everything through Chicago. Problem is, there's a five-day delay between when the deposits arrive and when they're credited to the fund. But I don't see where the earned interest is going in the meantime."

Crossing his arms over his chest, Ox leaned back and smiled in amazement. "You ever decide to switch sides and get in bed with the bad guys, corporate America had better look out."

I couldn't help but to notice his cut biceps, and mentally scolded myself for being so easily distracted.

Soup spun in the swivel chair to face us and grinned. "The memory storage device you found was actually a test run of Social Insecurity."

"Social what?"

"It's the name of the virus. Social Insecurity. The guy has a sense of humor," Soup said.

"What guy?" I asked.

"The guy or gal who wrote the code. I don't know who, or how many people are actually involved, but whoever wrote the virus is the brains behind it all."

Ox motioned for Soup to continue.

"The database of taxpayer names on the USB flash drive was dummy information. It was developed from a credit bureau database of random names, so the virus could have a test run before it was tried on the real thing. But the fields, coding, and security encryption are identical to Chesterfield's actual client databases." Soup paused to slurp some lumpy liquid from the coffee cup before explaining further.

"Social Insecurity is sitting quietly in Chesterfield's system. Patiently waiting for the first day of the quarter, when it becomes active. The first thing it will do is identify all clients who were processed as new SIPAs. The information is all there, but the accounts have a zero balance until the initial deposit from the government is made.

"On the target day, electronic transfers from Social Security will start flowing through the ACH, or automated clearinghouse system, and credit each individual SIPA account registered with Chesterfield Financial. The Social Insecurity virus will pluck one thousand dollars from every incoming transfer. The bumps, as I call them, are immediately routed to another bank account. And voilà! This guy will go to bed as a poor man and wake up the next day with millions and millions of dollars. He'll be able to check his balance shortly after midnight, to see exactly how rich he is. Those thousand-dollar bumps are going to add up quick."

"How many millions?" I said.

"Well," Soup said, studying the ceiling while he mentally calculated, "all the people that chose a SIPA and chose Chesterfield as their broker. From the eastern half of the country. A grand from each. But based on the applications that have been piling up in Chesterfield's system, assuming a fifty percent closure rate because some who chose a SIPA could have either changed their mind or forgotten to sign and return the authorization form to Uncle Sam . . . somewhere in the neighborhood of fifty million dollars. And that's conservative."

Stunned, I looked at Ox, who sat contemplating it all with a hardened expression. Fifty million dollars was a lot of money.

Even more astounding was that nobody would realize the money was stolen until a month later.

"It would be one of the biggest cybercrimes ever in history, from a dollar standpoint," Soup continued. "Even though the new law went into effect in January, July first is the initial transfer day for SIPA money. Six months' worth of baseball and apple-pie-loving individual marks, waiting in line to be screwed by an opportunistic pickpocket."

"Why only a thousand dollars?" Ox said. "Why not take more on each bump?"

"Good question," Soup said, professorlike. "Because Uncle Sam specified that the minimum initial SIPA transfer must be at least a grand. The majority will be considerably more. But the Social Insecurity creator didn't want to take a chance. If, for example, he set the bump amount at five grand and an initial transfer came in that was only four, it would create an alert. A negative number, kind of like when a check bounces," Soup said.

"Will it work?" I wanted to know.

"Shit yeah, it'll work."

"Can you stop it?"

Soup grinned wickedly. "Of course I can. But I've got another plan."

"What's that?"

"Lemme work on it. I'll let you know." He swiveled back to study lines of text that were scrolling up a monitor. "It's a brilliant virus. Damned brilliant."

"This guy wants to steal money from hardworking Americans," I reminded him.

"I'm not condoning what he wants to do. I'm just saying you've got to recognize that kind of talent."

"You're that kind of talent but you don't steal from innocent individuals," I said. "Just large conglomerates such as airlines."

"Yeah, well," Soup said. "Everyone draws the line somewhere. Anyway, the airline in question owed me two round-trip tickets' worth of frequent flier points."

"Why didn't you just redeem your points?" I said to his back.

"Much faster this way, and no blackout dates."

The jazzy ring tone of my phone sounded just as Ox and I were helping ourselves to a couple bottles of Coors Light at the Block. Although it was only eleven thirty in Wilmington, it was well past noon somewhere.

The caller was Dirk, who said a man claiming to be one of the kidnappers had just phoned the Chesterfields' home line. Samuel Chesterfield was out, but the caller let Lolly speak briefly to her stepson and she felt certain it was Jared's voice. The man told Lolly to have Chesterfield gather two million dollars in cash. Further instructions would come in a few days, he said, and hung up. Unfortunately, Lolly was too shaken and didn't attempt to keep the caller on the line as the agents had instructed, Dirk told me.

Nonetheless, the call was traced to a cell phone in Cincinnati, Ohio, and the phone was traced to a retired nurse. The woman was a victim of wireless fraud, the agents quickly determined. A cell phone had been modified to snatch account numbers from her service provider and the reprogrammed phone could make free, untraceable calls from anywhere in the country.

I'd barely flipped the phone shut when it rang again. Hal, the fourth in Spud's weekly poker game, explained that Spud's car was flooded out in the parking lot of the barbershop. After a pause, he admitted that the Chrysler wasn't only flooded out, according to Spud, but also partially submerged in a pond.

"Why'd he call you?" I asked him.

"Fool said he'd pay me fifty bucks to pull him out. Told me to put some rope in the wife's station wagon and get there quick."

"And?"

"And I told him I'm not a damn towing service. Plus I've gotta get to the internist's office for a doctor appointment. Besides that, I don't think the station wagon could pull a golf cart out of a pond. It's only a V-6 for chrissakes."

Unsure whether I should be angry or amused, I relayed the story to Ox and asked if he thought we'd need a tow truck.

"For sure," he said happily. "C'mon, we'll take your car and I'll drive. This should be fun." I always preferred to drive myself, unless it was Ox doing the driving.

It was nearing lunchtime, and the Block always did a good business between noon and two o'clock. But it would do a good business whether Ox was there or not and the employees could handle things just fine without him.

Hal was at the shopping center when we arrived, playing the role of a curious spectator instead of a concerned friend. The city cops had responded in their image-friendly solid-white cars with quaint blue lettering. But cops were still cops and these two were youngsters with an attitude. Spud wasn't helping matters.

"A witness from the barbershop said that your friend here drove the car straight into the pond," one uniform said.

"Ah, hell," Spud replied. "Bobby can't see too good. He was just trying to park. Ask him"—he pointed to Hal—"he'll tell you it was just an accident."

Hal instinctively took a few steps back to distance himself, showing his palms. "I just got here, you old fool. I ain't no towing service and I ain't no witness, either."

The cop started to question him, but decided to clarify things with my father first. "This is your car, but you say you don't have a driver's license?"

"No shit, Sherlock. That's why I wasn't driving, for crying out loud."

"Spud," I intervened. "Don't be smart-mouthed. Just answer his questions."

"My smart mouth says this stupid piece of scrap should've sunk the whole way, for crying out loud!" he cried, waving his walking cane in the direction of the sunken Chrysler. "The damn thing is gonna have water damage now."

I smiled at the uniforms and calmly asked if there were going to be any charges pressed.

"Guess you can't press charges for stupidity," the partner said.

Bobby produced an insulted look. "Aww, look here," he defended. "I was just doing what I was asked to do. Sink—I mean *park* the car. I can't help it if the pond is in the middle of the parking lot. I thought it was something I could drive right into. I mean, through."

"Excuse me?" the first cop said, taking a closer look at Bobby and then his license. "Are you on medication, sir?"

"He's just confused, Officer," I said, and if looks could slap a man, Spud and Bobby would have had stinging faces. "Bobby has had quite a scare. Now, if you're all finished with these elderly and harmless gentlemen, I'll see that everyone gets home safely. And I'll pay a tow truck to come for the vehicle."

Giving me the once-over, they didn't bother to conceal their skepticism. Even my government enhancements didn't help.

"Lieutenant Dirk Thompson is a good friend," I told them as a last resort. "He'll vouch for me."

The tail end of the Chrysler stuck out of the water, mooning us with its exposed underbelly. The front end was submerged enough to make the front tires invisible, and water crept a third of the way up the two front doors. Ox sat in the driver's seat of my car and, by the expression on his face, was thoroughly enjoying himself. My idiot father and I were his free entertainment for the hour.

Spud opened his mouth and pointed the cane to say something, but I silenced him with a menacing look. He was minus the barbershop trim he'd supposedly come for. Bobby leaned against the brick wall outside the barbershop, soaking wet up to his waist. Nearby, Hal was trying to suppress either indigestion or laughter. Probably laughter.

After some deliberation and a call to Dirk, the uniforms left me to deal with Spud and his partially submerged car. Figuring the show was over, Hal departed the scene, declining to give my father and his driver a ride, as he was running late for his doctor appointment. With a lot of muttering, Spud and Bobby pulled their bodies into the backseat of the Benz. I found an old blanket stashed in the trunk and made Bobby sit on it to keep the leather from getting wet. Ox called a tow truck.

"For crying out loud, Bobby!" Spud turned on his friend the instant we pulled out of the parking lot. "You took your foot off the gas too soon!"

"I did not!" Bobby shouted back at him. "Your stupid car bogged down in the mud the second it hit the pond. I could've put a fifty-pound weight on the gas pedal and the thing wouldn't have sunk all the way!"

"Now I'll have to pay a repair bill," Spud grumbled. "I have a thousand-dollar deductible."

"Don't blame me," Bobby fired back. "I was just trying to do you a favor. Can't help it if you have a front-heavy car."

"Gentlemen," Ox said, like the father on a road trip scolding two siblings in the backseat. "It's just a car. No big deal. Find another way to lose it."

I shot a sideways look at Ox, not believing that he'd just encouraged them to devise another plan. He grinned and I had the strangest desire kiss him. Or punch him.

We'd almost made it back to the Block when my phone played music again.

"You're popular today," Ox said.

"Jersey here," I answered.

"It's Chesterfield. I'm in the Lexus," he said and his voice was strained. "They're following me," he said.

"Who?"

"I don't know. But they're on my tail. They've bumped me once already."

"Where are you?"

He told me. I instructed him not to speed and not to stop, but to drive to the Water Street Restaurant. It was a trendy joint on a one-way street with a sidewalk café, and we were equal distances from it. I told him to pull right up to the curb and get out. I'd be waiting on the front patio. With Ox.

We made it to Water Street before Chesterfield did and Ox instructed Spud and Bobby not to budge from the backseat of the armored Benz.

When Chesterfield arrived with a screech of braking tires, Ox and I were seated at an outdoor table, beneath an opened umbrella. Chesterfield jumped out of the Lexus, leaving it half in the street and half on the sidewalk. A split second later, three men did the same. One of them grabbed Chesterfield by the back of the collar, forcing him to face the other two. The one who had him by the clothes was bald and short and had a gut beneath the suit he wore, but he was built like a tree stump. The other two were young with strong builds and wore jeans and T-shirts covered by blazers. All three were obviously hired muscle. I could see a bulge in the small of the first one's back; he had a weapon tucked into his waistband. My hand rested on the Glock in my shoulder holster, ready to draw.

Another outdoor table held some customers, two women. Sensing trouble but not leaving their drinks behind, they rushed to stand against the door of the restaurant and get away from the disturbance. In one fluid motion, Ox moved behind the stocky man in a suit, the one holding Chesterfield, and gave the guy a chop to the side of the neck. Stump dropped to the ground as though his body suddenly lost its bones. He never had a chance to go for his weapon.

The other two lunged at Ox while a staggered Chesterfield stood between them. With his hands on Chesterfield's shoulders, Ox jammed the heel of his boot into one of the men's knees at the same instant he threw Chesterfield to the side. The would-be attacker buckled and went down, his left leg jutted at an odd angle. The remaining guy threw a roundhouse punch at Ox's jaw. Ox ducked beneath the wide arc of the man's fist, and as he was coming back up, jammed a chop into the man's throat. He lurched but didn't drop, so Ox threw a lightning quick combination at the man's head, ending with a graceful uppercut that landed solidly on the chin. The final impact cracked loudly, sounding like concrete meeting bone.

The thing about watching Ox fight is that you have to watch closely, or you miss it. The entire tangle was over in about three seconds. It began and ended before I had a chance to join in. Not that I was complaining. I'd just gotten a manicure last week, when I thought I was retired.

"I'm feeling a little left out over here," I joked. Ox grinned, but then I saw his eyes narrow and move to a spot over my left shoulder. Reflexively, I squatted and spun to see a wiry-looking fourth man swinging a piece of pipe toward the space that my head had just vacated. I shoved my shoulder into his exposed crotch, then clipped him on the back of the neck with a double fist as the momentum of the pipe carried him around. He dropped to the ground with a moan and curled into a fetal position, clutching his groin.

Ox and I scanned the area to see if there were any more of them. There weren't. The two ladies tentatively returned to their patio table and, sipping their salvaged drinks, took in the scene.

"That's Hertz," Chesterfield said, pointing to the wiry one at my feet. Gary Hertz had been his property manager for the Bellington Complex. The one who'd taken him for fifty grand.

We heard the faint sound of sirens. "Let's roll," I said, assuming that a bystander or server had dialed 911. We all had better things to do with our time than answer questions for the next hour.

Ox tossed a twenty-dollar bill on the women's table telling them, "Drinks on me, ladies. Sorry for the intrusion." He slid behind the wheel of Chesterfield's Lexus, which still idled by the curb. Shakily, Chesterfield climbed into the passenger seat.

I retrieved the pistol, a Para .38, from Stump's waistband. Not wasting time to search the other two, I yanked Hertz to his feet and patted him down. He had a pocketknife and a pair of brass knuckles, both of which I tossed into a nearby trash can. I shoved him into the front seat of the car and ran around to jump in the driver's side. Still on the ground, the other three men were showing some signs of life as we pulled away from the curb, and when we turned the corner, we saw flashing blue lights heading their way.

"Unbelievable," Bobby said excitedly from the backseat. "Just like on TV!"

"Ah, I've seen better," Spud replied.

During the short drive, Hertz slowly came around and his eyes eventually focused on me. Although we were traveling at forty miles an hour, his hand inched toward the door handle.

"I wouldn't do that if I were you," I told him. He watched me pull the Glock from my shoulder holster and pass it back to Spud.

"Keep this on him, would you?" I asked.

"For crying out loud," Spud complained. "Lemme have that other one you picked up. If I have to fire this one, my arm will hurt for a week."

I pulled the .38 from my pocket and passed it over the seat as well. "Take your pick."

Looking pale, Hertz removed his hand from the door and slumped wordlessly in the seat.

"Can I have a gun, too? I'll help watch him," Bobby said.

"No!" Spud and I said in unison.

"Well, get me the hell back to your place, then. These wet pants are beginning to itch. There was some kind of slimy goo in that retention pond."

Ox, Chesterfield, and I sat with Hertz at my kitchen table. Bobby borrowed a pair of my baggy gym pants to replace his wet slacks, and he and Spud were at the Block eating fish sandwiches. Swimming always gave him an appetite, Bobby claimed.

"Tell me again why you and your girls were following Mr. Chesterfield today," I said.

"Can I have a Coke, or something to drink," Hertz said miserably. "I don't feel too good."

"You're going to feel a hell of a lot worse if you don't answer my question."

"We just wanted a key so I can get my stuff out of the apartment. Bastard had the locks changed while Melinda and I was at a movie."

Chesterfield nodded his affirmation. "After I was positive about the financials and knew they were stealing. When they found the locks changed and realized I was onto them, they skipped town. I thought they skipped, anyway."

"Rich asshole prick," Hertz spat out, eyes looking bright and jumpy.

"You sure talk a tough game," Ox said.

"Touch me again and I'll have you all arrested."

Ox laughed, an amused sound that was sinister at the same time. If I was Hertz and on the receiving end of that laugh, I'd have been shaking scared. Stupidly, Hertz believed that he had rights in this situation. I grabbed Hertz's hand, twisted it in a half-spiral, and pressed on a nerve at the back of his wrist. He winced with the excruciating pain and discovered that trying to move made it much worse.

"Lose the attitude," I told him calmly, "or you're going to make me angry."

I didn't let go of his hand, just waited.

"Look," he forced out between gritted teeth. "I just wanted him to let me into my unit. I got stuff in there. It's mine."

"Yeah?" I released his hand. He pulled it to his chest and cradled it there protectively. "Like the cash you embezzled?"

His eyes darted to Chesterfield and back telling me I'd guessed correctly. There was cash somewhere in the apartment. Chesterfield frowned when I asked what he wanted to do with his ex-manager. Most likely, he wanted to press charges but didn't want the negative publicity just as his book on real estate investment savvy was hitting the nonfiction market.

"Maybe we should check the apartment," Ox suggested. "Might find something interesting in there."

"I already went through it," Chesterfield said. "Nothing there except furniture and clothes. A television. A billiard table. I've called the Salvation Army to pick it all up."

"Let's take a look anyway," I said, trusting Ox's instincts. I cuffed Hertz, just to keep him from being annoying, and drove the three of us to the Bellington Complex. Chesterfield followed in his Lexus.

Looking very much like the keen Indian he was with the commanding presence of the colonel he used to be, Ox stood in the middle of the place and took a cursory look around. He nodded to himself and began a search by checking the cabinets beneath a built-in entertainment center. He tapped on the rear panels, checking for hollow spots in the wall. He removed several videos from their cases and examined them. Then he hit the eject button on the VCR. A tape slid out, and after examining it, Ox pulled a stack of bills from inside the hollow plastic shell. He smiled, slowly and without humor. If I were Hertz, I'd have started praying to whichever god I worshipped.

"Ah, screw you all," Hertz said with venom. Swiftly, Chesterfield moved in and punched him in the gut. It was a well-placed, solid punch that knocked the breath out of Hertz. He doubled over awkwardly, hands still cuffed behind him.

Ox's eyebrows arched up in surprise. "Nice punch."

"Thank you," Chesterfield said, shaking out his hand.

I thumbed through the pile of bills. They were hundreds and there were a lot of them. I passed the stack to Chesterfield. "That's a piece of what he owes you, anyway."

After a beat, Chesterfield folded the cash in half and pocketed it.

Ox methodically resumed his exploration of the apartment and ended up in the kitchen. He stood in the center of it for a few minutes, dark-skinned arms folded across his broad chest, eyes closed. If Chesterfield thought it was odd behavior, he didn't say so. The only noise came from Hertz. He still sucked air in an attempt to regain his breath.

Ox moved to the refrigerator and rummaged through its contents. He did the same with the freezer. Then he squatted and removed a black panel at the bottom of the unit. He slid out a wide tray that was designed to catch dripping condensation and both Chesterfield and I moved forward to look at the contents it held. Two clear plastic Tupperware containers were packed with miniature baggies of white powder, and several baggies of white sparkly rocks the size of small marbles.

"Cocaine, I'd think," Ox said. "Maybe some speed cut in."

Hertz slumped to the kitchen floor with realized defeat.

"What do you know about the children?" I demanded, using my foot to lift Hertz's head and make him look at me.

Confusion wrinkled his forehead. "What?"

"The Chesterfield kids. A boy and a girl," I said, using the toe of my boot to keep pressure on the nerve just beneath the soft spot in the underside of his chin. I'd included both of Chesterfield's kids, just in case Hertz had plans for the girl, too.

"I don't know what you're talking about." A fine layer of sweat popped out from his pale skin, but he appeared to be genuinely baffled. "I seen on the news about that Jared kid missing. But I don't know nothing about it, I swear."

I pressed harder against the spot between his chin and Adam's apple, putting my weight into it, and Hertz yelped in pain.

"I'm supposed to be retired and on my boat, but instead I'm here looking at your scrawny ass," I said. "On top of that, I've had a really long morning, and you're delaying my lunch."

His eyes were squeezed shut and he mumbled something incoherent. When he heard the slide action from my Glock as a round slid into the chamber, a wet spot appeared on the front of his jeans and urine slowly spread to make a puddle on the kitchen floor. Luckily for Chesterfield, his ex-manager's kitchen floor was ceramic tile and would be easy to clean.

"I don't know what you're talking about," Hertz repeated, crying.

I looked at Ox. Ox said with surety, "He doesn't."

They were two pieces of street scum, but the Hertz couple wasn't involved with the kidnapping. I called Dirk and he arrived fifteen minutes later with some boys from narcotics in tow. Satisfied that Gary Hertz was going to jail on drug-trafficking charges, Chesterfield kept the matter of the embezzlement to himself. A judge was called to issue a warrant for the arrest of Melinda Hertz.

Chesterfield thanked us, shook Ox's hand with unconcealed awe, and offered him a wad of cash as payment for his help. Ox declined. Anyone else would have taken the money and justified it as a finder's fee. Heck, I'd have taken it. After pumping his hand a second time, Chesterfield headed up to his penthouse.

Ox and I returned to the Block and ate an early dinner of fried catfish with homemade slaw that was sweetened with chunks of fresh pineapple, and chased the meal down with a couple of Yuengling lagers.

"You've got to find the kid soon, Jersey." He said exactly what I was already thinking. "July first is only eleven days away. SIPA transfer day."

I wasn't yet sure how it all tied in together, but I agreed with him. I had to figure out where Jared was being held and why. Were the abductors motivated by greed, revenge, or something else altogether? And would I get to Chesterfield's son in time?

Studying Ox's profile, soaking up his nearness, breathing in his masculine scent . . . something like gratitude—but more—washed through me.

Ox turned to look into my eyes. "What's on your mind, Barnes?"

"I'm glad we're working together one more time. I haven't changed my mind about retiring, but it makes me sad to think that we won't have any more adventures together."

Thumb at my temple, his hand caressed my face in a move that ended before I had a chance to fully enjoy it. "I have a feeling that there will be many more adventures in your life," he said.

I thought about that, unsure exactly what he meant. "Well anyway, I know I've told you several times before, but I really missed you all those years since basic training. I'm glad you're back in my life."

After a beat he said softly, "I'm glad, too."

"We're very good together," I thought aloud.

He turned my hand over, traced his fingers lightly against my palm. "Yes."

We drank another beer and watched a bevy of boats glide effortlessly up the Cape Fear River.

TEN

A week had passed since Jared's disappearance and, like a spent hurricane-force storm, the initial media buzz had weakened to lingering gale-force gusts of wind.

The "coordinated effort" of authorities hadn't produced any solid leads and Lolly told me that having an agent in her home twenty-four hours a day was beginning to get old. When I suggested that she play the good wife and keep the uniforms supplied with sandwiches and soft drinks, she rolled her enormous eyes with what may have been defeat or acceptance. It struck me that she seemed more concerned about the disruption in her life than her missing stepson, but I chalked it up to selfishness. She hadn't been ready to become a stepmother when she married Chesterfield and the children were just part of the package. For that matter, both his children were adults so he obviously hadn't chosen Lolly for her maternal instincts.

A grand-opening celebration for Chesterfield Financial's newest branch office had been scheduled for months and was going to happen as planned, tonight. Under the circumstances, Chesterfield wanted to cancel or postpone the bash, but the Feds counseled him not to. The evening might produce a lead, they said, and he should publicly continue his normal routine to show he wasn't intimidated. One criminal profiler, a psychologist by trade, convinced some of the higher-ups that the kidnappers might make an appearance. I wasn't so sure, but Ox and I decided to go anyway, with our dates in tow. Bill said he wouldn't have missed the opportunity to schmooze with celebs for anything, and Ox's date, Mindy, was simply along to stargaze. It was common for Ox to produce a date for special events, but strangely, a woman was rarely seen on his arm more than once. He immensely enjoyed female company, he'd told me once, but had zero desire for a relationship. A perfect complement to Ox, Mindy was longish and beautiful and thrilled to be out with him. But like the rest of his dates, I imagined that I probably wouldn't see her again. Still, a prick of jealousy flash-fired through my head when I saw them laughing together. I shook it off, thinking that retirement was messing with my head.

The party would be power-packed with politicians and Fortune 500 executives, and giant decorated tents were strategically positioned around gourmet food and open bars to accommodate them. To promote an image of hip sophistication, Chesterfield's PR people ensured that some prominent actors and musicians were in attendance to offset the predictably dull suits. The asphalt parking lot and surrounding areas had been transformed into a glitzy showplace and live entertainment was already gearing up in advance of people's arrival. There were even horse-drawn carriages waiting on standby for those who desired a historic downtown tour.

When I quizzed him about the party, Chesterfield explained that the expense of his trademark grand openings was well worth the media exposure and additional business from an upper class of investors. When people had millions to invest, they used Chesterfield Financial.

It was not quite seven o'clock, but the energy level was already palpable. Although only a few guests had arrived, hired security roamed the perimeter and federal and state agents were methodically spread out like sprinkler heads on a golf course, covering the entire area and ready to spring into action. Surrounding everyone, like ants searching for a grain of sugar, media swarmed purposefully through the tents and the office building, armed with cameras and digital recorders. Chesterfield had welcomed them to the party, despite the fact that half were probably there to rehash the kidnapping on the eleven o'clock news. The other half came with hopes of snatching celebrity photographs and interviews. I figured the latter half was way too early since the fashionably late wouldn't dare be seen before eight or nine o'clock.

In honor of the occasion, I did a full makeup application and wore one of my favorite Argentovivo satin bodices beneath a royal-blue cocktail dress and finished the look with a pair of spiky Italian heels. The knee-length dress had a sunburst of tiny rhinestones, which began at my waist and radiated upward to a scooped neckline. Upon seeing me, Bill said he had a desire to swing from a jungle vine and let out a Tarzan yell. The only bad part about my outfit was the Sig Sauer strapped to the inside of my left thigh. Although the calfskin holster was silky smooth, its buckle rubbed my other leg with each step and was irritating. I'd have preferred the Glock, but then I'd be itchy *and* walking bowlegged.

"What say we go find a copy room inside the building and rendezvous on top of the Xerox?" Bill said.

"Sorry, no hanky-panky right now because I'm working a case.

Sort of. But hypothetically, would we make single or double-sided copies?"

"The possibilities are endless."

"Hmmm," I said. "Let's wait awhile and see where the night leads. Anyway, didn't you want to meet Jennifer Lopez? She's in town filming a movie and rumor has it she'll be here."

"I hope she shows," Bill said, "but I'll bet she won't consider joining me in the copy room." His fingertips brushed the length of my exposed back, sending shock waves all the way to my toes. "You, on the other hand, might decide to give it a try."

A guest who must have been somebody arrived, because a swarm of media encircled her. As I stared into the mesmerizing show of camera flashes, an epiphany forced its way into my consciousness. Bill and I never talked about anything that really mattered. And then it hit me that I didn't *want* to share thoughts and dreams with him. Regardless of how wonderful he was, I'd be crazy to marry the other half of such a shallow relationship. On the other hand, maybe that's what marriage was all about. Progressing from the exuberantly sexual and carefree phase of the relationship to the intimate and trustworthy phase. It sounded a lot like work.

"What?" he said, staring at me.

Recovering, I smiled. "Nothing. Let's circulate and enjoy the party. Isn't that Lolly over there?"

Following the direction of my gaze, Bill strode off to mingle, saying that we'd have to make sure the automatic stapling device didn't puncture anything important should we go through with the Xerox plan. I watched his butt with appreciation as he disappeared, wondering how long it would take before Bill demanded more from me, such as an answer to his pesky proposal.

"Stapling device?" Ox said, standing beside me. I hadn't known he was there, and smiled at his stealthiness. He wore solid black jeans, a black silk T-shirt, black blazer, and black ostrich-skin boots.

The few women in our immediate area openly stared at him and a guy with a camera did a double take before consulting a list to determine whether or not he should be snapping shots of Ox. Walking up behind him, Mindy possessively took his arm.

"On the copier," I answered, smiling pleasantly at Mindy.

"This one is adventurous," Ox mused. "I'll give him that."

I looked at Ox, into deep mahogany eyes that danced with specks of green, and sighed heavily. "I'm not sure I can marry him, though."

"Yes, I know."

"Bill asked you to marry him?" Mindy said, squeezing Ox's arm.

I nodded. "Several times," Ox answered for me.

"Oooh, how exciting," she bubbled before her attention was caught by Kenny Rogers strolling through the tent. "I'll be right back!" She stretched on her toes to give Ox a cheek kiss and disappeared.

Ox turned the cheek to me so I could get a better look. "Lipstick?"

"Yeah," I said, wiping it off with a cocktail napkin.

"Why are you worried about Bill all of a sudden?" Ox said. "Didn't he first propose to you several months ago?"

"I don't know why," I said miserably. "Maybe because now that I'm retired—sort of—I'm supposed to do something more with my personal life. Bill is great but the wedding bliss thing sounds like an oxymoron. Why didn't I break it off the second he brought up the 'M' word?"

Ox reached out to untangle an errant strand of windblown hair that had tangled in my diamond stud earring. The brief touch of his fingers on my earlobe felt electric. "Because you convinced yourself that the formula might work once you retired. And because you were too busy to bother with finding another boy toy."

I punched him in the arm, harder than necessary to make my point.

"You want a quart bottle of beer to go with that clingy little dress and right hook?"

I would have punched him again but realized it wasn't the proper thing to do at such a social event. "Thanks, no. I'll stick with liquor tonight."

"You're gorgeous, Jersey Barnes, even though you want to punch me again," he near-whispered.

More guests began to filter in, their bodies draped in everything from cowboy hats and blue jeans to long designer gowns. While our dates socialized with the beautiful and famous, Ox and I surveyed the gathering, which now numbered around two hundred. Nothing and no one appeared out of place. On stage, an upbeat jazz band pumped out the type of horn music that made bodies subconsciously sway to the beat. On the ground, servers circulated with trays of epicurean finger foods. I sipped bourbon and Ox drank a glass of white burgundy. He emptied it and placed the glass on a nearby table.

"Nice," he said. "Very creamy with some citrus flavors and a toasty finish."

"I didn't know Lumbees drank wine. It could be bad for your image."

He left to retrieve fresh drinks and returned carrying a bourbon for me and a full bottle of wine for him.

"What if I slam it down straight from the bottle instead of using this puny glass? Would that help the image?"

The stemware did look inadequate in his huge hand. Like it might shatter between the strength of his thumb and forefinger if he weren't careful. "Yeah, but then you might get sloshed and I'll have to fireman-carry you to the car."

Ox laughed a deep rich sound that made people turn to see what they were missing.

Looking like a cop trying to fit in, Dirk approached us carrying a tiny napkin and a tiny plate covered with miniature hors d'oeuvres.

"I hate these social things," he said.

"Better than eating doughnuts," Ox told him.

"Can't argue with that. The smells coming from the catering trucks are making me drool. Just wish the damn plates were bigger."

The three of us found an unoccupied table and occupied it.

"Jersey," Dirk began, "we're all coming up dry on Chesterfield's boy. It might be a big help if you'd share what you've learned. Besides, I'll be up for captain in another couple of years. Helping break this case would look good on my record."

"Why are you so sure I know something you don't?"

Dirk responded with a give-me-a-break look.

"I really don't have much to tell," I said. "I haven't uncovered anything more than your boys." He clearly didn't believe me and looked to Ox for help. Ox just shrugged a shoulder and delicately drank his wine, from the glass.

"Look," Dirk said, planting his elbows on the linen-covered table and leaning toward me. "How about if we just compare notes. See if maybe we can help each other out."

"Okay," I agreed. "You go first."

He did, and I didn't learn much more than I already knew. Neither the ransom note, nor Chesterfield's home had yielded any suspect fingerprints or other usable evidence. The Feds had run background checks on virtually everyone within Chesterfield's organization and were still talking to people who knew Jared, including past professors and current friends. They hadn't uncovered anything unusual. No dusty skeletons had jumped out of any opened closets. And the consensus on Jared was that he was an honest, hard worker. Didn't take things for granted. Was intelligent, had made good grades. Achieved a perfect record of discipline at the Citadel, a notoriously tough South Carolina military academy. Was proud to be training with his father and had never wanted to do anything other than work in the family business. No steady girlfriends, rarely dated, and wasn't into drugs or drinking. Didn't smoke. Had a very bright future ahead of him.

When it was my turn, I told Dirk everything I knew. Except about the Social Insecurity virus, the reports of a problem by Eddie Flowers before he was shot, and the little embezzlement scam that the Hertz couple had pulled. Since I was working for Chesterfield, there were confidentiality issues.

"There were reports of a black Mercedes-Benz at the Water Street Restaurant during a disturbance," Dirk said. "Descriptions of a man and woman resembling the two of you were given by witnesses. In fact, a young lady would like your phone number, Ox. She's a bank teller. Said you were amazing to watch as you took down all the bad guys, and that you were polite, too. Picked up the tab for their drinks. Her exact words were, 'the gorgeous dark-skinned one with the tight ass.'"

Ox smiled.

"She didn't say anything about the other one?" I asked, insulted. Maybe she hadn't gotten a good look at me, as I took down Gary Hertz.

"Yeah. She said you stood there and watched the whole thing, staying out of the way," Dirk said. "Described you as 'the tall redhead with big boobs.'"

"It wasn't exactly like that," I said and Ox's smile got broader.

"Besides, my hair is more brunette than red. I believe the colorist at the salon called my latest shade a sun-kissed chestnut."

"Want to tell me about it?" Dirk said.

"Just a few thugs that Gary Hertz put on Chesterfield. He was mad about losing his job as the property manager for the Bellington Complex," I explained. "We didn't see any need to stick around after we reasoned with them."

"Why'd Chesterfield get rid of Hertz?"

"Suspected him of dealing drugs," Ox said. It was a good answer, since Hertz was now in jail on drug charges. And even though the answer didn't satisfy Dirk, it would satisfy his bosses at the police department.

"Yeah, well," Dirk said. "The three boys you left behind at Water Street all had priors. And the Hertz couple was a good bust for narcotics. Gary squealed and we picked up the wife yesterday. Captain said to tell you thanks. Off the record."

"Tell him no problem," Ox said, "off the record."

We sat at the table a while longer and surveyed our surroundings. Everyone seemed to be enjoying themselves, even the suits who tried to be inconspicuous in a crowd that had now grown to four or five hundred.

"Shall we go mingle?" I said to Ox when our glasses were empty.

"It is what you're suppose to do at one of these things," he agreed.

Leaving Dirk at the table to finish his food, we walked for several minutes before approaching Chesterfield and a group of men. After introductions, I heard the word "SIPA" and my attention span perked up and zeroed in.

"Senator Ralls serves on the finance committee," Chesterfield was saying. "We first met four or five years ago, when the committee had just begun discussing Social Security reform."

I made sure that the level of scotch on the rocks in the senator's cocktail glass never dipped below half and, by the time the featured band began playing, the senator and Ox were on a first-name basis and swapped stories like old war buddies. I learned that the finance committee had to give their blessing to all brokerage firms cleared to handle SIPAs. I learned that Senator Sigmund Ralls, from Georgia, owned a vacation home in Wrightsville Beach, which was less than half an hour's drive from the Block. I learned that his wife had darting, dark eyes and that I didn't much like her, even though she smiled and nodded at all the right times. Her expression was unattractively pinched tight, as though she were commanding a troop of one hundred men instead of just one. And I learned that Sigmund Ralls had a son, but was openly disappointed and critical of the kid. The same kid who coincidentally knew Jared.

"Damn kid is smart, Walton is," the senator said, taking special care to pronounce all of his words correctly so as not to appear drunk. "But he's damned lazy. Doesn't have any ambition. Got kicked out of school for a year, but instead of getting a decent job he's still sucking the tit, living at our beach house. I was hoping a good military college like the Citadel would straighten him out . . ." He took a hearty swallow of scotch, allowing some of the crushed ice to fall into his mouth with it. "I've often wished Walton could be more like Jared Chesterfield. That kid has got so much going for him, and now this. Kidnapped! Who would've thought?"

I wanted more details, but Ralls's wife was not going to let that happen.

"Darling," Hanna Lane Ralls gently interrupted. She clearly didn't want her husband airing the family's dirty laundry. "Let's go take a walk. I'm sure Mizz Barnes and Mister Oxendine would like to visit with some of the other guests."

Obliging her, the senator bid us good-bye. He was a bit

unsteady as the two of them walked toward the Chesterfield office building. That's where the bathrooms were, and a continuous stream of people flowed in and out.

I wanted to question Chesterfield on the relationship between Jared and the senator's son, but he was the center of a dynamic crowd. Getting him alone would be nearly impossible.

Ox and I roamed and ate and drank and chatted with the upper echelon for another hour. Deciding that the evening wasn't going to produce any case-breaking clues, we collected Bill and Mindy and were preparing to leave when Dirk caught up with us. His two-way radio crackled discreetly with blasts of anxious conversation.

"An employee was just found in one of the restroom stalls," Dirk said through a worried frown. "She's not breathing."

After asking Bill to drive Mindy home, Ox and I followed Dirk to the scene, weaving our way through an unknowing crowd of partygoers. Emergency medical technicians were unable to revive the woman, who another employee identified as Darlene, Chesterfield's personal secretary.

ELEVEN

Nobel Prize winner and late British philosopher Bertrand Russell once said that there is much pleasure to be gained from useless knowledge. The man was a genius but I must disagree with his assessment. There is much frustration to be gained from useless knowledge. Or, perhaps the knowledge I had at the present *was* useful but I just didn't know it yet.

The body count from Chesterfield's staff had now risen to two and there was no plausible explanation as to why somebody poisoned his secretary with a lethal dose of tranquilizers and sleeping pills. An empty, shattered glass was found in the bathroom, and another staffer recalled seeing her with what appeared to be an orange juice and vodka. But none of the bartenders remembered serving her. It would have been easy for someone to grind up the pills in advance and simply mix them into her juice, which would have masked the taste. Until they had evidence to the contrary, police were treating the death as an accidental overdose, but I didn't think so.

To make things even more baffling, the third time the kidnappers made contact was no more specific than the original note or the first phone call. Nine days had passed since the kidnapping and again, the call was placed with a doctored cell phone that was untraceable. This time, though, the caller was female. And when I listened to the recorded conversation, I figured two things. One, her voice was disguised. Two, the kidnappers were purposely stalling.

"*Listen*, asshole," she said when Chesterfield answered. "We told you no cops, but you didn't listen. So, now it's going to cost you more to get Jared back."

"Hey," Chesterfield said. "I spoke to a fellow before. Who are you?"

"It doesn't matter who I am. We got what you want. Jared. That's all that matters."

"Let me talk to him. I need to know he's really there with you. Otherwise, I could be talking to anybody."

"Piss off."

Chesterfield kept his cool. "Lots of people are claiming to be in on this," he lied. "You could be another nut wanting attention."

There was a pause before Jared's voice came across the line.

"Hi, Dad." He sounded very tired. "I'm okay, I'm not hurt or anything. I—" The phone was taken from him in midsentence and the woman came back on. She sounded around thirty, maybe older.

"Satisfied?"

"Tell me what you want. And, when do I see my son?"

"The price has gone up to three million. Three million dollars. Get the cash," she instructed.

"I've already got the cash. Ready to go," Chesterfield said, although he didn't have the money on hand. "How do I get it to you?"

"You'll hear from us in a few days."

The line went dead.

It didn't make sense. Chesterfield practically begged to give them the money and they didn't bite. Hungry fish always took the bait and greedy fish often snagged an empty hook. Was the real motive behind the kidnapping something other than ransom, and had Jared been in on things from the start? Even though he wasn't a computer whiz of the caliber to create such a virus, he could have provided the insider information from Chesterfield Financial. Whoever the culprits, they were stalling for time and my gut told me Social Insecurity must be the reason why.

As promised, Bill hadn't scheduled any modeling jobs for the entire week and declared that he was going to spend it with me, even if I was working. We stopped by Chesterfield's penthouse to check on developments with the agent stationed there. Because it was a shift change, there were two and they were comparing notes. I'd brought a container of hot steamed oysters, a pack of saltines, cocktail sauce made with freshly grated horseradish, and a six-pack of Corona beer. Although the on-duty agent chose not to drink, the rest of us washed the feast down with a brew while Lolly treated Bill to a tour of the penthouse.

I heard snippets of their conversation and determined they were chatting about home accessories and fashion designers and Bill's latest modeling gigs. They may as well have been speaking French for all I could understand.

My mobile rang, and it was Spud asking for a ride to the automotive repair shop. They'd sucked all the water out of his car, checked the engine compartment, given it a tune-up, repaired the damaged front fender, and prepared an invoice for nine hundred and ninety-eight dollars. His insurance deductible was one thousand. He was positive that the car repair people were in cahoots with the insurance people.

To respond to his telephone tirade would have been paramount to pouring Wesson oil on a stovetop grease fire, so I ignored it. "Sure, I'll take you to get the car," I told him. "But who's going to drive it back?"

"Oh, I got Bobby with me. We're at home."

Bill massaged the back of my neck as we drove to the Block to retrieve Spud. The tips of his fingers pressing into my neck muscles felt so good that my eyelids wanted to shut in ecstasy and I had to remind myself I was driving. I needed to keep my eyes open. I asked him what he thought about Chesterfield and Lolly's place.

"It's gorgeous," he said, "especially for a short-term thing. Makes me wonder what their permanent home in New York looks like."

"Did Lolly tell you anything about Jared? Friends, funny stories, that kind of thing?"

"No, not really. She's as surprised by the whole kidnapping thing as everybody. She said Jared has always been polite to her, even though she's the new wife."

"Anything else?"

"He's a vegetarian. Or is it a vegan? Anyway, he doesn't eat any meat except seafood." I didn't see where that tidbit of information would help lead me to Jared, so I let it pass.

"Anything else?"

"Don't think so. From all the photographs I've seen though,

he sure is a handsome kid. My friend Tommy would go crazy over him."

"Tommy? Like a guy Tommy?"

"Yes, a guy Tommy," Bill said with exasperation, as though I'd asked a dumb question. "Jared is good looking, smart, polite, *and* wealthy. He'd be the catch of the century for somebody like Tommy."

"Jared Chesterfield is gay?" It opened up a whole new realm of possible motives for the kidnapping. "How do you know he's gay?"

"You didn't notice his room?" Bill said, as though there was a flashing neon sign hanging on the wall that declared, A HOMO-SEXUAL SLEEPS HERE.

"Of course I noticed his room. I searched it," I said.

"Green and mauve cabana stripes, coordinating lamps with Tiffany inlay? Ceiling fans in the design of palm leaves? And it's neat, for another thing." Bill quit massaging my neck and turned his attention to the contents of his blazer pocket. He fished out a sleeve of Dentyne and offered me some before tossing a few squares in his mouth.

"You deduced, just by seeing Jared's room, that he is gay," I half-stated and half-asked.

"I assumed you would have picked up on the obvious, you being a trained professional and all," he chided. "But Sam doesn't know, of course. Lolly said that Jared is *very* deep in the closet."

"But Lolly knows," I thought aloud, "and Jared knows she knows?"

"Of course," Bill said, repocketing the chewing gum. "It's just something they don't discuss. Lolly figures it's not her business. If Jared wants to tell his dad, he will." Maybe Lolly was smarter than I'd given her credit for. She knew when to stay out of something.

On the other hand, she should have come forth with the information when Jared went missing.

"Jared probably thinks his dad would disown him if he knew," I mused. "And to think that the kid went to a military academy. They'd have tied him to a tree naked and painted him pink if word got out on campus."

"It wouldn't have been good," Bill agreed.

"What about boyfriends? Is Lolly aware of anyone special?"

"I asked her that because I was thinking of setting him up with Tommy if they ever find him, and she said no, definitely not. Jared doesn't date at all. He hasn't brought anyone home since they moved into the Bellington Complex. Males or females."

"If the modeling and actor thing ever falls through, maybe you should consider investigative work," I said, wondering once again if my few hours of retirement had turned my brain to mush. Had any of the suits assigned to the case uncovered what Bill figured out during a ten-minute tour of the Chesterfield place? And how would Chesterfield react if he learned that his only son may never produce heirs?

Bill replied that he would happily be an investigator, but only if it was a character in a blockbuster movie.

"Did Lolly ever talk about her parents or her family?" I wanted to know.

"Well, I didn't know her before college and we lost touch afterward. I remember that she used to visit her mother during breaks, but she never talked about her dad. I assumed her parents were divorced or something."

"Hmmm," I pondered aloud. "Lolly said earlier that her parents were traveling in Europe. But if they know about the kidnapping, why aren't they here to help her deal with it? For that matter, why isn't Lolly sticking close to her husband's side, to help him deal with things? She seems to be gone a lot."

"She always was one to do her own thing. Selfish, I guess. In school, we use to tease her about how the world revolved around her. Like, if the football team lost a game, she'd swear they did it to make her lose the five-dollar pool." He shrugged. "Anyway, I really wish you would drop this thing with Chesterfield. And why won't you tell me what it is that you've found?"

I couldn't stop the annoyed look that tightened my features. "I already told you, Bill, that there isn't anything solid to tell you. Besides, you know I don't discuss my work."

"Not even with me?"

"Especially not with you," I retorted.

"Sorry," he muttered. "You don't have to bite my head off."

The two of us never argued and I didn't feel like starting now. He continued massaging my neck and we dropped the topic of my work.

Spud and Bobby were ready and waiting when we got to the Block. With a melody of old-age grunts, they climbed in the backseat and we headed to the auto repair shop. Jersey's Faithful Taxi, at your service.

"Got your checkbook, Spud?" I couldn't resist asking. Bill gave me a reprimanding slap on the leg and Spud muttered something about where I could put his damn checkbook. Then he added something about how the state ought to provide the Vaseline when they were going to screw someone.

"You've got to be careful about letting friends drive your car," I said, egging it on.

"Aww, you all know it wasn't my fault!" Bobby cried.

"A thousand damn dollars. For crying out loud," Spud grumbled. "Anyway, there won't be no need for a deductible next time."

"What next time?" I eyed my father in the rearview mirror.

"Nothing. All I'm saying is that, when I get rid of the stupid car, I won't have to worry about any more deductibles."

"If you kept the Chrysler out of retention ponds," I said, "you wouldn't have to worry about a deductible right now."

Spud's car was parked near the front door of J.J.'s Auto Repair Shop, and appearance-wise, you couldn't tell it had been sunk. It looked close to brand new. We waited while a grumbling Spud and a defensive Bobby ambled inside to pay the invoice.

Laughing at them, Bill found my left hand and isolated my ring finger, massaging it between his. "It wouldn't ever be dull, being married to you, Jersey."

Oh, man. He'd sprung the "M" word on me again.

He mistook my look for something other than dread and forged on. "As soon as you get this Chesterfield thing under wraps and your official retirement begins, I'll ask you for real. With a ring and all. And you can pick a date and—"

"Bill. Stop planning my life."

"Our life," he said.

"I don't want to talk about marriage," I told him, gently removing my hand from his, the ring finger burning as though scalded by association. "It's not you, it's just that I don't want to marry anybody. As good as we are together, I think you're ready for the next stage in your life. A family and kids and all that. But I'm not sure I am."

Bill's flawless face fell into a moment of incomprehension. "You don't want to marry me? Seriously?"

"Seriously."

"Wow. That comes as a surprise. What woman wouldn't want me all to herself, forever?"

I might have laughed aloud at his enormous ego if it weren't a serious conversation. "This woman. I'm truly sorry, Bill, but I'm still not ready for a commitment."

He shrugged at the paradigm, laughed. "Hey, it's cool. Don't worry about it. We still have major good times together, right? So we'll stay like we are and I'll give you time to come around. Maybe you'll change your mind."

I didn't know if he'd said it to save face or if he was seriously intent on keeping me in his life until I succumbed. But I sensed that the quick conversation was the beginning of the end for me and Bill. Oddly, I didn't feel too bad about it, especially after he captured my mouth with his and delivered a long and tantalizing kiss.

We broke the embrace when Spud emerged from the shop, shaking his head and talking to himself, just like I remembered him doing after he'd paid a stack of monthly household bills when I was a kid. He shuffled to the Chrysler and raised the hood.

"What's he doing?" Bill said.

"Beats me. Checking out the job they did, I guess." I was about to go take a look myself when Spud's head emerged and he shot a thumbs-up signal to Bobby. The two of them climbed in the LHS and merged into the flow of traffic with Bobby behind the wheel. Bill and I fell in behind them.

We'd been driving about ten minutes when I noticed black smoke snaking from beneath the Chrysler's hood. Strangely, Spud and Bobby high-fived each other after they pulled off the road. They ambled out of the LHS and we came to a stop behind them.

I pulled the Chrysler's hood release and Bill opened it to reveal a mushroom cloud of opaque, pungent smoke. In the next instant, darting flames appeared. The engine was on fire and everyone instinctively moved away from the burning car.

"Well, this is ironic, Spud," Bill said. "You just got it fixed and now this!" The fire grew and flames licked at the sky. I pulled out my phone to call 911 and ask the dispatcher if any tank trucks were in the area. We needed portable water for the surrounding grass and a dry chemical extinguisher might work on the car.

I flipped open the phone and checked the signal-strength bars. "I'll call the fire department. That's about all we can do." I barely got the 9 punched in when Spud snatched the cell phone from my hands.

"What did you do that for?"

"For crying out loud! Just let the stupid chunk of metal burn! That was the plan," he yelled.

"The plan?"

"Yeah." Bobby backed him up. "Hal and Trip told us how you could cut the fuel line to burn up your car. Just a little snip, then drive until the engine gets hot and there you have it."

I felt like a mother looking at two eight-year-olds who'd just told me they climbed a water tower and spray-painted graffiti in bright orange neon because their friends told them to send a message to the aliens. They both acted as though sabotaging your own vehicle was a perfectly logical thing to do.

"Good grief, Spud!" I yelled at him. "What were you thinking?"

"I was thinking that a man ought to be allowed to drive his car!" Something hissed and popped and abruptly the fire flared, sending us a few more steps away from the burning car. Still, the intense heat permeated the distance and seared into my skin.

I snatched the phone back from Spud. This time I got two numbers punched in before I was interrupted by the piercing whoop of a siren. A pickup truck screeched to a stop in front of the LHS and two young guys jumped out. One grabbed an extinguisher from an equipment box in the bed of the truck.

"Our timing must be good," the first kid said. "Lucky for you, we happened to be driving by! We're volunteer firefighters." That explained the siren on an unmarked truck.

Spud jabbed his walking cane into the ground, barely missing his own toes. "Oh, damn it to hell! For crying out loud! They've got a fire extinguisher!" He threw out a few more curses and the kid looked confused. His buddy was already dousing the flames with sweeping motions from a chemical foam extinguisher. They went out within a matter of seconds.

"What's the problem, sir? We're *helping* you," the first kid said, spreading a flame-retardant blanket on top of the engine compartment to prevent the fire from flaring up again.

"For crying out loud," Spud muttered, deflated. Even the previously animated walking cane hung limply at his side.

Bobby sighed. "I guess we'll need a ride from you, Jersey."

"You were planning on a ride from me, anyway, weren't you?"

"Well, yeah. That's why we did it when you were already behind us. That way we wouldn't have to stand around on the side of the road waiting for you to come and get us," Bobby explained. "At the barbershop pond, it took you half an hour to get there."

I threw my arms in the air and did a mini-pace. Not only did they want to destroy the Chrysler, but they didn't want to be inconvenienced while they did it.

"You're both grounded," I told them. Bill started laughing and each time he tried to stop, he'd look at the expression on Spud's face and start up again.

"What's going on?" one of the volunteer firemen asked.

"You wouldn't understand," I answered, and dialed a phone number.

"J.J.'s Auto Repair," a mechanic answered.

"Jersey Barnes here," I said into the phone. I told him yes, it was me again and yes, Spud had just picked up his car, and yes, they had done a super job on it. Then I explained what I needed. I told him yes, it was the same cherry-red Chrysler LHS, and yes, use the same towing company to haul the thing back to their shop.

When I hung up, Bill burst out laughing again. "Sorry," he apologized, trying to catch his breath between spurts of laughter, "I can't help it. You've got to admit, it's funny."

Then Bobby joined in, and even the two firefighters, who were not exactly sure what was so humorous, began laughing.

"For crying out loud," Spud said and waved a dismissing hand at his amused audience. Without another word, he jabbed his walking cane into the ground and plopped himself into the backseat of the Benz. Grunting with the effort, he slammed the door hard enough to rock the vehicle, a valiant effort considering how heavy the hidden armored plates were. Bobby got in on the other side. I thanked the two kids for stopping and asked if I could reimburse them for the blanket that they were leaving with the car. They refused money but handed me a business card with the address of their volunteer fire station and said donations were always welcomed.

Bill and I slid into the front of my car. As we pulled back onto the road, I could see the corners of his actor's full lips curve up. "You should reconsider my proposal, hon. I think it would be fun to have Spud for a father-in-law."

TWELVE

An unknown man and I were sprawled on an oversized hammock that was strung between two perfectly spaced coconut palm trees. A cushy pad covered the woven rope hammock and we sank luxuriously into its depths. The beach was deserted.

We were completely nude, the sun hot on my skin, a caressing breeze blowing as if a sultan's harem were fanning us with palm leaves. A bucket of iced champagne sat on the ground, and between sips of the bubbly, the stranger fed me whole strawberries. As I savored the sweet ripe flavor, he morphed into a darker skinned and more heavily muscled man. Grinning impiously, Ox poured cool champagne into the crevice at the center of my stomach and was licking it out when I woke up.

It was the kind of dream that one did not want to end prematurely and I wished to know what Ox would do next. But more sleep was not to come and the vivid dream quickly discolored until it was a thin memory. Cursing, I went straight into a hot shower.

As usual, Spud was already up and reading Monday's newspaper by the time I reached the kitchen in search of java. Even though he usually drank a cold Yoo-hoo, brewing a pot of coffee was part of his morning routine. I poured myself a cup, grabbed a store-bought muffin and a banana, and joined him. Hearing the crinkle of the plastic wrapper, Cracker immediately positioned himself strategically below my mouth.

"What is the big attraction to driving a dumb S-U-V, for crying out loud?" my father said, pronouncing each individual syllable of SUV as though it were a disease. "It says here that the craze is hybrids and these crossover SUVs. People don't want regular cars anymore."

"Morning, Spud," I responded. I stopped momentarily to stretch in my chair and appreciate the view of the river, which was one of my favorite things about living at the Block. It was an overcast morning but the sky had a wispy layer that promised to allow sunshine through by noontime.

"You tell me, kid, because I just don't get it. They're bastardized station wagons, is all. And they're so big, you can't see anything when you get stuck behind one." I almost told him that he couldn't see anything anyway when he was driving. That's why his driver's license wasn't renewed. But I resisted, not wanting to get him started on the state of North Carolina's unjust policies so early in the day.

"I guess that's why people like them," I said, peeling the banana and giving Cracker a small piece. "Because they're big."

"My Chrysler is a much better ride than some stupid S-U-V." He polished off the last of his Yoo-hoo and threw the automotive section of the newspaper toward the trash can.

"You hear anything from J.J.'s?" I asked, referring to the shop that was repairing Spud's fire-blackened car.

"Yeah. Sal called and said that Jerry's got all the rubber hoses and stuff replaced, but Mike had to order a couple of parts. So it'll be a few more days before it's ready. Sal's a good kid. Good mechanic, too."

Spud was becoming well acquainted with the entire family at J.J.'s. If things kept up the way they were going with his mission to get rid of the car, he'd be joining them for the company party at Christmastime.

I alternated bites of muffin and banana. The good thing about not cooking is that it forces you to eat a relatively healthy breakfast. I'd much rather pig out on a steak and cheese omelet with hash browns and bacon than the fruit and muffins I usually eat. Unless Bill was around and made us breakfast, Spud always ate the same thing every morning. Toast with apple butter, prunes, and a chocolate Yoo-hoo. If he was feeling adventurous, he'd substitute a strawberry Yoo-hoo in place of the chocolate one.

"You learn anything more about the accountant, the one who took a slug between the eyes?" Spud wanted to know. If there was nothing interesting in the newspaper, he would turn to me for his fill of daily gossip.

"Not much," I told him, dropping another pinch of banana into Cracker's ready mouth. He swallowed it noisily without bothering to chew. "Chesterfield hired a firm to do an internal audit and told them to focus on the SIPA stuff. But so far, they haven't uncovered anything unusual. They can't find whatever it was that Eddie Flowers found, which got him killed."

"What about the secretary lady?"

"Nothing there, either. They found a bottle of mixed pills in her handbag. Even though she didn't have a prescription for them, they're still treating the death as an overdose."

"And the kid?"

"Well, he's alive, or at least he was when they put him on the phone. Oh, and I found out that Jared is gay."

"What the hell does that kid have to be happy about right now, for crying out loud?"

"Gay, as in homosexual, Spud."

"The kid don't like girls?" Spud said. "When I was twenty, a girl could just look at me and I'd get a boner."

"Thanks for the visual."

Spud shook his head. "That just ain't normal for a boy his age."

"I don't think age has anything to do with it. Anyway, he's deep in the closet." At Spud's confused look, I continued, "Jared doesn't want anyone to know, so he keeps it a secret. The public doesn't know and Chesterfield doesn't know."

I turned my attention to refilling my coffee cup and Cracker's food bowl. The dog danced in anticipation. I always fed him each morning and Spud fed him at night. By splitting the duty, if either one of us ever forgot, Cracker wouldn't go hungry. For that matter, we could probably both neglect to feed him for a week and snacks from customers at the Block would keep his belly full.

"So, maybe you should go find some of the boy's, ah, boyfriends. See if they know where he is," Spud suggested.

"That is my plan, to find out who the boyfriend was, or is. Bill has a friend who might be able to help me out, an art museum curator."

"How come Bill has gay friends?"

"A lot of people have gay friends. Especially models and actors."

Spud pursed his lips in distaste, like I'd just fed him a bug. Trying to penetrate his old-school mentality was futile. He'd contentedly spent his entire career with various small-town police departments. He got to pal around with the boys, serve warrants, investigate an occasional vandalism or burglary, rarely saw a homicide, and probably never encountered any gay rights issues.

The phone rang, saving us from further discussion on the matter. It was Bill, who gave me the information on the museum curator. As I jotted it down, Bill said he was spending the day at Kure Beach, catching some rays and memorizing his few lines for an upcoming movie.

"Are you going to the museum to ask about Jared Chesterfield?" Bill wanted to know.

"Probably. Or I may just shop for art."

"Bring your high-limit plastic," he said and added something about loving me bunches before hanging up.

"Have a good one," I said, wondering why he kept saying he loved me even though I'd never replied in kind. Like trying to leave the house without a weapon during my one day of retirement, telling Bill that I loved him wasn't going to happen. At least not anytime soon. Why couldn't a relationship just stop at its second or third month of maturity and remain there, happily carefree and uncommitted?

"When do we leave?" Spud asked me.

"We who?"

"You and the twins and me," he said. "I don't have anything going on until the poker game tonight. So I'll go with you to talk to the artsy-fartsy fellow."

"Quit animating my breasts, will you?"

I chugged the cooling remains of my coffee, Spud grabbed his mermaid walking cane and put on a purple plaid beret that he thought made him stylish, and we headed for Bradley and Slate's Art Gallery and Interior Design. Fortunately for me, the curator knew everyone who was anyone in the gay circle.

A woodsy aroma mingled with the heady scent of blooming magnolias beckoned us through the open front door. The gallery was housed inside a historic building that featured plenty of windows and skylights, a recent renovation to provide natural light. Viewing benches were placed tactically throughout the joint, from which patrons could sit and admire paintings. Some displays featured special lighting with spots and dimmer switches so the viewer could experiment to find just the right amount of light. Apparently, there was a technique for gazing at art.

I stopped in front of a particularly flashy statue of a nude woman leaning against a tree. It was solid black and angular to the point where you had to study it a few seconds to figure out what it was.

"It's called *Mother Tree,*" a man said, materializing out of nowhere. "Would you like to see it in a low-light environment? The accents smooth out nicely."

Spud harrumphed. "I'd like to see it come to life, for crying out loud."

"We're here to see Cameron Slate," I said to ward off further commentary from my father.

"He's in the office, but I can help you with anything on the floor."

"Please tell him Bill's friend is here," I said. "I am curious, though. How much is this piece?"

"Ah, this young artist is especially fond of Gullah-influenced art. You have fine taste. The piece is thirty-six hundred dollars." Spud whistled surprise through his teeth and I silently agreed. I'd figured it to be priced in the hundreds, not thousands.

"Thanks," I said. "I'll think about it."

He gave me the once-over, shot a sideways look at Spud, and showed some teeth in what might have been a smile. He moved off as silently as he'd arrived.

Minutes later, we were ushered into Cameron Slate's office.

Although he wore an expensive suit, he had the look and build of a man who knew how to fight, and the calm precise movements of someone who probably wasn't afraid to do so. I'd warned Spud on the drive over to let me do the talking.

"I'm here to learn what you know about Jared Chesterfield," I began. If the name meant anything to him, he didn't show it. His face remained pleasant, expressionless.

"You don't look the type to be shopping for art." It may have been an insult.

"Do you know Jared?" I tried again.

"I watch television and read the newspaper."

"I need to know more than what is public knowledge."

"What is your interest, Miss Barnes?" he asked.

"I've been hired by his father to bring him home. So far, I've been unable to determine where he is," I said.

"And you think, once you find him, you can simply bring him home?"

"Yes, I do."

He nodded, but didn't offer more, like a sheet of written instructions on where to find Jared. Spud began to fidget. My method of questioning someone was most likely much different than his had been during his career with the cops.

"Hmm," Cameron said. He studied me, perhaps trying to get beyond the fact that I did not look like someone who could retrieve a hostage from bad people.

"Bill said you might be able to help," I prompted.

"How, exactly?"

"I'm not familiar with Wilmington's gay community. I've just learned that Jared is gay and I'd like to talk with some of his friends."

"How will that help you?" His questions in place of answers were beginning to annoy me.

I met his eyes, smiled. "I won't know that until I talk with them."

"Do you have any idea how much a tabloid would pay for such a juicy story? Especially right now, when the Chesterfield family is a regular part of the evening news?"

"Yeah," I said. "I have an idea. I also have all the money I need. My only interest is in locating the kid, and to do it soon."

"Why?" Another question. Spud began to drum his fingers on the small table that separated our wingback chairs.

"I can't tell you that."

"Does Jared's father know?"

"That is son is gay? I don't think so."

"Are you going to tell him?"

"Rousting someone out of the closet is not my thing. It may become apparent to Chesterfield, depending on what I uncover," I said. "But what do you think he'd rather have? A heterosexual dead son or a homosexual live one?"

Cameron Slate made a decision. "I don't personally know Jared. But I do know who he was seeing, unless something changed in the past month."

Spud's fingers stopped tapping the wood.

"A bartender in the historic district. I think he works the day shift. His name is Steven Meyers. His father is Michael Meyers. You may have heard of him? Big real estate developer in South Carolina?"

I nodded. I'd check the name later.

"Anyway," Cameron continued, "Steven's father found out Steven was gay when a guy he dumped went a little crazy and wanted retaliation. The ex showed up at the real estate office and told all. Now, Steven has been disowned. His trust fund, which was his as soon as he completed college, has been revoked. Supposedly it was somewhere in the neighborhood of a million and a half."

Spud leaned forward in his chair to listen. Things were finally getting interesting.

"So, Jared's boyfriend was set, financially," I said. "Until a jilted lover tattled to daddy. Tough situation." Jared may have been worried that the same thing could happen to him.

"Steven is still young. He wasn't using good judgment in choosing his friends. But he's tough. Bartending to put himself through school and planning on going into occupational therapy."

"Thanks for the information. It might be a big help."

He revealed the name and location of the bar and we shook hands.

"Good luck," he said.

Our next stop was the pub where Steven Meyers worked as a bartender. From the outside, it looked like a dive but the interior was tasteful with lots of dark wood and colorful artwork on the walls. A rectangular bar was built in the middle of the place. Besides one kid working behind the bar cleaning glasses and whoever did prep work in the kitchen, Spud and I were the only people there. It was barely eleven in the morning and the pub had just opened. I suspected that barflies seeking their first drink of the day would soon filter in and the lunch crowd would arrive shortly after.

We pulled up bar stools. Spud asked for a Coke with a slice of lemon and I had an iced tea. The kid behind the bar was the right age to be Steven. Maybe we'd gotten lucky on the first try.

"Are you Steven?" I asked him. He studied me for a few seconds to see if he knew me. He was tall and slender and had the build of a basketball player. His face was clean shaven, with an open expression. He looked like the proverbial all-American boy next door.

"Yeah, but sorry, I don't recognize you. Have we met?"

"No," I said. "My name is Jersey. I'd like to talk to you about Jared Chesterfield."

His eyes clouded and he lost the friendly smile. "Whoever you are, and whatever you want, I can't help you."

"If you care about Jared, you'll talk to me. I'm trying to find him while there's still time."

I'd gotten his attention. "Are you a cop?"

"No. Jared's father has employed me to find his son."

His face went pale. "He knows?"

"About the two of you? I don't think so. I do, though, and have some questions."

He scanned the bar to see if we were still alone. "What makes you think I can help?"

"I know the two of you were, maybe still are, an item. I'm not here to judge anyone or blab secrets. I'm only trying to find Jared and any information you have can be very useful."

Steven moved down the bar to retrieve a box of fruit. He came back to where we sat and began cutting lemons into slices on a small wooden cutting board.

"Are you going to talk to me about Jared or not?" I said.

"How'd you get my name?"

"From Cameron Slate. He and I have a mutual friend."

"Cameron Slate knows who I am?"

"Sure," I told him. "Just like you know who he is. You don't personally know each other, but you know of each other. You're both well respected in your own way. You, apparently, have caught the eye of Jared Chesterfield. Good-looking, single, millionaire several times over. Big news, I'd think, in gay circles."

Steven thought about that while he efficiently sliced another lemon and flicked the pieces into a plastic bin. "What do you want to know?"

"You were Jared's boyfriend?"

"Still am." Another lemon.

"Has he made any contact since you heard about the kidnapping?"

"No, nothing. I've been so worried, I can't stand it. But who could I tell?" The first bin was full, so he switched from lemons to limes and began cutting them with a bit more vigor. The sharp knife sliced cleanly through the thick skin and hit the cutting board with a hollow thunk. *Slice, thunk, toss.*

"You tell whoever you can trust, if you must tell. But, since we're dealing with the son of Samuel Chesterfield, I suppose it's hard to know who you can trust."

"Tell me about it." *Slice, thunk, toss.* "Both of us with imposing fathers who couldn't possibly understand. My father won't speak to me. Doesn't acknowledge that I exist."

"I'm sure it can't be easy," I said softly, urging him to tell me more. Spud was about to interject something from a father's point of view, but I gave him a *shut-up* look.

"It's not. It's not easy," Steven said. He'd gotten a faraway look in his eyes. "I can't stand not knowing what's going on with Jared. He could be hurt, or worse."

"When did you see him last?"

"We cooked dinner at my apartment two days before he disappeared."

"Did he seem worried about anything?"

"Nothing out of the ordinary. His bio-mom wanted money again."

"Bio-mom?"

"Barb Henley, Jared's birth mother. A horrible bitch."

"I thought Lillian Chesterfield died."

"She did. But Jared's biological mother's name is Barb. Mrs. Chesterfield was never able to conceive children, so they used her eggs fertilized by Mr. Chesterfield's sperm and a surrogate mother.

Jared's sister was born to a twenty-year-old law student. And Jared came out of the womb of Barb Henley. She was a young secretary at Chesterfield Financial in New York and volunteered to be the surrogate because she needed money." Steven filled another small plastic bin with the limes and started on an orange. *Slice, thunk, toss.*

"She delivered Jared, went to work for some other company, and that was it. Jared and his sister knew they'd been delivered by surrogate mothers since they were teenagers because it was in their medical records, so it was never a big deal."

"Then what happened?" I asked.

"Jared told me that when he was like, maybe fourteen, Barb appeared out of nowhere and said she was his biological mother. She told him that Mr. Chesterfield had an affair with her and when she got pregnant, it was really her and Samuel's baby."

Spud's mouth had fallen open, and even I was shocked. It sounded like a daytime soap opera. "Go on," I said.

"So she wanted money. Told Jared that she was really his mama, after all, and deserved something more than the hundred grand Chesterfield had paid her to be a surrogate."

"For crying out loud," Spud said with disgust. "You people sure have screwed-up families!"

"A lot of people have screwed-up families, Spud," I said, thinking of my own.

Steven scanned the bar again for customers. "Anyway, she wanted a few hundred here, five hundred there. A thousand to get herself a new washer and dryer. Another two grand for new furniture. That kind of thing."

"Jared gave her the money?"

"Yeah. He wanted to keep her quiet, because he couldn't stand the thought of his mother—his real mother—finding out that he was the product of an illicit affair."

"Unbelievable," I mumbled, angry that Chesterfield hadn't

told me about his kids' surrogate mothers and thinking that maybe he held other secrets, too.

People began filling seats at the pub's tables and a server appeared to take their lunch orders. Steven disappeared momentarily to pour several glasses of wine and blend a frozen drink. When he returned, we asked for two lunch specials—a grilled ham and turkey sandwich with Dijon mustard and melted provolone cheese on sourdough bread.

"So Jared never told his father what was going on?" I said, after he'd placed our order.

"No, never. How could he?" Steven said and I thought, very easily. Barb was most likely lying.

"Where'd he come up with the dough, without making his folks suspicious?" Spud asked. I wondered the same thing. No matter how wealthy a family was, parents tended to notice the spending habits of their children.

"From money he made working for his dad part-time. He also sold a solid gold antique pinkie ring with an awesome emerald in it. Family heirloom. He told his folks that he'd lost it in the ocean. He has a trust account, but he can't access it until he's twenty-five."

I eyed Spud, thinking of all my growing-up incidents that we could never look back on and laugh about. Like the time I pawned my mother's microwave oven when I was fifteen and later claimed to know nothing about its disappearance. My father hadn't been there to discipline me for that stunt, much less share the important times like birthdays and proms. I looked back at the kid behind the bar and hoped he might reconcile with his father, before too many decades passed. "How long have you known Jared?"

"Since his sophomore year at the Citadel. A little over three years."

"What happened with Barb? Did she go away?"

"She found out that Jared liked guys. When Lillian Chester-field died, Barb no longer had anything to hold over Jared's head so he told her to bug off. That was when he was a senior in high school. But then, after he started college, the bitch hired a private investigator to follow him around, on speculation, just to see what she could dig up, I guess. The guy managed to get pictures of Jared kissing a boy."

I swallowed some tea. "Do you know where Barb lives?"

"Somewhere in New York. She demands money by phone."

"How long have you lived here?" I asked, wondering if the kid had followed Jared to Wilmington. Steven noticeably blushed. He explained that he'd lived in Charleston, where he first met Jared, and moved to Wilmington when Jared graduated. He didn't say who actually followed who to Wilmington. Jared could have asked Chesterfield to put him in charge of the Wilmington branch office. Either way, it wasn't my business.

"Has Jared ever had a DNA test?" I wanted to know.

"I don't think so," he said with a crinkled forehead. "You mean a DNA test could prove if Barb was lying?"

"Of course."

Spud and I were silent while Steven moved off to take orders from two businessmen who'd sat at the bar. Returning, he picked up where he'd left off without prompting. "There was something else, too."

"For crying out loud," Spud said, almost choking on a swallow of soda. "There's more?"

"Jared told me about an old roommate at the Citadel. I think the guy knew Jared was gay. But he was cool with it, like, it was no big deal and the secret was safe with him, you know? But then, right around the time of graduation last year, he wanted Jared to give him some information from Chesterfield Financial. His reason was that he wanted to go to work for a brokerage firm, and having inside information would help. When Jared told him he wouldn't do it, the guy threatened to out him." So not only was Chesterfield's ex-secretary and surrogate mother blackmailing the kid, but an ex-roommate was, too. Greedy people seemed to be feeding on Jared.

"What information did the roommate want?" I asked.

"Jared didn't tell me but he knew it wasn't the right thing to do. He couldn't figure what the guy wanted with the information, anyway. But after he thought about how my father pretends I don't exist, he gave in."

"Who's the kid? The Citadel roommate?" I asked.

"Jared never said a name. He told me about it, but didn't want to talk about it. You know, like he was sorry that he'd confided in me to begin with? So it never came up again until last month. Jared said he would make up for what he'd done. He got the memory stick back—the same one that he shouldn't have given out to begin with." Bingo! "But then he couldn't open the files on it, so either it wasn't the right memory stick or it had been changed. He was going to talk to some accounting guy to determine if there was a problem before he told his dad what he'd done."

Eddie Flowers. The accountant must have surmised that there was, in fact, a problem.

"Do you know anything else about the roommate?"

"All I know is that the father was some sort of big politician, or something. Like maybe a congressman?" he said and headed to the kitchen.

Walton Ralls. The senator's son. The one who got himself kicked out of the Citadel. I'm pretty sure the Citadel always has several students whose fathers are politicians, but the fact that Senator Ralls was on the finance committee that oversaw SIPAs, and Chesterfield's and Ralls's sons were enrolled at the Citadel at the same time was certainly curious. Plus, since Jared was being groomed to work alongside his father in the business, he would have had access to the SIPA databases at Chesterfield Financial.

Steven came back with four sandwiches. Two went to the businessmen at the end of the bar and the remaining two were mine and Spud's. They smelled delicious. He studied me with worried eyes. "Can you get Jared back?" It was the same sound of desperation that Samuel Chesterfield displayed when he asked the same question.

"Going to do my damnedest."

Steven nodded and I figured he was what he appeared to be—a bartender and a boyfriend—but I'd do some checking to be sure. I quizzed him further while Spud and I ate. Steven said he couldn't think of anyone who would want to kidnap Jared, except maybe Barb Henley, because she was money hungry.

"*Feel* like a ride to Wrightsville Beach?" I asked Spud when we were back in the car.

"Sure, why not?"

I called Soup and asked for an address on a home in the Wrightsville Beach area. I gave him a name. He put me on hold, got into the tax records, and had an answer in less than five minutes: a street address for the only home in the area owned by a Sigmund Ralls. Soup also gave me the permanent mailing address in Georgia and, just to show off, rattled off the purchase prices, property taxes, and heated square footage of both. Since the permanent address was in Georgia, it had to be the senator. The one from Chesterfield's grand-opening party who was on the finance committee, and whose son got kicked out of the Citadel.

I jotted down the information before telling Soup I needed medical information and a doctor's name for Barb Henley, who used to be a secretary for Chesterfield Financial. I told him why.

"Your tab's growing faster than a kudzu vine, Jersey," Soup warned me. "You weren't pestering me this much before you retired."

As usual, I could hear computer keys clicking in the background. He slurped on something and the telephone handset amplified the sound of him swallowing. "You know I'm good for it," I said.

"I can mosey back into Chesterfield's system, see if personnel has an address on her. The quickest way to get her doctor's name would be to get into the pharmacy's system where she fills her prescriptions. They'll have the prescribing doctor's name and her insurance information. From there I can get into the insurance files, check on claims, too. See if anything interesting turns up," Soup said. "Do you want her current doctor's name or the doctor she used when she was still with Chesterfield Financial?"

"Whomever she used twenty-three years ago," I said, since Jared was twenty-two.

He slurped again. "Might take some time," he said. "If we get lucky, a few hours. If not, probably tomorrow."

I told Soup that I owed him.

"No shit," he said and hung up.

The overcast morning had blossomed into a gorgeous afternoon. A cooling breeze held the humidity at bay and a partly cloudy sky kept the temperature from surpassing the high eighties. Traffic flowed nicely as I drove to Wrightsville Beach with Spud riding shotgun. Many drivers had their windows down and sunroofs open and their bodies moved to music blaring from their favorite radio stations.

"If I'd known we were coming to the beach," Spud grumbled, "I'd have brought my fishing rods."

I didn't understand the appeal of surf fishing, other than the fact that the fisherman could enjoy the beach under the pretense of partaking in a sport. When Spud did it, he rarely came home with any fish.

Wrightsville Beach, a small island that was home to less than four thousand people, was typical of the state's many beaches. Multicolored and multistyled raised beach cottages and scattered community shops and restaurants decorated the strip. Rolling sand dunes peppered with long wispy sea oats, clumps of seagulls resting at the high water mark, and pelicans skimming the water for schools of fish were a common sight. And nothing could compare to the first deeply inhaled breath that smelled of warm sun and sea as we approached the beach from a block away. Best of all were the brilliant sunrises: a free gift of pure art available to anyone who cared to look. As soon as I retired, I planned to relish many sunrises.

We found the address without trouble. Even though a Mustang convertible sat in the driveway, indicating an occupant, Spud and I took the liberty of walking the perimeter. The home was an oceanfront wood-framed two-story with wraparound porches and two levels of covered outdoor decks in the rear. Like most neighboring houses, it was plain in the front but elaborate in back with lots of glass to enhance a coveted view of the Atlantic. The lower deck sported a hot tub and lots of outdoor furniture. One corner housed a summer kitchen with a built-in grill and wet bar. The upper deck contained tables with umbrellas, several chaise lounges, and a lone sunbather. He spotted us and did not return my friendly Southern wave.

"Hi, you must be Walton," I called up to him. "Your father told me you'd be here," I lied. Spud and I made our way up the first flight of stairs and didn't have to navigate the second up to the upper deck because the kid hurried down. He wore nothing except a pair of baggy shorts and a nervous expression as he pushed too-long stringy bangs out of his eyes. He asked who we were and

I caught the faint but unmistakable odor of pot clinging to his skin. He'd been on the deck smoking a joint. I explained that we were friends of the senator and wanted to see the house.

"What for?"

Since he didn't question the senator comment, I knew we were at the right place. Without asking, I walked through a glass sliding door into a large family room and motioned for Spud to follow. He did. After a puzzled moment, Walton did, too.

"What do you think you're doing?"

"Since your father is thinking of selling the beach house, he said we were welcome to take a look around before he decides to list it with an agent," I improvised.

"Dad is selling the beach house?" the kid said, buying into my lie.

"Yeah, and I may want to buy it. I been thinking about getting me a beach pad," Spud explained with a wave of his walking cane, happily joining my ruse. "They're good babe magnets."

"Dad never said anything to me about selling," Walton said.

"What's that I smell on you?" Spud said to throw the kid off guard, even though he knew exactly what the odor was. You work as a cop, you learn what dope smells like. "You smoking that funny weed up there on the deck? Your daddy wouldn't like that." Walton tried to decide whether or not he should be scared.

"I don't do drugs," he said defensively. Checking out the large room, I spotted a huge flat-screen television. A news anchor was blurbing the upcoming evening news and a photo of Jared flashed on the screen above text that read FULL REPORT TONIGHT. Perfect timing!

"Hey," I said, pointing at the TV. "Your dad said you attended the Citadel. You didn't know that Jared kid, did you? You know, the boy who was kidnapped from some financial firm? I read in the paper that *he* graduated from there."

"Uh, yeah, I guess. I mean we were actually roomies for a little while."

"You're kidding! How wild is that?" I said, turning on my dumb blonde—or in this case, my dumb brunette—appeal and looking at him with wide eyes. "I'll bet that the cops will want to talk to you, then. The newspaper said they're talking to everyone who knew him at school."

"Well, yeah." Walton grinned and stole a long, stoned look at my tits. "I already did talk to them and they were real assholes, you know?"

Spud and I started touring the home, trying to look like interested shoppers. Not knowing what else to do, Walton followed.

"Cops can be such jerks," I said, stretching my lower back and jutting out my chest. "They're all on a power trip, or something. What did they do to you?"

"Kept asking me the same questions over again, just in a different way, like they were trying to get me to change my answer or something, you know?"

Spud made exclamation noises as he opened kitchen cabinets and closet doors and turned on and off lights. He could play a role, I had to give him that.

"Oh, man." I gave Walton the wide eyes again. "So what did you tell them?"

"I told them that I didn't know anything about the kidnapping, you know? Except what's been on TV, I mean. We weren't even good friends or anything. I just roomed with him for one semester, right before I got kicked out."

"I heard that military academy is really tough. What did they kick you out for?"

"Well, I didn't really get kicked out. Officially I'm suspended for a year." He lowered his voice so my father couldn't hear. "For smoking pot. But I never wanted to go there anyway. My dad made me, for the discipline and all that bullshit," he said.

"Yeah," I said, going for empathy. "Parents can really suck sometimes." Spud shot me a squinty look from beneath raised bushy eyebrows.

Walton pushed the bangs from his eyes. "Well anyway, getting snatched was just a bad break for Jared, I guess. I mean, those kind of things happen to really rich people, right?"

I nodded, agreeing.

"What do the utility bills for a place like this run each month?" Spud said.

"Uh, my dad takes care of all that," Walton said. "Bills go to his house in Georgia."

"Wow," I said, going for awe. "You've got it really good! Living right on the beach, the house all to yourself, and no bills. You want to trade places?"

He grinned at his good fortune.

Spud and I continued forging our way through the house but didn't see anything unusual until we got to Walton's room. It held a desk with a computer and a bunch of equipment similar to the stuff in Soup's efficiency apartment and I spotted a few flash drives lying next to the keyboard. But memory sticks were becoming like cell phones—most everybody had one.

"Wow," I said again. "Were you majoring in computer science or something? I can barely work the remote for my TiVo. I'd never know what to do with all this stuff!"

He blushed. "No, I just, uh, use it for the general stuff. You know. Internet surfing and all that. I want to design video games, but my dad said I was going to law school and that was that. I told him he was crazy, so he enrolled me in the Citadel to straighten me out. Guess I showed him, huh?"

I asked to use his phone, and he pointed to a cordless home phone that sat on an end table.

"Can I use your cell phone? I'm thinking of getting a new wireless service, and I thought I'd see how your reception is here on the beach."

"Help yourself." He retrieved the phone from a baggy shorts pocket and gave it to me. On cue, Spud motioned Walton over to a bathroom to ask about the water pressure. I ducked outside and installed a tracker on the kid's phone. Then I pressed a few buttons to see his preprogrammed speed dial list. There were only three numbers and I jotted them down. I hit the redial button, and made a note of that number when it appeared in the window. I ended the call before it had time to connect and punched in a random telephone number just in case Walton wanted to see who I'd called. I got a recorded message telling me that the number I dialed was not in service. Perfect.

"Because, my friend Hal's water pressure is so damn lousy," Spud was gesturing with the cane when I came back in, "that he can hardly get the shampoo out of his hair. But he don't even have any hair, except a teeny row around the back of his head and it's thinner than a cheap potato chip. He shouldn't even spend money on shampoo."

Walton stared at Spud with a half-stoned, half-confused look on his face. I thanked him for use of the phone and continued leading the tour. We ended up in the garage, which was really just a closed-in space beneath the house. Spud opened and closed some windows while I changed the topic of conversation back to the Citadel.

Walton said he wasn't ever going back to the military academy and didn't give a rat's ass who knew it. He was just staying at the beach house until he found a place of his own, he explained. And no, he wasn't working anywhere, but that didn't matter. I wondered why it didn't matter. Everyone had to earn spending money somehow.

I nodded to Spud to let him know I was finished with the kid.

"Ah, I don't know," Spud muttered after looking inside a storage room that was built into the oversized garage. "I think this pad might be a little too big for me. Tell your daddy when you see him that I'll get back to him."

We were pulling out of the driveway when Walton realized that he'd forgotten something. "Hey," he called. "What're your names, anyway?"

Spud mumbled something unintelligible that ended in "-field" and we drove off.

I gave Spud a squeeze on the shoulder. "You did good, Spud. Bill ought to get you an acting job!"

"Thanks." He patted my knee. "You and the twins did pretty good yourselves."

I scolded him with a sideways look.

The sun was sinking gracefully and had metamorphosed into a deep golden yellow with startling streaks of orange, giving the sky a lazy, late-afternoon glow. One of the most incredible things about living in Wilmington is watching the sun materialize over the ocean and watching it disappear into the river.

"I don't think that kid's elevator goes all the way to the top," Spud announced.

"He's having a tough time living up to the senator's expectations and he's angry at the world."

"Hiding something, too," Spud said.

"Yep," I agreed.

"But it ain't the rich boy, least not inside that house." Spud had been very thorough during his pretense of shopping for real estate. He had searched every possible space where a person could be.

"Nope."

"You think he's smart enough to have written the computer virus? He had that big computer setup and all."

"People are smart in different ways. Walton doesn't appear to have an ounce of common sense, but he could be a genius like Soup on the computer. Hard to say."

We picked up a twelve-pack of beer and a box of fried chicken with biscuits for Spud's poker game.

"Thanks for your help today," I told him when we pulled into the Block.

"No problem. But next time you say you're retiring, remind me to laugh, for crying out loud."

THIRTEEN

The countdown readout in my head was revolving much too quickly and there were only five days left until our patch of earth rotated into the consequential calendar square of July first. I couldn't help but think of it as an execution date for someone, most likely Jared Chesterfield. Not to mention the momentous occasion when the biggest cybercrime in history would occur, if Soup didn't stop it.

With nothing better to do at the moment, I made an appearance at the Barnes Agency. Although Rita bitched and moaned about the heavy workload since I retired, she appeared to be handling things just fine. I'd driven Spud and Hal—who was still blessed with a driver's license—to pick up the Chrysler at J.J.'s Repair Shop and stopped at the agency afterward. Rita shot me a *don't-you-feel-sorry-for-me* face. I almost heard weepy violin music playing in the background.

Our secretary had a baby boy, she told me, and it weighed seven pounds, seven ounces. She couldn't tell me what Suzie had named the kid, but Rita knew its weight. Baby Seven-Pound-Seven-Ounces received a blanket and a sport stroller compliments of the Barnes Agency.

Looking like an excited kid with a new toy, Rita sat at her desk testing a gadget. It looked like an ordinary fountain pen but contained a radio-frequency detector and would alert her with a slight vibrating mechanism if someone within a ten-foot radius was wearing a wireless microphone. The pen was a much more subtle way to tell if someone was wearing a wire than patting them down. Surprisingly, it was an actual ink pen encased inside a Montblanc shell. You could write a note or sign a restaurant tab with it.

Trish had borrowed the agency's surveillance van for a few hours and, through an office window, I saw her pull into the driveway. She was one of the few people I allowed to use the van for jobs other than my own, but she was good with the electronics and smart enough to stay out of trouble. The agency also allowed her to run a tab for use of the van, and she paid it off by working for us when we needed her. It had been a pretty good setup for both of us.

"Hey, Jersey," she said, breezing through the door and tossing the van's keys to Rita. "What are *you* doing here? You miss the place?" Trish is petite and usually wears her waist-length blond hair pulled back in a ponytail. When sitting in the driver's seat of the big Chevy van, she could pass for sixteen.

"The boss came by to check up on me," Rita answered. "I think she feels guilty about dumping everything in my lap."

"What are you working on?" I asked Trish, ignoring my partner's barb.

"The usual. This lady's pit bull lawyer hired me to get some skinny on the husband, who filed for divorce. He's an orthopedic surgeon and graciously offered to let her keep the Beemer and the beach house," Trish explained while folding a piece of Juicy Fruit into her mouth, accordion style. "Thanks to me and your clunker of a van, Pit Bull is now armed with audio and video of the good doctor bumping bellies with another woman. Even better, the girl is only seventeen and a patient of his. She's the star of her high school tennis team. He scoped her knee last year."

"You're calling my van a clunker? I've been through a lot with that van. She's a classic."

"*She's* twelve years old and backfires at the most inappropriate times. By the way, you owe me for an oil change. Six quarts and a filter. Labor was free. My boyfriend said the oil hadn't been changed in so long, it had the consistency of chocolate syrup with coffee grounds mixed in."

I pulled a twenty out of my wallet. "Chocolate syrup? He must've been hungry, thinking about food when he was draining the oil pan. Don't you feed the poor fellow, like a good little missy?"

Trish took the twenty and pocketed it. "No, he feeds me," she retorted. "I dumped the dentist. This is a new one. He's a mechanic *and* he knows how to cook. A biological male miracle. I'm in heaven."

Trish had a knack for attracting boyfriends whose particular skills she just happened to need at the time. She claimed it was co-incidence, but Rita and I knew differently. In the past year, she'd dated a carpet distributor, a building contractor, and a dentist. She now had brand-new berber carpeting throughout her condo, a screened porch addition behind it, and laser-whitened teeth that blinded you when she smiled.

I asked Trish to keep tabs on the senator's beach house during the next two days. If my visit had frightened the kid, Walton Ralls would make phone calls and stir things up. I wanted to know what, or who, surfaced when he stirred. Since he wouldn't want the calls on the phone bill that his father paid, he would most likely do his calling from the wireless phone that now had a tracker in it.

"I want to know when someone else is in the house besides the kid—friends, delivery people, whatever," I said. "They'll probably spend time on one of the outside decks. Use the directional zoom and let me know if you hear anything interesting. Also, there is a tracker on the kid's wireless. Number three." Trish needed to know which tracker I'd used so she'd know which preset phone number to dial in on. Since it was a residential neighborhood with a lot of beach home rentals, she could slap on the fake flooring company or locksmith door magnets and the clunker would blend right in.

"No problem, Jersey. I really enjoy doing your shit work," she said and took the keys back from Rita.

"You're well compensated for doing my shit work."

"You mean use of the clunker? That's good compensation?"

"How much did you earn from Pit Bull? You always work on a fee-plus basis. How much 'plus' will you get for the skinny on the surgeon doing the tennis star?" I challenged.

Her lips stretched into a sly smile. "Yeah, yeah. I know. I couldn't have gotten what I did without your clunker. In fact, I've grown quite fond of the van. When I leave it here at the agency, I get separation anxiety."

"Why don't you just make yourself a set of keys?" I said, ignoring her sarcasm. Between jobs for us and her own, Trish had possession of the surveillance van more than Rita or I did. Neither of us liked to do surveillance, but it was a necessary evil and Trish was good at it. Plus, she had something I didn't—a lot of patience.

"Sure," she said, dropping the van keys into a handbag that was slung canteen-style over her body.

"While you've still got the mechanic boyfriend," I added, "why don't you see if he'll give the old girl a tune-up? I think she needs a new fuel filter, too. And the tires are probably due for a rotation."

Trish produced a smirk and aimed it my way. "I'm not dating him for his mechanical abilities."

"Sure you are," Rita and I replied in harmony.

"What does your Honda need?" I said.

She looked sheepishly at the floor. "He's fixing the air conditioner and installing a power sunroof."

"You go girl," Rita said, waving her pen in front of a desk chair that was wired with a microphone. I couldn't see or hear the pen's vibration, but Rita motioned me over to check it out. The pen vibrated just enough for my fingers to detect the movement.

"Where'd we get this?" I asked.

"From Steroid. I traded him some stuff we don't use for the pen and a really cool digital camera. It's smaller than a pack of chewing gum," Rita bragged.

Steroid, so named because he has no neck and more bulges of muscle than any man ought to, is in the gadgetry business. Rita loves to drop in on him and haggle, like other people get off bargain hunting at Saturday morning garage sales.

"Hey, can I borrow the camera sometime?" Trish wanted to know.

"Sure," I said. "But if you'd dump the mechanic and date Steroid," I told her, "you could probably get your own camera. Maybe a vibrating pen, too."

Her middle finger went up. "Vibrate this."

"Actually, dating Steroid might not be a bad idea, Trish," Rita said. "Then you could talk him out of a wiretap and return the one you borrowed back in January."

"Crap," Trish said, smacking her gum. "I thought you forgot about that."

Rita never forgot anything. She shook her head from side to side, once, in answer.

"Listen, I've got to scoot," Trish told us, smart enough to realize when it was time to vacate. "Retirement agrees with you, Jersey. I dig that paisley shirt. You blend right in with the geriatric crowd." She smiled brightly and closed the front door behind her.

I updated Rita on the Chesterfield case and she updated me on her two cases in progress. Although she pretended otherwise, I think she enjoyed being in charge. As if to prove that nobody— not even the founder of a business—was indispensable, everything flowed smoothly. The bills were being paid, the new business was coming in, and the existing clients were happy. Plus, Rita was relaxed, at least on Mondays, Wednesdays, and Fridays because she'd made good on her threat to hire a masseur instead of a clerical temp. I knew because his massage table was set up next to the coffee machine.

"I guess you'll be glad to get the Chesterfield thing wrapped up," Rita said, "so you can get back to the business of retirement."

"Absolutely," I answered, puzzled by a tinge of regret. I was definitely ready to be on the boat with a hunky man and without phones, responsibilities, or guns. Well, maybe one gun. But I'd expected to be missed at the agency, at least a little bit. I asked Rita how the search was going for a new partner.

"Haven't found anyone worth talking to yet. But we've got some feelers out."

"Good," I told her. "Stay in touch."

I went out the way Trish had and stepped into a sunny morning. The air was crisp and the birds sang. It was the type of day to get things done. Not wanting to disappoint Mother Nature, I got busy.

I was in my car heading to the Bellington Complex when Soup called with the skinny on Barb Henley. I pulled off the road, put on my wireless headset, and found a pen and notepad.

He gave me the name of her doctor when Jared was born and the name of her current doctors. She had eight of them. Either she had some major health problems or she was a hypochondriac. Or, she might have been addicted to prescription drugs and found it necessary to rotate doctors to keep herself in ample supply.

Soup gave me her previous three addresses and her current address. She worked part time at a retail store and I wondered why, if she was in such desperate need of money, she didn't work full-time. A late-model Porsche 911 Turbo was registered in her name and her driving record revealed two speeding tickets and one DUI. A person with a history of drinking and driving shouldn't be behind the wheel of that much raw power. And since she was toting herself around in a new Porsche, she either had very good credit or she had a source of funding other than the petty cash she was blackmailing from Jared.

"Get this," Soup said, saving the best for last. "She had a condition called tubal infertility. Both of her fallopian tubes were blocked up. Even though everything else worked fine, her eggs couldn't get through. So there's no way she got pregnant by Chesterfield having sexual intercourse with her." He paused to slurp something.

"Anyway," Soup continued, "medical records don't show any pregnancies except the one where she had the egg implanted as a surrogate and the time frame is consistent with Jared's birth. She's single, no children, doesn't claim anyone as a dependent on her tax return." He paused and the faint sound of fingers rapidly punching computer keys came through the telephone. Soup always worked on two or three things at the same time. "Oh, and check this out. Chesterfield Financial has been providing her with insurance all these years, even though she's not on the payroll."

Why would Chesterfield pay medical insurance for an ex-secretary, even if the woman did lease out her uterus to carry Jared? I wondered if Barb Henley had something on Chesterfield, and was blackmailing the father the same way she was blackmailing the son. Or, perhaps continuing medical insurance was part of the original surrogate mother agreement. I supposed that if one wanted children badly enough and one had wealth, they would pay just about any amount to have a baby.

Flipping the notepad shut, I looked in the rearview mirror to see a small white car pull off the road behind me. I couldn't tell whether it was a Ford or Chevrolet. For that matter it could have been a Kia or a Hyundai. Brands of cars were no longer easily distinguishable by sight, and it was angled so I couldn't make out the logo on the grille. A slender man wearing a cowboy hat and baggy T-shirt emerged and approached my car. Longish hair flowed from beneath the hat, mirrored sunglasses concealed his eyes, and a flaky skin condition covered his cheeks above a scraggly mustache. As he walked up from the passenger side, he motioned for me to roll down the window. I reached for my Glock instead.

"You're going to have to put me on your payroll, Jersey," Soup was saying in my ear.

"I don't have a payroll," I told him, loading a round into the chamber. "I'm retired, remember?"

"Shit," he said, and drew the word into three syllables.

From ten feet away, the stranger shrugged at my noncompliance, pulled a revolver from the waistband of his jeans, and fired two shots into my passenger window. They pinged off, leaving pockmarks on the bulletproof glass. A third shot hit before it dawned on the shooter that his bullets weren't penetrating the glass. He emptied two rapid shots into my right front tire and ran back to his car. A professional would have known how to defeat bullet-resistant glass by firing three shots in a tight triangle pattern, but this guy's shots were all over the place. It's why I didn't chance an accident by peeling out and forcing a merge into traffic.

"What was that?" Soup said. "You in the surveillance van? You really ought to get the backfiring thing fixed."

"Listen, I'll catch you later." I clicked off my headset, jumped into a crouched position behind the door, and fixed the Glock's sight on the runner, waiting for him to turn and fire at me again. But he didn't and as his car squealed into traffic, cutting off another driver, I couldn't safely take aim at his wheels and I didn't get a tag number.

Sighing, I opened the hatchback to retrieve a jack and the spare. With the government, I always had run flat tires on the Mercedes, but now I had plain off-the-shelf Michelins. I should have spent the extra money, I thought, removing a lug nut and wondering who'd just tried to kill me. In the instant the shooter pulled a handgun from his waistband, I had caught a glimpse of hips that looked curvy beneath the baggy denim fabric. Whether male or female, the black hair and flaky skin was most likely a disguise.

I called my travel agent and had her book two seats on the next flight into New York's LaGuardia Airport. We'd have to connect through Charlotte, but then, you had to connect through somewhere to get anywhere out of Wilmington. She also reserved a room at the Hotel Sofitel, a thirty-story French joint in Manhattan's theater district that had a super view of the city and a fully stocked minibar in every room. Next I rang Bill, thinking that an overnight trip would be a good test of his promise not to push the marriage thing. Plus, I hated to eat out alone.

"Hiya, gorgeous," I said. "How'd you like to accompany me on a quick trip to New York? Have a nice meal with a big city view."

"Love to, but only if I get to choose the restaurant."

"Deal." I had just enough time to pack an overnight bag, see Spud, and have a talk with Chesterfield before Bill and I headed to the airport.

Forty-five minutes later, overnight bag in the backseat of the Benz, I sat with Chesterfield in his office. A new assistant who was probably a temp sat at Darlene's old desk in the lobby and the office across the hall, the one designated for the branch manager, sat empty. A Citadel jacket was thrown over a chair in one corner and a trio of marina prints hung behind it. I dove right in by asking Chesterfield about Barb Henley and the question totally threw him.

"My, my. You have been busy," he said with a touch of anger. "The FBI agents already quizzed me about Barb, but they came up with nothing on her. What does she have to do with anything?"

It was my turn to be a little angry. Samuel Chesterfield's son's life could be on the line and he withheld pertinent information from me.

"Maybe nothing," I said. "Or, maybe everything. I'm working for you, remember? I'm the good guy. And when I agreed to work for you, you agreed to my terms. Tell me about her."

He told me everything I already knew and some I didn't. She'd gone to work for him right out of high school. Was sweet and friendly but underwent an immediate change as soon as she was carrying his and Lillian Chesterfield's child. Began making demands that were unreasonable, but Chesterfield chalked it up to hormones. She immediately quit her job and demanded full pay, even though the original agreement was for her to work until her third trimester. She had plans to start college after the baby was born.

"Tell me how this surrogate mother thing works," I said.

"Well, you know that Lillian couldn't bear children, even though her eggs were fine. A doctor took my sperm and fertilized one of Lillian's eggs, then implanted it in Barb's uterus. Basically, we hired Barb to carry our child for nine months. We paid all of her medical bills, and believe me, she had the best medical care. We also continued paying her full salary and benefits, even though she quit work immediately—said she had to rest. She got a fee of one hundred thousand dollars after Jared was born."

"What did she have to do, other than let her body take over?"

"She signed a contract and agreed to not smoke, drink, or do drugs. She had to follow doctor's orders and couldn't do anything to harm herself or the baby during the term of the pregnancy. Also signed a confidentiality agreement and signed papers stating that she understood that she had no rights to the baby." Chesterfield rubbed his eyebrows between thumb and forefinger as though he had a headache. The jacket of his custom-tailored suit hung on a coatrack and I noticed that he wore silver-and-ruby cufflinks. Not too many men wear cufflinks anymore, but Chesterfield was sticking to his routine. Despite the circumstances, he was continuing to function as best he could. He ran one of the most powerful brokerage firms in the country and he still dressed the part. It was what he did.

"Where is she now?" I wanted to know.

"Jared was born healthy, I paid Barb, and that was it. For whatever reason, she sends a Christmas card every year, to the family. Last card came, she was living outside of Manhattan."

166 / T. LYNN OCEAN

"Yeah, she still is," I told him. "I'm going to pay her a visit tomorrow morning. By the way, I add travel expenses to my fee."

Chesterfield dismissed the travel expenses with a wave of his hand, but after a beat, did a double take. "You think she's involved?"

"Let's just say she's involved with your family more than you know. I can't elaborate, but I'll tell you everything I've found out when the time is right. For now, you're in a holding pattern and I'm trying to find your son."

Chesterfield blew out a frustrated sigh. "I don't think the agents are getting anywhere. They've been talking to a bunch of Jared's old classmates and instructors at the Citadel. And they've interviewed just about everyone at Chesterfield Financial. They've spoken to my clients and past clients. That's a lot of people."

"They find anything?"

"Nothing that they're telling me." He looked out a window and rubbed his forehead again. "What's going on, Jersey? Give me something."

"How about you give me the rest of the story on Barb."

"There is no more."

I waited. Chesterfield met my gaze for a few seconds, then sighed and looked out the window. "It's just hearsay, but one of the other secretaries said that Barb fantasized about marrying me. The girl walked up on her in the employee lounge—this is over twenty years ago, you realize—and Barb was writing out a name on a napkin. Mrs. Barbara Chesterfield." He shook his head to dismiss any significance. "There were a few incidences when Barb was carrying Jared. She told me that she wished it was really our baby—mine and hers—and that she would have made me a good wife. Maybe I shouldn't have, but I just kind of played along. I didn't tell her she was totally nuts because I didn't want to upset her and cause something to happen to the baby. Plus, I just chalked it up to the hormones. You know, food cravings and irrational mood swings and all that? I read a book on it."

"Did you have an affair with her?"

"Heck no!" he said in a hushed voice. "She was barely nineteen when she gave birth to Jared. . . . She kissed me once at a company party. I might have kissed back, I'm not sure. But that was it. That was after Jared was born. She wasn't even working for us anymore, she just showed up at the party. I made it very clear that I did not fool around on Lillian and that was that."

I asked Chesterfield if Barb had been in touch with anyone in his firm or his family recently. As expected, his answer was no. I'd gotten all I was going to out of him for the time being. I had just enough time to hook up with Bill and make the New York flight.

Approaching LaGuardia, we had a snapshot view of New York City from the sky. The night was sliding into dusk and Bill had a hand cupped around his eyes, shielding the glare from cabin lights as he peered through the miniature window at a buffet of twinkling lights. I cringed at the idea of occupying the claustrophobic window seat, but Bill loved it.

He swiveled in his seat. "This was a great idea, Jersey. We might just have to stretch out in the hotel room before we change clothes and head out to Times Square. You know, to test out the bed."

Already, New York City's energy was an aphrodisiac and luckily Bill seemed to be back to his old self, the one who was looking for a good time instead of a wedding chapel.

"Always important to check out the bed first thing," I agreed.

"I'll make dinner reservations for nine thirty or ten? That gives us plenty of time for you to have your way with me."

"Perfect," I told him. "When in New York, do as the New Yorkers do. It's posh to eat late."

"It's posh to eat anytime," he said, "if it's you I'm eating."

There was a slight bump when tire tread met runway and the brief swaying motion caused us to do a mini synchronized tango in our seats.

FOURTEEN

The next morning, I left Bill lounging at the hotel and hired a car to take me to the address that Soup had given me.

It was evident that Barb Henley was at one time a knockout. Her facial features were perfectly proportioned—wide mouth with full lips, dainty nose, and eyes that turned up at the outer corners just enough to give them an exotic appeal. But her skin had an unhealthy pallor to it and her nose had the bloated, reddish look of someone who drinks way too much booze. Her eyes were bloodshot and at least an inch's worth of dark growth at her scalp stood in contrast to the rest of her bleached hair. There was something familiar about her.

She lived on the fifth floor of an apartment building that wasn't upper class, but respectably had a doorman and a nicely decorated lobby with a security guard. When he called her on an intercom, she promptly told the guard to let me up as though strangers called on her every day.

"My name is Jersey, and I'd like to talk to you for a few minutes," I said when she opened the door to get a look at me. Without asking why, she shrugged her shoulders and headed back into her apartment, leaving the door open. I took it as an invitation to enter. When we were seated across from each other in her living room, she asked who I was. She wore cutoff jean shorts and a long-sleeve cardigan sweater over a tight tank top. A half-drunk glass of what appeared to be a Bloody Mary, complete with a wedge of lime and ground pepper floating on the top, rested beside her. It was not quite ten in the morning.

"I'm working with Samuel Chesterfield and I think you can help." I'd often found the direct approach worked best when I wasn't sure where I wanted to go with something. Things had a way of playing out, telling me what I needed to know.

She didn't act surprised. "Another cop? I've already spoken to those dreadfully boring people from the FBI. At least this time they sent a woman instead of a stiff suit." She looked me over from beneath morning-puffy eyelids and I didn't correct her assumption that I was a cop.

"What can you tell me about Jared?"

"Nothing, except what you probably already heard. I was the surrogate mother for the kid. Gave birth to him. Got paid to do it. What else do you want to know?"

Why you're blackmailing him, I wanted to ask.

"When's the last time you spoke with him? Or had contact with him?"

She took a long drink from the glass and wiped her mouth with the back of her hand. "I've kind of kept up with the boy, see how he's doing and all that. I may have spoken with him on the phone two or three months ago." Sure, I thought. To blackmail another thousand dollars out of him. And she was fibbing on the time frame. It had to have been more like two or three weeks ago, according to Jared's boyfriend. The Feds would have checked her phone records, but she probably called Jared from an outside location.

"So the two of you are friends, then?"

"I wouldn't say that, exactly. But you give birth to someone, you kind of want to see how they turn out, you know?"

"Sure," I said. "You been doing any traveling lately?"

A glance around her home told me that she wasn't into computers. A built-in desk on one wall housed an electric typewriter and a few stacks of mail. I didn't know anyone who had a personal computer and continued to use a typewriter. To a hacker smart enough to write a computer virus like Social Insecurity, a typewriter was a fossil. It was something that belonged in a museum, right next to the eight-track tapes and slide rules.

We conversed some more and I got the sense that there was a side to the woman she tried to hide. Manipulative came to mind. I envisioned her craftily doing whatever she had to, including blackmail, to keep herself living in a comfortable high-rise apartment and driving the late-model Porsche she kept parked beneath it. But I didn't see her masterminding a kidnapping, plotting to steal millions of dollars overnight, or both. I debated whether or not I should confront her on the blackmail issue with Jared, but decided I could be more effective in putting an end to it if I waited and thought the situation through. I wasn't flying totally blind, but close to it.

"What do you do for a living, Barb?" I asked, changing subjects. Before answering, she lit a menthol cigarette, inhaled deeply, and blew the resulting smoke over one shoulder, away from me. Twenty years ago the action may have been polite, or even sexy. Now, it made her look like a washed-up actress in a B movie.

"I work part-time at a clothing store. And I date rich, old men," she challenged, going for the shock value, possibly expecting a reprimand on her lifestyle. "To someone in his sixties, seventies, I'm still pretty damn hot."

"I'm sure you are," I said, noticing that she had finished her drink. Although she didn't appear to be getting drunk, she also wasn't worried about making a positive impression. She wore an attitude like another woman might wear a flashy piece of jewelry—to make sure that it got noticed.

"Is there anything else you'd like from me?" She leaned forward, and slowly licked a celery stick from her drink while she blatantly checked out my breasts.

"No, thank you, except answers to a few more questions," I said politely, as though she hadn't just come on to me.

"Cops," she said with disdain, like she dealt with the law on a regular basis.

"Do you have any ideas on where Jared could be? Do you know of anyone who'd want to harm him?"

"Don't you think that if I did, I'd have called Sam? I am, after all, kind of a mother to the kid."

She was about as maternal as one of those spiders that fed on their young. I thanked her for her time and let myself out of the apartment.

City sounds and bright, hazy sunlight greeted me when I left the building. I took a deep breath, not knowing whether to feel sorry for Barb Henley or categorize her with the crooks and creeps. Either way, I'd found out what I needed to about the woman. I felt sure that she wasn't a kidnapping suspect or a computer hacker, but I also wasn't eliminating her from my list. There was always the possibility that she was sleeping with someone who was a computer genius. And in her case, it could be a man or a woman.

I caught a cab back to the hotel. Bill and I didn't have to catch our return flight until five o'clock and until then, the city had our names written all over it. There was plenty of time for some power shopping and a leisurely lunch.

FIFTEEN

The man's slurred words carried up the stairs as I walked from my home down to meet Soup at the Block. It was an obnoxious customer, ordering Ox to serve him a drink and ending the drunken demand with a particularly offensive racial slur against American Indians. Our thoughts in synch, Ox's grinning eyes met mine. We both wanted the privilege of escorting the jerk out.

"Flip you for it," I said.

Ox pulled a quarter out of the register and tossed it in the air before catching the coin and holding it against the back of his other hand. I called heads and won.

The man swayed against the bar. "I said, gimmie a bourbon and Coke, you—"

"Excuse me," I said politely from behind him.

He turned and his eyebrows went up. "Whoa and *whoa.* Get a look at you."

About forty years old, he was well dressed and well groomed. He looked like a banker or perhaps a manager. Some people simply shouldn't drink. "Did you walk here?"

He nodded, ogling my chest. "In town for a convenshun and got a room with a big bed," he said thickly. "Come back to the hotel with me and I'll slow it to you. Shoo it to you. I mean, show you."

"How about you head on back to your hotel by yourself and sleep it off. Tomorrow's a new day."

He grabbed my breasts and squeezed. "How 'bout you take these tits behind that bar and mix my drink."

I eyed Ox, wondering if the man had gotten so drunk at our place. Ox shook his head. "He was drunk when he got here. Just came in."

"Right." I removed the guy's hands from my breasts and kneed him in the balls hard enough to cause pain but not incapacitate him. When he bent over, I gripped his upper arm and led him to one of the open industrial-size garage doors. "Your wife wouldn't appreciate you groping a stranger. Go to your hotel and go to bed."

"Bitch!" The man spun and caught me across the jaw with a backhanded slap. Suppressing the urge to crank his neck and put a permanent end to his drunken binges, I grabbed the hand he'd hit me with and held it in a reverse wrist lock while punching him hard in the abdomen. Just to give his fellow conventiongoers something to talk about tomorrow, I followed the moves up with a palm jab that would most certainly result in a black eye.

As he sat crumpled on the cobblestone and concrete floor, I rummaged through his wallet until I found a hotel key card, complete with an address. Ox phoned for a cab and I removed a twenty to pay for it.

Soup arrived just as the cabbie carted off the drunk. "Did I miss something?"

"Nothing much. I just won a coin toss with Ox," I said, wiping a drop of blood from my lip. A mere seventy-two hours remained until money would begin transferring into SIPA accounts on July first. Three days until Jared would either be exposed as a scam artist or killed by those who were the scam artists.

Ox handed me a Ziploc bag of ice for my jaw. He knew I hated bruises. "Are you one hundred percent sure that you can stop Social Insecurity from activating?" I asked Soup, holding the ice to the side of my face. Finding Jared Chesterfield was my main priority, but I didn't want to see innocent taxpayers get robbed. If the virus achieved its goal, e-commerce would be scarred forever. While most crimes quickly faded into yesterday's news, the repercussions of Social Insecurity could last for years.

"Sure," Soup answered lightly.

"One hundred percent?" I repeated. The first day of the new quarter, the first day ever in history for the electronic transfer of Social Security funds into privatized accounts was knocking at the door. Not only did I want to prevent the virus from activating, but I also didn't want the Feds to discover that I had known about the virus but kept the information to myself. They tend to frown on that sort of thing, enough to throw my butt behind bars.

"Yup," Soup nodded. I'd known the man a long time and he'd never been wrong with a declaration that pertained to computer technology. Still, he'd never been involved with a computer scam with this kind of potential. The stakes were so high, they needed oxygen to breathe.

"Can you find out who's behind it?" I asked. "Track the hacker without letting him know we're on to him?"

"Not unless we let the bug bite and do what it was designed to do. We could determine where the receiving bank account was established and go from there. Then there's a slight chance."

"Not an option," I mused aloud. We sat at the bar, pondering, and I traded my bag of ice for some hot wings with carrot sticks and blue cheese dressing. The Block's menu didn't offer soup, but Soup didn't mind. He ate real food as long as he wasn't in front of a computer screen or on a surveillance run. The spicy sauce immediately caused us both to sniffle, but a runny nose and burning lips was half the enjoyment of eating hot wings. We ate and thought some more, going through paper napkins and Bass ale draughts at about the same rate.

"Bottom line is, Jersey, this guy won't be found if he doesn't want to be. At least not through the electronic dimension. He's too good. The only way he'll trip himself up is if he were to start bragging about what he's going to do. You know how people will talk, to impress a friend or a chick."

As usual, the Block's garage doors were open and a breeze that smelled of river and marsh and thriving estuary life moved through the bar, caressing its inhabitants with a comforting earthy scent. Cracker lay on the ground between me and Soup, snoring. He knew from experience that I would not give him a buffalo wing, so he didn't even try.

"Doubt he would brag until after he had the money in his pocket and was out of the country, anyway," I said. Nodding in agreement, Ox pulled up a bar stool and joined us.

Soup tossed a stripped chicken wing bone onto the nearly empty platter, wiped his mouth with a fresh napkin, took a swig of beer, and grinned. It was the grin of a Cheshire cat who'd just eaten the prized canary.

"No bragging is going to happen, at least not after the fact. Some crying, maybe," he said, victorious.

"Who will be crying?"

"I don't know *who*," Soup said, the cocky grin bigger. "But I sure know *why*."

Speaking to us like a neurosurgeon explaining a hemispherectomy to a six-year-old, Soup described how he'd spent the last three days doing a type of counterhacking. He hadn't slept much and had been surviving on minestrone and Red Bull energy drinks, he told us, but he hadn't felt a high this good since the time he helped Interpol stop a twelve-year-old Japanese kid from shutting down the New York Stock Exchange.

Because the first day of SIPA electronic transfers had not yet occurred, no money was missing. Yet. Soup had written and planted code in Chesterfield Financial's system that would catch the stolen thousand dollars from each individual SIPA and reroute it back to the original account. Social Insecurity would do its thing, but Soup's program would snatch the funds before they made it to the thief's designated account. If it worked as expected, the bad guys would have no idea their bank account remained empty until they checked the balance the following day.

"This will work?" It was a pretty big gamble in my book.

"Did I write it?" Soup answered.

"You're a wizard, man," Ox told him. "Is Jersey paying you anything?"

"Hell, no," Soup said at the same time I answered, "Of course."

"This little morsel of your handiwork will be worth quite a bit to Chesterfield," Ox said, stating the obvious, which neither Soup nor I had the foresight to think of. Soup probably did have a nice thank-you paycheck coming from Samuel Chesterfield after it was all over with—if we got his son back alive while saving his company's reputation at the same time. To a man in Chesterfield's position, such an achievement would be priceless.

I munched a final carrot stick, letting the chunky blue cheese dressing cool my tongue. "Why even let the SIPA money come out, only to reroute it? Why not just kill Social Insecurity to begin with?"

"This way will be so much more entertaining," Soup said merrily.

A commotion grabbed our attention and I hoped it wasn't another repugnant drunk. Thankfully, it wasn't.

"Son of a bitch! Damn fools don't know when a gift horse is looking them in the mouth, for crying out loud!" Spud said, using a cane to move as fast as his arthritic amble would allow. Bobby and Trip followed him into the Block. To say that Spud was agitated was an understatement. The walking cane stabbed the concrete floor with each step. Bobby and Trip followed at a safe distance so the cane's angry tip wouldn't inadvertently catch one of them on top of a toe. Bobby was offering words of encouragement while Trip had laughed himself into a coughing spell. Everyone in the Block stopped what they were doing to stare at the three stooges.

"I think you mean, 'don't look a gift horse in the mouth,'" Trip told Spud.

"What?" Spud demanded.

"Never mind," Trip said, showing a display of near-pain as he tried to hold in another belly laugh. With much shuffling, the three of them situated their aging bodies at an empty table.

Soup chugged the last of his beer and disappeared with a wave, leaving me with the tab. I always paid my tabs, even though profits from the Block ended up in my pocket anyway. Mine and Ox's. I dropped some money into the register and carried the plates of bare bones and the pile of used napkins to the kitchen before joining Spud and his buddies.

"What's up, gentlemen?"

Spud's arms waved in emphasis or maybe irritation. "They

drove the Chrysler and wrecked the damn thing! The bumper's all messed up, like it was backed into a pole or something."

Ruby, a fifty-year-old waitress and veteran at keeping customers in line, ignored Spud's tirade. She delivered three glasses of ice water and efficiently took orders. Spud wouldn't shut up about his car long enough to talk to her, so Bobby ordered beers for everyone. Ruby returned with four frosty mugs of beer and a basket of steaming hush puppies. I waited for someone to explain what was going on.

"Your daddy here wanted to get his car stolen, so we parked it in the bad district," Trip explained, eyes watery from laughing. "He left the key in the ignition and the doors unlocked. Even made sure they had a full tank of gas and left a twenty-dollar bill on the dashboard, to get their attention."

"Whose attention?" I said.

"The hoodlums who were supposed to steal it, for crying out loud!" Spud interjected.

"You left your car in a bad neighborhood, hoping that it would get stolen by *hoodlums*?" I asked.

"Yeah," Trip answered for him between contained giggles. "They stole the car all right but then they brought it back!" His words trailed into a full-blown belly laugh.

Bobby wanted to laugh, too, but didn't want to further piss off Spud. He looked uncertainly at me, the corners of his mouth twitching. "They parked it about a block from where we originally left it. We had driven back to make sure it was good and gone before we called the cops to report it stolen, and there it was! They left the key in the ignition, but cleaned out the glove compartment and the trunk. Went through about half a tank of gas and dinged up the rear bumper when they took it for a joyride." He ate a hush puppy and almost spit some out when he started laughing. "They took the twenty, too!"

182 / T. LYNN OCEAN

Flabbergasted, I wondered if I was really Spud's birth daughter. I tried to summon up some anger but Ox started chuckling and the laughter was contagious. Everyone joined in except for my father.

"Oh, to hell with you all! Every last one-a-yas," Spud said as though we'd betrayed him. He reached down, feeling blindly for his cane. Sensing that my father needed some companionship, Cracker trotted up to him and pushed an exuberant nose into his hand, demanding to be petted. Spud scratched a spot behind the dog's ears and mumbled something unintelligible about being unable to find decent thieves these days. As though he understood and was sympathetic, Cracker tilted his head sideways and studied Spud. The attention from man's furry best friend had a calming effect and Spud scooted his chair back up to the table. "Guess they needed some written instructions," he grumbled to nobody in particular.

"Good hoodlums are hard to find," Ox said.

"Spud," I told him, "cars stolen by juvenile delinquents are usually recovered within a couple of weeks. You should know that from your days on the force. Your insurance company wouldn't have paid off until after their mandatory waiting period. Chances are, the Chrysler would've turned up before then anyway."

He sullenly stared at the tabletop and I felt like a parent scolding a child.

"Jeez, we didn't think of that," Bobby said. "So then basically, Spud would have just loaned out his car for a month to some thieves? For free? Then it would turn up, like they're giving it back to Avis or something?"

"Yep," I said, and ate a hush puppy. It was still warm and melted in my mouth. Ox had a cook who made the batter with the usual cornmeal, but added beer, honey, and freshly grated sweet corn. The Block's hush puppies were decadent. Spud methodically chewed one of the cornmeal morsels, concocting a new plan.

"I'll just hire somebody," he finally proclaimed.

"To do what?" Trip asked.

"Steal the car, that's what!" Spud answered. "If your average street criminal doesn't have enough brains to steal a car when it's handed to him, I'll find me someone who will. And pay him to make sure it's not recovered." Bobby nodded his head in agreement and Trip shrugged his shoulders as if to say, *why not?*

"Don't mean to be a spoilsport, Spud," I said, "but I'm pretty sure that'd be illegal."

"Illegal-schmegal! Not renewing a man's license ought to be illegal, for crying out loud." His face reddened as his blood pressure rose. I couldn't argue with his logic and wasn't sure I wanted to hear any more about his newest caper to rid himself of the LHS, so I left my father to consort with his buddies and found my best friend.

Ox gently turned my face to look at the side that had been hit. "A little red, but no bruise," he said, giving my cheek a quick caress before bringing up the impending SIPA transfer date. I brought him up to speed on Barb Henley and her ongoing blackmail with Jared and we discussed Soup's counterhacking skills.

"Good that the virus will be quelled, but you've got to find the kid beforehand," Ox said. "I don't know why exactly, I just know." Maybe his protective spirits had followed the Chesterfield case. Or maybe he had some clairvoyant abilities. Either way, when Ox made a definitive statement, I treated it as fact.

The cordless phone behind the bar rang. Ox answered and spoke for a minute before handing it to me. It was Dirk, calling to inform me that the kidnappers had made contact with Chesterfield again. The caller was the same female as before and this time she gave instructions for a drop of the cash. Her stated place was near the museum at Fort Fisher, a Civil War landmark just outside of Wilmington. When the money was retrieved, Jared would supposedly be released in a nearby public place. The drop location made sense since Fort Fisher was wide open and accessible by foot, vehicle, chopper, and boat.

"When?" I asked.

"Three days from now. Five thirty in the afternoon." Right after the SIPA transfers were scheduled to finish. It couldn't have been coincidental and confirmed my suspicion that the Social Insecurity creators were the alleged kidnappers.

"Why not sooner?" I said into the phone.

Dirk said that Chesterfield tried to schedule the trade for tomorrow, but the caller wouldn't bite. Again, she let Jared speak briefly to prove he was alive and again, the call was made from a doctored, untraceable cell phone.

They were stalling. Fort Fisher was the perfect place for a drop that would never be picked up. It was all just a diversion because they had no intention of collecting a ransom. Why bother with three million when you thought you had fifty million coming? If Jared was a hostage, the kidnappers would have no reason to release him, either. He could ID them.

I passed along the information to Ox and he agreed that nobody would show to collect the ransom. The real issue was locating Jared. There was still the possibility that Jared was in on the scam from the beginning. But, more likely, the Social Insecurity creators snatched Jared to keep him from talking. According to the bartender boyfriend, Jared had given out a flash drive with Chesterfield Financial information to an old roommate, but then got it back. Which would explain the device I'd found hidden in the gym bag. But was he in on the plan? Had Eddie Flowers found out about the virus before taking a slug in the head? Had the secretary caught a whiff of the scam before dying of an overdose?

I finished my beer and grabbed a handful of hush puppies from Spud's table as I walked out. I caught a snippet of their conversation even though I willed my ears not to hear. Bobby and Trip were making arrangements to take Spud's car back to J.J.'s repair shop to fix the bashed-in rear bumper and Spud said there was no need to fix it since it was going to get stolen soon anyway. Trip countered that no self-respecting car thief would steal an automobile with body damage, even if he was being paid. Bobby suggested that they sell raffle tickets at the senior center and give away the car as the grand prize. I made myself keep walking.

I headed to the agency to do background research on Barb Henley and learn more about Senator Ralls, his wife, and his pot-smoking son. Politicians with too much power have been known to develop a sense of omnipotence. Did Senator Ralls believe that he was entitled to take whatever he wanted? Had he lost the family fortune? Was it possible that the senator and his son were in on Social Insecurity together? Or was I completely in the wrong ball court? Maybe none of the Ralls family was involved. I had to get some answers soon. Jared was running out of time.

As I sat at my desk in the agency, contemplating life and my immediate role in it, Lolly appeared in the doorway.

"I wasn't sure I'd catch you here, but I was out running errands and thought I'd stop by."

"Lolly," I said, surprised to see her. I wasn't aware that she knew the address of the agency. It is unpublished and not listed on our business cards. "How are you holding up?"

"Okay, I think, considering everything," she said, settling herself into a chair across from my desk. Despite her situation, she looked fresh and pampered, as though she had just departed from a day at a beauty salon. Her short blond hair had been recently styled and the white sundress she wore was crisp and unwrinkled. "I'm just worried about Sam. This kidnapping is taking its toll on him. And of course I'm worried sick about Jared. There's still an agent always hanging around the penthouse. I don't know what to think anymore."

Other than a sympathetic shoulder to cry on, I couldn't ascertain what she wanted. There were plenty of other shoulders in Wilmington. "You'll get through it, Lolly. Right now everything seems overwhelming, but we'll get Jared home safely and put the bad guys in jail."

She looked skeptical. "Have you found anything out? I mean, who *are* the bad guys?"

"You're as up to date as anyone," I told her. "I'm talking daily with your husband he's keeping you informed, yes?"

"Sammy and I talk. But I think he keeps things from me so I don't worry."

"Such as?"

"What's the real motive behind them taking Jared? Sam said something about it being odd that they didn't jump sooner at the ransom money. If I kidnapped somebody, I'd want my money, you know?"

"It does appear that Jared's disappearance may be a cover-up for something else that's going on."

That got her attention. She leaned forward and blinked long, mascara-darkened lashes over worried eyes. "Something else? I thought they were just after Sam's money."

"I can't discuss hypothetical situations, but I can tell you that things are close to breaking wide open."

"Have you told anyone else this? I mean, are you and the agents on the same page?" she questioned.

"I don't have anything substantial to tell them, yet," I said. "Besides, I'm not acting in any official capacity. I'm simply a hired hand, trying to help find Jared."

"So Sam is paying you?"

"Of course. You didn't know?"

"Well, no," she said and tilted her head in thought. "It's just weird how I hired you to follow Sammy. Well, I mean you did it for free so I didn't really hire you. But now you're working for him."

The comment struck me as odd. It would seem that since they were a married couple in the middle of a family crisis, I would be considered as working for them. Not *him*. I didn't answer.

"I guess I'm just getting stressed out," she pouted. "Not knowing what's going on makes everything worse."

"Lolly, you just be there for Samuel and leave the worrying to all the people working on this case."

She peered at me through teary eyes. "Okay."

"Before you go, I have a question. How well do you know Senator Ralls?"

"Senator Ralls?"

"Yes, Sigmund Ralls from Georgia. Samuel knows him quite well."

"I've met him but I don't really know him. His wife is nice."

"What about his son, Walton, who attended the Citadel at the same time Jared did?"

She studied her shoes for a moment. "Same as the senator. I've met the boy but I don't really know him. I heard he got suspended for smoking dope. Jared never mentioned him so I don't think they were good friends or anything."

I asked a few more questions that revealed nothing and eventually the conversation reverted to polite, small talk. I hate small talk. Lolly left with a dramatic, impassioned plea for me to save Jared.

SIXTEEN

One thing I know from my time in the military is that it is tough to keep anything secret when you live in a dormitory environment. Near impossible, in fact. I drove Highway 17 down the coast from Wilmington to Charleston, South Carolina, and reached the Citadel in about three and a half hours.

The school has only two thousand cadets enrolled in any given year, but boasts a hundred-and-fifty-year history of prestigious higher education in South Carolina. There are four classes with the freshmen, or knobs, sitting lowest on the totem pole and the senior class ranking the highest. And while Charleston has a reputation of being one of the friendliest cities in America, the Citadel has a reputation for being one of last remaining good ol' boys schools that take care of their own and discourage outsiders from poking around in academy business. Undeterred by the intimidating reputation, I waltzed in, acting like I was a long-standing alumni, even though the academy hadn't started admitting females until 1995, the result of losing a lawsuit.

After flashing a fake Federal Bureau of Investigation identification card to three different faculty members, I found myself waiting to speak with some students in the lobby of the admissions office. I possess stacks of identification that officially declare me to be anything from a cop to an inspector for the Department of Agriculture. All of my identification is to the exact standards— shape, size, and color—for that particular agency, so the trick is to have the attitude to back up the plastic. Today, I was a Fed investigating the Chesterfield kidnapping. The folks around the military college had already been questioned by several of them and one more was just another annoyance to be dealt with.

I explained that I didn't want to speak with instructors or staff, but rather anyone who had been in the same dorm with Jared and Walton Ralls while they were roommates. I also wanted Walton's previous roommate, if the boy was still enrolled.

An hour and a half later, I had spoken with four kids and hit pay dirt with the last, Michael Stratton. As a senior, he'd developed a cocky attitude and made it clear he didn't like talking to me. He was a stocky kid with a baby face, shaved head, and green eyes. He wore the traditional military uniform that all the young Citadel men wore.

"Are you planning on going into the military?" I asked him.

"Yeah. Air Force. So?"

"So you'll be working for the government. I work for the government. We're all on the same side," I told him. "No need not to help each other."

"You're the one asking questions. I don't see how that's helping me."

"For starters, I won't have to explain to your commanding officer that you are an insubordinate little shit. Secondly, I won't have to tell your parents that you purposefully impeded a federal investigation. That's against the law."

If anyone was breaking the law in this situation, I was. Impersonating a federal officer could land me in jail, but then I never had been one to shy away from a felony if it was for the greater good. Fortunately, the threat of talking to his parents got the boy's attention and he instantly became cooperative.

"Sorry, ma'am," he said. "I know you're just doing your job."

"My associates have already spoken with you?"

"Sure. They talked to everyone who had anything to do with Jared. I mean, I didn't even know him that well and they questioned me for almost an hour."

"Well," I told him in a confidential tone, "the person I want to talk about today is Walton Ralls."

"Walton? Well, he got kicked out, you know. Zero tolerance on drugs. Even his dad couldn't get him out of that one."

"Tell me everything you know about Walton. And about how Walton and Jared got along when they roomed together."

He hesitated. "You know, there's like this code of ethics around here. A good person doesn't go around talking about his buddies, especially behind their backs. I . . . I'm just not sure—"

"Let me give you another code, son. It's a code to live and help live. You don't leave a teammate, or in your case a fellow cadet, behind," I told him, inwardly smiling at how easy it was to bull-shit a twenty-year-old. "Sometimes when you look at the big picture, you have to break the little rules. What I'm asking you to do is help us find Jared. Not leave him behind."

"Talking about Walton can help you do that?"

"Yes."

We strolled the campus while Michael Stratton gave me a lot to mull over. I learned that Walton was a computer geek and a

192 / T. LYNN OCEAN

good enough hacker to have broken into the school's system to change some grades for a friend. He enjoyed a little pot now and then and didn't care if he graduated or not. His only goal, according to Michael, was to embarrass the senator. He did just enough at the military academy to get by and his daddy was called on more than one occasion to get Walton out of trouble.

"I probably shouldn't bring this up, but it's not like I'm the only cadet who knew about it," Michael said as an afterthought. Music suddenly reached our ears and when we walked around a building, a marching band came into view. The music was stoic and upbeat with a rhythmic background of drummers. The seventy or so students carried an assortment of instruments including bagpipes.

"That's the Regimental Band and Pipes," Michael explained. "They're practicing."

We stopped to enjoy the show for a few minutes before continuing our walk. "You were talking about something that several cadets knew?" I prompted.

Michael hesitated, lowered his voice. "Oh, yeah. It was just a prank, you know? Me and Walton were taking candid Polaroid pictures of other cadets. Stupid stuff, like surprising them on the toilet or whatever. So anyway, we caught Jared in, uh . . . a very compromising position with another kid in the shower. We didn't know the other guy, but it was Jared for sure. Walton told Jared later that he threw the picture away, like it was no big deal. But I think he really kept it because he told me it might come in handy someday."

I could still hear the sound of horns and drums, faintly carried with the breeze. On a verbose roll, Michael said that Walton constantly bragged about rendezvousing with an older woman. Laughing, my informant confessed that he and all the other cadets figured Walton invented the fantasy woman, since nobody actually ever saw her.

I'd gotten what I needed and thanked Michael Stratton for his time. Not bothering to inform the higher ups that I was done with their students, I hit the road and grabbed a roast beef sandwich from the Arby's drive-through. I set the cruise control on sixty-five and wondered why Jared had attended the Citadel in the first place, knowing in advance he'd never fit in.

It grew dark by the time I reached the Block and Cracker greeted me with bubbly enthusiasm. He eagerly sniffed my shoes and legs to determine where I'd been. Satisfied that I hadn't been disloyal by visiting another dog, he sat and waited to see if I'd brought him a surprise. I hadn't, but I fed him a shelled peanut and he was just as happy with that.

Ox slid onto the bar stool next to me and we indulged in a couple of bottled Coors Lights. Since I hadn't yet cut down on my beer intake, I figured I could at least go to a lower-calorie product. From our vantage point, we could see Spud's car in the rear driveway. The bumper hung at an awkward angle and there was a sizable dent in the center of it.

Although Wilmington's falling sun was filtered by a row of stringy clouds, the air remained dense with heat. The Block's overhead ceiling fans spun at top speed and customers drank more iced tea than profit-generating booze.

"J.J.'s Auto Repair is sending a tow truck to pick it up in the morning," Ox said. "Complimentary, this time."

"Has he hired someone to steal it yet?" I asked.

"Don't know. Your father is one hell of a thinker," he said, and I couldn't decide whether the comment was flattering or insulting. Maybe neither. It was probably just an observation.

The early evening crowd of customers was the self-sufficient type that wouldn't need much for the next hour. They were locals who, content to watch sports on television and catch up on the latest neighborhood gossip, would get around to ordering appetizers or dinner later.

"I think you've been ruffling somebody's feathers," Ox said after a healthy swallow of beer. I noticed with dismay that, according to the silver label on my bottle, I was drinking one hundred and two calories. It wasn't even a longneck. I'd have to run in the morning. I'd also have to quit drinking so much beer, I thought, and wondered if my malted beverage intake classified me as a borderline alcoholic.

"If I'd said that to you, about ruffling feathers," I told Ox, "it would have been a politically incorrect faux pas, or racial discrimination, or something."

"Yeah, and then I'd have to tomahawk chop you up top the head," he said in a deadpan voice. I smiled. There were very few things that could get Ox riled up, and a reference to his Lumbee Indian heritage was not one of them. Tonight he wore a white cotton shirt with the sleeves rolled up and navy shorts with heavy socks and hiking boots. He looked as though he were about to depart for a safari.

"You got something going on tonight?" I asked him. "Maybe a gator hunt in the swamp, or a trek along the river?"

"Never know," he said.

I'd learned to accept the mysteries in Ox's life and didn't press further. There was a real possibility that he *was* going for a midnight hike. "So, whose feathers have I ruffled?"

"Not sure. But a couple of bruisers came in this afternoon asking about you. They weren't locals and they weren't tourists." Wilmington has its share of vacationers throughout the year, and while sightseers might stop in the Block for lunch, they certainly wouldn't have reason to ask about me.

The men told Ox they were friends of mine, looking me up for old times' sake. They asked if I lived upstairs and if I was home.

"They look like friends of mine?" I said.

"You have friends?"

"Ha, ha."

"I told them you were probably out with your grandkids—" he grinned at the cut on my age, "—you being retired and all. They didn't flinch. They obviously don't know if you have grandkids or not. Doubt they even know what you look like."

"Definitely not friends," I said.

"Nope."

Apparently, I'd been poking around in all the right places. A couple of thugs had come calling, which was good news. It meant that I hadn't been wasting my time with a somewhat primitive, albeit effective investigative technique: when you don't know who you're after, keep poking around until you stir someone into action. Many criminals would never be caught if they didn't act impulsively after their hot buttons were pushed.

"You happen to get an ID on the vehicle?"

"They walked in. Probably parked several blocks away," Ox said, grabbing a handful of roasted peanuts from a bowl. He shelled one and offered the insides to me before eating them in one smooth motion. "I'd have followed them, but it was lunchtime and the place was busy. Ruby was off today and we were one short in the kitchen."

As in many downtown areas across the country, parking was at a premium in the historic Wilmington district. Well-traveled sidewalks, which connected more than two hundred square blocks, were often busier than the roads.

I thought about eating dinner, but settled for some peanuts instead. The only way to learn more about the visitors was to wait for them to return. I just hoped they did it soon.

SEVENTEEN

When the numbers came into focus as I woke up, the clock on my nightstand told me it was just after three o'clock in the morning. I'm not sure if it was an unnatural noise or a sense of intrusion, but something awakened me and rang my internal alarm. A squirt of adrenaline pulsed through my veins and I instantly went into combat mode. Cracker, asleep at the foot of the bed, suddenly lifted his head and stared toward the bedroom door with intensity. The outline of his alert ears and perfectly still wide head was barely visible by the streetlight filtering through my bedroom windows.

"Shhh," I whispered to the dog. Reaching for the Glock, which was on the nightstand, I rolled off the mattress into a crouch. I waited for eight, maybe ten seconds and didn't see or hear anything. Still, the feeling of unease did not dissipate and Cracker continued to stare into the darkness, his nose working. As it had done countless times before, my index finger rested lightly on the trigger, ready to inflict deadly force with less than a half-inch worth of movement.

"Stay," I told the dog softly. I didn't want Cracker involved with an intruder, especially since he probably wouldn't offer help. If burglars were to hit the Block when Spud and I were away, Cracker would lick them in greeting and watch them cart off the goods with his tail wagging.

In spurts of quick, silent movement, I made my way through our kitchen and into Spud's efficiency apartment without turning on lights. A pair of Frederick's of Hollywood satin sleep shorts and matching cotton tank top were my pajamas of choice, and bare feet allowed me to move noiselessly. Spud's bedroom door was open and I could just make out the rumpled covers of his bed. He wasn't in it.

I jumped through the doorway, moving the Glock in a searching arc in front of me and came face-to-face with the barrel of a gun. It was one of Spud's and he held it steady with both hands, pointed at my chest.

"Son of a bitch!" He exhaled quietly, as recognition registered in his brain.

"Sweet Jesus!" I whispered, thankful my father didn't have a jumpy trigger finger.

We breathed deep and instinctively moved together so that our backs were flush against the bedroom wall. Once a cop, always a cop. And, once a marine, always a marine. Father and daughter shared the same genes and apparently, some of the same instincts. Something had awakened Spud, too, and he hadn't liked whatever it was, either. A search of his room and the immediate hallway revealed nothing.

"You almost scared the piss out of me, for crying out loud," he muttered. "My prostate ain't what it used to be." Spud had taken the time to don a robe and eyeglasses after he'd gotten out of bed. We paused to regroup, our weapons pulled in to our bodies, pointed at the ceiling.

"Stay here," I told him.

"Like hell," he said.

He would do what he wanted to anyway. "Okay, then, cover me."

The house was eerily silent and in a heightened state of awareness, I could hear blood coursing through my arteries. I didn't even detect the usual sounds a two-hundred-year-old building makes. It was as though the Block held its breath with indignation, waiting to see who had rudely invaded its upper level so early in the morning.

Spud and I made it to our shared kitchen when deep growling erupted and settled into sharp, spitting barks of warning. Cracker sounded like a lethal German shepherd instead of a perpetually happy, trusting Labrador. The next sound my ears processed was a gunshot. The explosion of gunpowder was reduced to a compressed whistling sound and echoing pop—the bullet had been fired from a small or medium caliber gun equipped with a silencer. The muffled sound ricocheted off the Block's exposed brick walls and the barking stopped.

Wondering how badly Cracker was hurt or if the animal was dead, I resisted calling out to him. With Spud on my heels, I moved to the living area.

"Stay here," I whispered again.

"Like hell," he said again.

At the same instant we crossed into the living room, clicking sounds reached my ears. Cracker's toenails dug into the hardwood floor as he ran at full speed toward the fireplace. I silently said a word of thanks to the man upstairs. We were all in immediate danger, but a nanosecond of relief washed over me when I knew Cracker hadn't been hit.

Movement caught my eye as I searched for Cracker's destination. Squatting on the elevated brick hearth, a bulky form aimed a gun at the dog, preparing to fire again. Several shots pierced the night at the same instant Cracker barreled into the man's stomach with ninety pounds of canine force. The stranger's body slammed against the brick wall of the fireplace and hung there for a frozen second before crumpling to the floor in slow motion.

Weapons ready, we scoured the living quarters for another intruder. There wasn't one. Spud flipped on a light and I squinted as my eyes adjusted. Fur raised along his spine, Cracker stood over the man on our floor, a steady growl emanating deep from inside his belly. I kicked the gun, a Smith & Wesson Model 19 .38 revolver, away from the man's hand—even though there was most likely not a need to.

I had aimed for the intruder's shoulder area and the two rounds of .45 hollow-point ammunition from my Glock disabled him. But the single shot from Spud's Ruger punched a hole squarely in the center of the man's forehead. He'd landed on his back when he slid to the floor and the opening in his face looked small and perfectly round. The back of his head, though, would reveal a grisly hole the size of a baseball and I was glad we couldn't see it. Just to be positive he was no longer among the living, I felt for a pulse on the man's neck. There wasn't one, and I immediately got the willies.

"Oh, man. I *hate* being around dead people." Backing away in revulsion, I studied Spud with raised eyebrows, wondering why he hadn't aimed to disable like I had. It was tough to get information out of a dead man.

"He was going to kill my dog, for crying out loud," my father said.

I hadn't realized Spud considered the dog his, but then I guess from a domestic standpoint, we had joint custody. And one thing was certain about Spud. Although his eyesight had deteriorated and his arthritic joints continued to thicken, his aim with a weapon was still dead-solid perfect. A gun collector and shooting enthusiast even before he'd become a cop, Spud taught me how to shoot at about the same time the training wheels were hammered off my bicycle. By the time he walked out of my life when I was nine, I could put a tight circle of holes through the center of a paper target with a .22 revolver at thirty feet. He'd taken his other guns, but left the snake gun with me. I still had it.

"Can't say I blame you," I said, petting the dog to calm Cracker's stressed nerves. And mine. "But when they ask, tell the cops the guy was aiming at us."

Spud didn't flinch. "He was aiming at us."

We studied each other for a beat.

"Look, kid," my father said, gesturing with his gun, "that man didn't break in to shoot a dog, for crying out loud. And since I can't think of anybody who wants me dead, I figure the guy planned to shoot you, as soon as he took out Cracker."

Still, he could have put his round into the man's shoulder instead of his brain. "Your point is?"

"I don't want to lose my daughter, for crying out loud."

It was as close as he'd ever come to saying how he felt about me. I'd take what I could get. "Thanks, Spud."

It suddenly occurred to me that my sanctuary had been invaded. Since I'd opened the Barnes Agency, no one had ever come after me at home. The overwhelming majority of my jobs were nowhere near Wilmington and I'd come to think of the Block as my peaceful refuge. Although I'd installed a nearly impregnable security system when I first bought the building, nobody ever bothered to use it. Waking up to find an armed killer in my home stung like an unpredicted slap in the face. I felt foolish and vulnerable.

Cracker threw a final growl at the dead man before trotting to stand by Spud's side.

"Way to kick some ass, you too-white fool," Spud told the dog. Like me, he hadn't believed the animal had any guard-dog instincts in him.

"You okay?" I asked Spud.

"Sure. You?"

"Sure," I said. "Except for the minor detail of a dead man in our home."

Glock in hand, I jogged down the stairs to search the Block's lower level. There were no more bad guys hanging around, but one of the industrial garage doors had been pried open and was raised just enough for a man to belly-crawl through. The shooter had come in the same way he'd entered the previous day, when he'd spoken to Ox—right off the sidewalk, through the door, and into the pub. Only this time, he continued up the stairs that led to my home. I was in the habit of locking only the doorknob instead of the dead bolt above it, and that was just to keep an errant customer from wandering in. It was an easy lock to pick and once again, I mentally scolded myself for not taking precautions like setting the alarm system, especially considering current events that included getting shot at on the side of the road. Complacency could get you killed.

I flipped on the Block's outdoor floodlights and grabbed the cordless phone from behind the bar to call Dirk. Oddly, it rang before I had a chance to punch any numbers.

I answered before the first ring stopped. "Hello?"

"What happened?" Ox said, the words rushing out. "You okay, Barnes?"

"A man tried to kill me, but he's dead. How did you know something happened?"

"A dream woke me up. Are you hurt?"

"No."

"Spud?"

"He's fine. Cracker is, too."

"You search the guy?"

"Not yet," I said.

"Need to search him before police arrive."

The mere thought of squatting next to a dead person repulsed me. "Think to yourself that it's just a body," Ox continued. "An empty shell that can't hurt you."

"Okay," I said, not at all comforted.

"See you in a few minutes. Meanwhile, do the search."

"I haven't called the cops yet. Can't you search him when you get here, then we'll call?"

"Somebody else may have already called," Ox said patiently.

Knowing it would take police ten minutes to get to the Block regardless of who summoned them, I disconnected from Ox and immediately dialed Dirk at his home number.

"Thompson here," he replied automatically through a sleep-laden haze. Since he was a detective on the force, phone calls in the middle of the night were probably more common than he'd like.

"Got a dead man inside my house," I told him, "and it's completely creeping me out. Would you please send somebody to haul the body out of here?"

"Jersey?"

"It's me."

"Somebody came after you at the Block? Is Spud okay?"

"Yes, and yes. But if it's the same boys who came looking for me yesterday and spoke to Ox, there were two of them. I've only got one."

"You see the other one?"

"No."

"You dial nine-one-one?"

"No."

"I'll take care of it. You'll be flooded with blue lights in no time," he said.

I walked back upstairs and forced myself to take another look at the body on my floor. I didn't know him but felt positive Ox would recognize him from the day before. In case I'd need them later, I snapped two photographs with a digital camera, one wide shot and one close-up of the face. Next, holding my breath and reminding myself that being frightened of a dead person was absurd, I slipped on a pair of latex gloves and did a rapid search of his clothing. He didn't have another weapon on him nor a wallet. All I found were a set of car keys, half a roll of Tums antacids, a money clip holding less than a hundred dollars, and a matchbook from Club Capers. I wasn't familiar with the establishment, but from the etched silhouette of a naked dancer on the cover, I imagined it could be an adult club. Scrawled in blue ink on the inside cover was what appeared to be, "*collect*" and below that, "*5th St. left.*" There was also "*4:30*" and tomorrow's date written on it. I returned the money, keys, and Tums to their rightful pockets, went to my bedroom to get dressed, and practically ran back downstairs to get away from the body. Within minutes, the Block turned into a blue-and-white flashing circus. Ox arrived immediately after and when he encircled me with broad, warm arms, the rapidly cooling body on my floor ceased to panic me.

EIGHTEEN

I thought about the man that Spud killed while I grunted with the effort of bench-pressing one hundred and five pounds. I was at the Kingsport Health Club enjoying a free visit. I'd told the anorexic girl behind the counter that I was thinking about joining and wanted to try the place out. She gave me the once-over and, smiling with what she thought was a glamorously healthy look, told me to help myself and call her if I had any questions about the equipment. Although it was a beautiful smile, her face looked gaunt, as if the skin were stretched too tightly over her chin and cheekbones. When she handed me a towel and locker key, I noticed that her collarbones protruded enough to rest a pencil on top of them, and I experienced an urge to feed her. Instead, I returned the smile and toured the facility.

I'd already been once, to ask the manager a few questions after

I found the encoded flash drive hidden in the same gym bag as a Kingsport Health Club aerobics schedule. The manager was happy to cooperate but all I learned was that the Chesterfields had a family membership. Jared and Lolly, separately, would work out occasionally.

I wasn't accustomed to using Nautilus equipment instead of free weights and decided I didn't much like the machines. There was something satisfyingly puritan in placing heavy metal discs on a bar and pumping it without the controlled stability that a Nautilus machine provided. But Kingsport didn't have a free-weight room. I missed the odor of clean sweat and the grunts of exertion and the words of encouragement from spotters forcing one more repetition out of their partner's exhausted pectorals. And I missed the cold beers that were drunk afterward, not to mention that I was often the only woman in the place. Kingsport was a gym for the beautiful people of Wilmington and its social-friendly atmosphere came complete with televisions, sofas, and a juice bar. The sounds of electronic beeps, blended with smooth hydraulic swishing sounds blanketed the room. It was almost hypnotizing.

Shaking out my arms, I maneuvered myself into an incline leg machine and set the pin to one-fifty. Lying on my back, focusing on the rhythmic tones as I methodically pushed the foot panel out and slowly allowed it to return, I noticed a fellow in the wall mirror looking at me. I gave a nod of acknowledgment before doing two more sets of twelve. I was looking forward to getting back to my regular gym for the next workout, even though there were better-looking men at this one. I managed to extricate myself from the machine with some grace and was wiping my face when he approached. He was younger than I with a slim, well-toned body and a dark, perfectly uniform summer glow that must have been gained by lying inside a tanning bed. Flirting with a regular might be a good way to pick up some useful information about Jared.

SOUTHERN FATALITY / 207

I gave him my charming smile. "Feel free to work in with me," I said, even though there was an identical—and empty—leg machine right beside us.

He returned the smile. "Thanks."

"Actually, I think I'm finished with this one so you've got it all to yourself. Lying nearly upside-down to do squats makes me a little nervous," I said.

He laughed knowingly. "I know what you mean. It took me a couple months to get used to this club after always doing free weights. But it's like drinking skim milk. Once you get used to it, you don't like the regular stuff anymore. Free weights now seem archaic. I like having my pulse automatically checked, and knowing how many calories I've burned, and the total amount of weight I've lifted."

"So you're a regular here, then?"

"Sure am. Name's Matt."

I touched his arm. "Perfect, Matt! I'll buy you a smoothie at the juice bar and you can tell me all about the place, since I'm thinking of joining."

"Sounds good. Half hour?"

"Works for me." He wasn't as hunky as Ox by any means and he didn't have Bill's model-perfect face, but if I were in the dating market, I'd share a dance floor with him any night.

We went our separate ways and in my peripheral vision, I caught him discreetly watching as I navigated the machinery, expanding and contracting muscle groups in my body. I showered in the locker room and threw on a pair of white flare-leg jeans, the Sig in an ankle holster, a black tank top, and the same sandals I'd worn in. After returning the locker key to Anorexia, I found the juice bar and slid onto a seat next to Matt. He'd showered, too, and donned a clean tee and jeans.

I would have preferred my customary glass of water chased by a Bass ale but we ordered two fruit smoothies with powdered protein, ginseng, and vanilla. Surprisingly, mine tasted good—similar to orange sherbet with a bit of grit and spice in it. I felt healthier after the first few swallows, like I was making up for all the salt, grease, and booze I'd dumped down my gullet during the past week.

"Are you new to Wilmington?" he said.

"No. I work out at a different gym, but heard about Kingsport and thought I'd check it out."

"I thought you might be a gym rat," Matt observed. "Great muscles, but not too bunchy for a woman. I'd have trouble hanging out with a girl who could kick my ass, like one of those female bodybuilders?"

I thought about informing him that I could kick his ass. "Thanks," I said, instead. "So what can you tell me about the gym? You must like it here."

He sucked some smoothie through a straw. "Sure. I've been a member for two years."

"You probably know everyone here, then. Do you happen to know Jared Chesterfield?"

He studied me with renewed, perhaps skeptical, interest. His expression fell into sad disbelief. "Yeah, he's a member here. Shame what happened. I've been following the kidnapping on the news."

"Maybe you can help me out then," I ventured. "I'm working for his father."

He frowned. "I thought we were sitting here because you liked me. And because you were thinking about joining Kingsport."

I showed him my most charming smile. "Always good to keep your options open."

His face softened. "Are you a cop or something?"

"Or something. I'm trying to learn what I can about Jared. On a separate note, you seem like a terrific guy and I probably would like you. But hey, at least you're getting a free smoothie out of the deal."

He laughed. "I might just have to get a wheat bran and flaxseed energy bar, too."

"Done."

"I'm probably not going to be all that helpful, but what do you want to know?

"Anything you can tell me. Such as how often you saw Jared here. And who he worked out with."

"Do you have a steady?" Matt asked, changing the subject.

"Yes, I do."

"Too bad," he said, giving me an appraising look.

We discussed Jared while I finished my nutrient-packed shake. Matt told me how he first met Jared when the family moved to Wilmington and how he was shocked to discover that Jared's father was Samuel Chesterfield. He knew Jared was gay because a lot of gay men worked out at Kingsport and Jared palled around with them. But he never worked out with anyone in particular, Matt said, and he never spoke of a boyfriend. The disclosures covered ground I'd already traversed and I started to think I'd wasted my time when Matt mentioned the roommate.

I perked up. "Roommate?"

"No big deal. I just happened to be at the juice bar talking to Jared when one of his old college roommates stopped in. They'd gone to school together. You know, small world and all that. Jared seemed really surprised to run into him."

"You remember a name?"

He studied the bottom of his glass for a moment. "Walter, maybe?"

"Walton?" I said, mentally keeping my fingers crossed.

"Yeah, I think that was it. Jared called him Walton. Used it as a greeting. You know, like they weren't good friends or anything."

Several people had drifted into the gym's juice bar and it was beginning to resemble the Block during happy hour. Only this crowd was partaking in health drinks instead of booze and they all looked like they'd walked right out of *People* magazine. But the familiar camaraderie was there.

"So what happened?"

"Nothing really. Jared and this guy Walton talked for a while. They agreed to get together later and that was about it."

"Did Jared seem pleased to see Walton?" I asked.

"I'm not sure. He didn't ask the guy to sit down and join us."

"Where were they meeting later?"

"Umm." He paused to think. "A bar I think. I remember that the roommate said drinks would be on him. Club something."

Club Capers. The same bar imprinted on the outside of the matchbook I'd found in the shooter's pocket. I'd checked the phonebook and there were no other bars that began with the word "club." Had Walton conspired to trick Jared into a meeting, only to kidnap him? Or were Jared and Walton working together? Either way, Walton's father had access to crucial information, which may have fueled the scam. The senator was the head of the finance committee and used a laptop. All the senators had one, compliments of taxpayers. There was no telling where the computer had been and who had access to it.

I finished my smoothie, put some money on the counter, thanked Matt for his time, and headed out.

"You ever decide to get back in the dating game . . ." the sentence drifted off as he raised an eyebrow at me.

Like a jazzy heartbeat, the dynamic group Foreplay pulsed from Bose speakers in Bill's place when I picked him up for our lunch date. He never got bent out of shape over my independence, odd occupation, or propensity to be the person behind the wheel. Sprawled on the sofa, he was reading a movie trade magazine. Celebrity weddings was the cover story.

"Hey!" he said and pointed to a candid paparazzi photo. "This gown would look incredible on you, don't you think?"

The thought of stuffing my body into layers of white satin and chiffon made me nauseous. I changed the subject to something more palatable: food.

"Hey, yourself," I said, planting a kiss on his mouth. "We still on for lunch?"

"I'd love to eat with you," he said, pulling me onto the sofa. "Or, we could skip lunch."

If it weren't for the Chesterfield case and the sickening vision of a wedding dress he'd wedged in my head, I would have skipped lunch in a second. Delayed it, anyway. "Save that thought," I told him. "Right now, you and I and Ox are going to dine at Club Capers."

"Seriously?"

"Yep." I was sure I hadn't been followed after leaving the health club, but took a quick look at the street below Bill's condo anyway. Somebody had sent the shooter and could easily send another one after me. In addition to the Glock strapped to my side, I had the Sig in place around my ankle and a razor-sharp Browning knife in my pocket. The pocketknife was perfectly weighted for throwing, a skill Ox had taught me. The three-inch blade was the perfect length to quietly drop someone at close range, a neat trick the U.S. government had taught me. I'd also put the CAR-16 assault rifle in the rear floorboard of the Benz. With thirty rounds per magazine, a short barrel, and collapsible stock, it was a perfect combat weapon to conceal in a vehicle. It was entirely too much firepower for a civilian to be carrying around, but both times I'd chosen to use it in the past, it had come in quite handy.

212 / T. LYNN OCEAN
If Ox and I were correct about Jared's life being tied in to the SIPA transfers, the grim reaper wasn't knocking on the door, it was pounding. Tomorrow was July first. I wasn't sure what I was up against and I damn sure wasn't going to be caught unprepared.

If Ox and I were correct about Jared's life being tied in to the SIPA transfers, the grim reaper wasn't knocking on the door, it was pounding. Tomorrow was July first. I wasn't sure what I was up against and I damn sure wasn't going to be caught unprepared.

The only comforting thing about the man Spud shot was that he must have been an amateur. Ox confirmed it was the same person who'd come looking for me a day earlier, and agreed the man was a novice assassin. Had he been a professional, he never would have tried to hit me in my home. Besides that, a pro would carry a different weapon. Revolvers equipped with silencers were much louder and drew more attention than semiautomatics. And if he was a hit man subversive enough to do the job in my own house, he probably would have succeeded. On the other hand, amateurs took lives everyday. Being hit by a high-paid professional didn't make you any deader than being hit by a two-bit street thug. Dead was dead.

Bill shot me a quizzical look. "Isn't Club Capers a titty bar, Jersey?"

"I'm not sure. But if the menu doesn't look appealing, we'll just have a drink while you admire the dancing, then go somewhere else for chow."

"I bet this has something to do with the Chesterfield case," he mused, replying to a text message on his phone. "Not that I'm complaining. I haven't been to Club Capers since a bachelor party last year."

I watched to make sure he set the alarm and locked the dead bolt. If Bill thought I was acting strangely, he didn't mention it. He was probably too energized by the thought of lunch at Club Capers to notice oddities.

We collected Ox at the Block, and during the half-hour it took us to find Club Capers, we didn't pick up a tail. During the fifteen seconds it took us to be seated inside Club Capers, we picked up a young dancer. Assuming that two guys and a woman entering a strip joint were looking for action, she shimmied into a seat at our table and introduced herself as Honey. She wore a short silk robe that was held shut by one minuscule button at the waistline. There were no garments underneath except a G-string.

Ox nodded pleasantly, as though she was a shopper in line at the grocery store rather than a nearly nude girl who oozed sex appeal. "Thanks, but we're just here for some lunch. Is this the only Club Capers or is there another location?"

"We're the only one I know of," she said, leaning forward to reveal lots of pale, unblemished skin before nodding in the direction of the back corner. "The Capers bar is back there. It's got televisions and a separate entrance. That way, men can tell their wives they're at a sports bar."

"Don't do this any longer than you have to," he told the dancer, slipping her a ten-dollar bill. "It'll make you age pretty quick."

"You're probably right," Honey answered, tucking the money into something beneath her jacket. She sauntered off in search of another mark, putting her time to good use until it was her turn to dance on stage again.

Capers bar sat on the other side of double glass doors and, as promised, it resembled a sports bar strewn with ESPN-tuned television screens. An assortment of bistro tables were sandwiched between a U-shaped bar and a wall laden with cozy sofa and chair arrangements.

We situated ourselves at a table in the far corner where Ox and I had our backs to a wall and could see both entrances. We could also see who came and went through the swinging kitchen doors. Although he appeared completely relaxed, Ox was as tuned into our surroundings as I was. Enjoying himself, Bill was tuned into the circulating dancers.

The darkened bar was unusually busy for a Sunday afternoon and to my surprise, the majority of customers were eating lunch. I supposed the ambience made a cheeseburger well worth the twelve-dollar menu price. We ordered iced teas and three hamburger platters with hand-dipped onion rings and hoped for the best. I pulled the matchbook out of my pocket and passed it to Ox.

"You make anything of this?" I asked him.

He studied the scribbles on the inside cover for a few seconds, looked at the cover that read CLUB CAPERS with an etching of a nude woman, then returned his gaze to the writing.

"It's today's date—" he glanced at his watch "—and about four thirty. Don't know about these other scribbles. Looks like 'collect'?"

"That's what I thought. But collect what? It could be a collect call, but there's no telephone number."

"The 'Fifth St. left' looks like directions to somewhere," he said. "Fifth Street?"

"That's not enough information for directions," Bill pointed out, half-listening. "There'd be a house number or something."

"What else could 'St.' stand for?" Ox said.

"Saint? Stop?" Bill brainstormed.

Our teas arrived and we toasted to a successful recovery of Jared. Looking around, I noticed that the bar stools were perfectly spaced, in contrast to the Block, where bar stools ended up everywhere by the end of the evening. The Capers bar had large, leather-covered swivel stools that were affixed permanently to the ground by a single pole support.

"Bar stool. Could it be the fifth bar stool?" Ox said at the exact same time I thought it.

I nodded. "But from which left? It would depend on which door you came in."

He downed a third of his tea with one smooth gulp. "Maybe the guy hired to hit you was supposed to come here to collect his fee."

"What?" Bill demanded. "Somebody tried to kill you, Jersey?"

"You haven't told him," Ox said.

I shook my head.

Bill stopped staring at a dancer. "When?"

"A guy broke into the Block last night," I told him. "To eliminate me. Probably to keep me from investigating the Jared Chesterfield case, since that's all I'm working on right now."

"A guy? What guy?"

"We don't know who, or why."

"I only wanted you to help Lolly with the cheating-husband thing. I never expected that you'd get so involved and that you could get hurt." He shook his head and went back to watching the dancer with a vertical worry line creasing an otherwise smooth forehead.

"It's what I do, Bill." The burgers arrived, preempting further explanation.

Frowning, he sprinkled salt on his onion rings. "You mean, what you *used* to do. You're retired, remember?"

"Retired or not, it's one reason why you shouldn't want to marry me." I was actually *glad* I'd stumbled into the Chesterfield mess, even though it threw a curve ball at my retirement plans. Putting away bad guys always has given me a euphoric high. I just prayed that we caught them in time.

Ox unceremoniously dug into his burger.

"Well, soon you really will be retired and done with this stuff for good," Bill said and ate an onion ring. "Then you'll come around and deal with your gamophobia. That's a fear of marriage. I read an article on it."

The corners of Ox's mouth went up, just a little, as he took another bite of hamburger. To stop further discussion of my impending nuptials, I dug into my food, too. The burger was great—juicy and served on a freshly baked bun. It may have been worth twelve dollars, even if not delivered by a topless waitress.

"Think I know which side the fifth bar stool is on," Ox said between bites. Without making a show of doing so, my eyes scanned the bar area. A burly man in his early fifties was settling himself onto the fifth bar stool from the left, if viewed from the bar entrance. He glanced from his watch to the doorway and back to his watch. I questioned Ox with my eyes.

"He's the friend of the guy that made Spud angry." It was thug number two. The one who hadn't stumbled across Cracker and gotten himself shot to death in my home.

I drank some tea. "He paying any attention to us?"

"Not yet," Ox said.

"Bill, why don't you go back to Club Capers for a little while? Enjoy the entertainment on the other side of those swinging doors," I said.

He started to protest.

"She'll be fine," Ox said. Wordlessly, Bill stood and walked out of the bar.

Our server stopped by to check on us. We assured her everything was good. Even in his preoccupied state, the man on the fifth bar stool took a few moments to admire the server's bare breasts and afterward, her retreating backside. Then his eyes swept the room and fear registered when he recognized Ox. He shoved himself off the stool and ran to the door. Ox, moving more gracefully than any two-hundred-and-twenty-pound man ought to be able to, caught up with the guy before he made it outside. Right behind them, my hand tightened on the grip of the Glock as Ox used one of the man's arms as leverage to shove him outside to the sidewalk.

The man jerked his head backward into Ox's chin and frantically drew a gun from his jacket pocket. Ox's hold on the man's forearm strengthened to a bone-crushing force. Wincing in pain and unable to turn his body around to face us, he dropped the gun and stopped struggling. I retrieved the weapon while Ox instructed the guy to keep walking. A couple of kids on skateboards gave us a wide berth as they wheeled past.

"Fellow tried to pull a gun on me," Ox said, unconcerned, as though commenting on the weather.

"Well, that was a crazy thing to do," I replied.

The three of us made our way to the rear of the Club Capers building and, after I patted the thug down and found no more weapons, Ox slammed him against a Dumpster.

"You've made a mistake," the man stammered as he struggled to remain on his feet. "I don't know what you want." He wore an off-brand polyester suit with a white button-down shirt and no tie. His body bulged beneath the disheveled fabric, but the mass was soft weight with no solid muscle behind it.

"I think you do," I said.

"I don't even know who you are!"

"I think you do," I repeated.

Breathing heavy, his eyes darted back and forth from Ox to me.

"I'm the woman you and your buddy were hired to drop. Problem is, I'm not ready to check out just yet."

Leaving me to deal with the rent-a-thug, Ox headed back inside the club. Our guy had come to meet someone at Club Capers, and that someone could very well have shown up. Walking into a club, even an adult club, Ox was about as unobtrusive as an elephant. But whomever hired the shooter might recognize me.

I studied the heavyset man more closely. His demeanor verified that he wasn't a professional hit man. "Tell me who hired you and this encounter will be easier for us both."

He turned to run. I threw a low side-kick to the back of his knee. The instant he went down, I cuffed one of his hands to a thin metal pole that ran vertically along the corner of the Dumpster, and pressed on his damaged knee with my foot just because he'd angered me.

"I don't know what you're talking about." His free hand raked across a balding head.

"Don't make me lose patience. My hamburger is getting cold while I'm standing here by this stinking Dumpster. The longer you make me wait to finish my meal, the madder I'm going to get."

Sliding the captive bracelet along the pole, he slowly stood. "Seriously, chickie, you've got the wrong man." I punched him in the lower gut, but angled my fist upward sharply enough to penetrate his diaphragm. He made a long, sucking hiccup sound and fought to breathe.

"We can do it your way and your wife won't recognize you when she comes to bail you out of jail. Me, I'll just be a little sore tomorrow and I'll need a manicure." I looked around to make sure we hadn't drawn an audience. "Wait a minute . . . why should I beat the stuffing out of you and have sore hands for my trouble, when my friend can do it for me?" I made a move as though going back inside to get Ox.

"I never saw her," he said, still gasping for air. "It was a woman, she talked to Hank, my partner, to set it up. Said to get rid of you, and if we did it by yesterday, there was an extra five grand in it. We was supposed to meet here for the cash."

"Go on."

"She gave us your name and the address of that bar where you live. Price was ten grand, plus the five bonus. But you was a harder case than we figured."

How insulting. My life was only worth fifteen thousand dollars?

"How'd she find you?"

"I guess she asked around. Hank and I, we do some . . . security type work now and then. Rainbow fixed it for us to meet her at Club Capers to begin with. But only Hank came because I had to take the wife to the doctor."

Rainbow was a small-time Wilmington bookie who probably didn't know the woman wanted a professional hit. Although I knew of him because my partner Rita liked to bet on college football, Rainbow didn't know me. In his world, men like these were utilized to scare someone into paying gambling debts. Most likely, the bookie had pocketed a few hundred bucks for arranging the meeting and gone happily on his way, not realizing his referral would get one man killed and land the other one in jail.

"Where were you the night Hank paid me a visit?"

"I was there, outside the place. Keepin' a lookout. We didn't know about the dog or the old man bein' there. Thought it was just you," he said, still working to fill his lungs with air.

A professional would have known exactly how many people and animals lived in a building and what their typical routines were. For that matter, a pro wouldn't work with a buddy, especially one who'd run scared at the sound of a barking dog. Even for amateurs, they'd done a pretty lousy job. Not that I was complaining.

"And, you came to Club Capers why?" I asked incredulously. The job wasn't done. Did he really think someone would arrive with a bundle of cash for a job well-botched?

"She called me. Said we missed but the price was up to twenty grand if I finished the job alone. She was supposed to give me five as a deposit." He studied a kitten that picked at some stray garbage near the foot of the Dumpster. "I needed the money. I'm into Rainbow for five alone, and the ex is after me for back alimony . . ."

His voice trailed off as he realized the absurdity of what he was telling me. That paying off his petty debts was justification for trying to take my life. Looking at him with disgust, a thought nudged its way into my conscious. How had the woman known I was still alive? And that Hank was dead? It hadn't been in the paper.

"She called you on your cell phone?"

He rubbed the cuffed wrist with his free hand. "Yeah. I called the number back to ask her a question, but some dude answered. It was a pay phone at an Exxon station."

"How did you know who to look for today, to collect your advance?"

"She said for me sit on the fifth stool at the bar, same as we was supposed to do to collect our fee anyways. And she didn't say it would be her meeting me today. Just that somebody would bring me the money."

"What's your name?"

"Horace."

"Horace, I've got a nice present for you." I flipped open my cell phone.

"Why did I listen to Hank? We're not hit men. I can't do time again. I can't."

I uncuffed Horace from the Dumpster, recuffed his hands together, and walked him back into the Capers bar. Bill had rejoined Ox at the table and they were finishing their hamburgers. Horace and I joined them.

"Ox, Bill," I said, "meet Horace." He situated himself awkwardly in a chair, hands locked behind him, and stared into nothingness. If surrounding patrons thought it odd to see a handcuffed man at our table, they didn't show it.

"Go screw yourself, Horace. Better yet, wait and let your cell mate do it for you," Bill said.

Ox and I looked at each other with raised eyebrows.

"Guess he doesn't like the thought of some slob trying to kill you, Jersey," Ox said.

"I really don't," Bill agreed. "It's so unrefined."

I surveyed the club and didn't see anyone or anything unusual. Nearly nude girls circulated, working the lunch crowd for tips.

"Nobody else showed," Ox said.

Bill asked for tea refills. Ox finished his meal and mine. I called Dirk and told him there was a package at Club Capers with his name on it. More specifically, the partner of the last package that he'd removed from my living room floor.

"This one still breathing?"

"Yep."

"Your retirement is turning out to be rather eventful, Jersey. If you keep serving up criminals on a china platter, we're going to have to put you on the staff roster."

"Thanks for the offer, but no thanks," I told him. "I would appreciate it, though, if you'd return some of my handcuffs. I think you owe me four or five pairs by now."

"A cruiser will be on the way to collect the package and I'm about ten minutes behind them. The handcuffs may take a bit longer. I'll have to requisition them."

NINETEEN

Rainbow was easy to find and Ox said he'd enjoy accompanying me to pay the bookie a visit, on the hunch that the woman who had hired Hank and Horace was also one of Jared's kidnappers. If nothing else, Rainbow could give us a description.

We had dropped an unusually subdued Bill at his condo after lunch and I didn't get the usual good-bye kiss. He may have been rethinking his wedding wishes. I hoped he was. It would make things much easier.

Rainbow's hangout was a sports bar called Tippy's, and he was there often enough to claim a corner booth as his own. People called him Rainbow because his hair ranged from blond to bright orange to red. He paid out quickly when he lost, Rita told me, but he also had a reputation for collecting quickly when he won. According to my partner, he took sports bets from fifty up to two thousand dollars. On request, he would take much larger bets, which indicated he had a financial backer—possibly someone based in Atlantic City.

When Ox and I slid into his booth, a man resembling a mature Redwood tree instantaneously appeared, hand beneath his jacket, prepped to draw a weapon. He stood, waiting on instructions from Rainbow. Ox raised an eyebrow in amusement and I wondered why a small-time bookie needed a bodyguard. Maybe in his world it was a prestige symbol, like wearing Gucci loafers.

"This is Dick and I'm Jane," I said to Rainbow. Up close, his hair was an even brighter shade of orange than it had first appeared. His skin looked pale in contrast, but his greenish eyes were alert, calm. I guessed his age to be around fifty. "We need your help," I told him.

He nodded his head, indicating the Redwood could leave before returning his attention to us. "I've had a few threats lately. Just being cautious," he explained. "How can I help you?" There was a slight hint of an Irish accent behind a smooth voice.

"We're here because you recently hooked a woman up with some hired muscle. Hank had the misfortune to point his gun at my dog while he was trying to kill me and got himself shot to death. His buddy Horace fared a little better—he landed in jail instead of the morgue. I want to know who hired them."

Rainbow got whiter beneath his already blanched skin.

"Excuse me?" He sat up with genuine disbelief. "Hank and Horace tried to kill you?"

I kept my eyes on Rainbow. There was no need to repeat myself. A cheerleader type appeared at our table, wearing a skimpy top and tight black bike shorts. Ox ordered beers for us. Sensing tension at the table, she retreated quickly. Taking in the scene, Ox's eyes roamed Tippy's. It was a comfortable place with a clientele

of men watching sports on strategically placed televisions and
women flirting with the men who watched sports.

Rainbow sank down in his seat, arms crossed defensively across
his chest. "Look, if you know who I am, then you understand I
don't deal in that kind of thing. I'd never hook somebody up for a
hired hit. I don't even *know* any professional hit men."

I imagined that he probably did, but didn't pursue the matter.

"Perhaps the woman didn't make it clear to you what she
wanted," Ox said.

The cheerleader returned with two mugs of beer and a bowl of
pretzels. She'd also brought Rainbow a bourbon on the rocks and
a cola in a separate glass. He downed half the glass of cola in one
take before sipping the whiskey.

"Don't like them mixed," he explained. "Ruins the carbonation."

I wasn't interested in his drinking habits. "You want to tell us
about her?"

"I tell you what I know, you'll leave me out of it?" Rainbow
was accustomed to negotiating. A man with his career never gave
up something for nothing. Instinct told him it would behoove
him to cooperate, so he wasn't going to ask for too much. But he
had to ask for something.

"Sure. No hassles for you."

"The woman showed up at my booth one afternoon, like you
two just did. I'd never seen her before. Said she needed somebody
to help her out with a—how'd she phrase it—a *security problem*.
She needed help with a security problem." He did the double-
glass drink thing again. "Said she needed someone who didn't
mind breaking a few rules and that she needed them immediately."

"Why did she ask you?" Ox said.

"Don't know, didn't ask."

226 / T. LYNN OCEAN

A couple of guys wearing denim jeans and Duke University T-shirts approached the booth to place a bet, but stopped short when they saw Ox. "We'll catch you later, man," one of them said.

"I'll be here," Rainbow agreed and turned his attention back to me. "She was a looker, you know? I figured she had problems with somebody stalking her. An ex maybe. Something like that. So I turned her on to Hank and Horace. They work as a team and have taken care of me when I needed to, ah, persuade someone to pay up. I'm real sorry to hear about Hank. He was a good guy."

A good guy who didn't minding shooting a complete stranger. "I'm sure."

"What did she look like?" Ox asked.

"Tall, curvy. Never took off her sunglasses. Long jet-black hair, bangs. A knockout. Even beneath all that hair and the glasses, she was beautiful. I got a woodie just talking to her."

"Could she have worn a wig?" Ox said.

Rainbow shrugged by cocking his head.

"What color were her eyebrows?"

"Not sure. Lighter than the hair, maybe? They were mostly covered by the tinted glasses. Plus, I wasn't looking at her eyebrows, if you know what I mean." Rainbow finished his cola and bourbon, separately. "Anyway, that was it. I told her how to get in touch with the guys, she pressed a couple of C-notes into my pants pocket, and she left."

"Your *pants* pocket?" I asked.

A faint smear of pink appeared across each pasty cheek. "Yeah. She leaned across the table, like she was going to kiss me or something, and stuffed the bills into my jeans pocket. I haven't seen her since."

"When was that?" I said.

"Lemme think. Atlanta was playing Florida, lost by two. It was four days ago."

The three of us sat in silence, drinking and contemplating. It was something to go on, but not much. Wilmington was full of beautiful women, but we only needed the one who was furtively moving pieces on Chesterfield's game board. The one who wanted me dead and out of the way. Or, perhaps the beautiful woman who was working for someone else that wanted me dead and out of the way. There wasn't any more information to be gleaned at the moment, so we finished our beers and stood to leave.

"I'm out of it then?" Rainbow said, wisely choosing not to ask why somebody wanted me dead. He earned his living by taking people's bets, not nosing his way into their businesses.

"As long as you've been straight with me," I said.

"I've been straight with you."

I handed the bookie a card. "You hear from her again, call me."

As we walked away, Rainbow said, "By the way, I think her name might be Theresa or Alecia. Maybe Lisa. I definitely heard an 'isa' in there. Somebody called her mobile and I could hear them through the headset. A guy. He was talking real loud before she hung up on him, which was right after she realized who it was."

Another morsel of information to process. I thanked him. The streaks of blond, orange, and red hair nodded in acknowledgment.

"So, what's your guiding spirit telling you now?" I asked Ox as he drove us back to the Block in the Benz. It was yet another delightful summer day in Wilmington—the kind of day that put people in a good mood—but I wasn't appreciative of the weather. All I could think about was the possibility of facing Samuel Chesterfield after he'd learned that his son was dead. I hoped it wouldn't come to that.

"I don't know what my guiding spirit thinks about the mess you're in, but I'm thinking that this Social Insecurity virus is going to activate tomorrow. You'd better hurry up and figure out something soon."

"Gee, thanks," I said.

"Anytime." Ox showed me his brilliant smile, the one that gave me a warm feeling every time I saw it, even if he was being sarcastic.

"I'm wondering about the time frame, when the woman contacted Rainbow."

"Four days ago. That was after the accountant took a bullet," Ox said.

As usual, we were on the same wavelength. Darlene was murdered for no apparent reason, but she might have known something since she was Chesterfield's personal assistant. Eddie Flowers was killed because he *had* discovered something amiss at Chesterfield Financial. I was next on the list because I was getting close to figuring out what that something was. Probably, it was the same person—or people—who wanted the three of us out of the way.

We broke free of heavy traffic and Ox stepped on the accelerator. "Is Trish still keeping an eye and ear on the senator's beach house for you?"

"Far as I know. I haven't heard anything from her lately. But I usually never do, until she has something worthwhile." Trish was good at what she did because nobody ever suspected that she was an investigator. Just like me, she could play the ditzy, helpless female role to a tee. Unlike me, she could happily do surveillance for days.

"I think you'll be hearing from her soon," Ox said.

On cue, my mobile rang. The incoming number on the display told me it was Trish. I eyed him, wondering how he knew. He shrugged, as though making a prediction that metamorphosed into fact was no biggie.

"Hello?" I said into the flip-phone.

"Two women paid a visit to the Ralls kid at the senator's beach house about half an hour ago. They arrived together in a white Buick LaSabre. Both were maybe in their late thirties, one bleached-blond and the other had on a floppy hat so I couldn't tell what color her hair was. I didn't get a great look at either one of them through the binoculars," Trish reported.

"What else?" I asked. She wouldn't have called unless there was more.

"What's weird is that the car isn't in the senator's driveway even though there is plenty of room. It's parked three doors down, in front of a vacant rental house."

"You get photos?"

"Of course I got photos. And a read on the plate." Trish recited the number to me. "Incidentally, Jersey, my boyfriend tuned up this clunker van of yours. You owe me forty-seven dollars for parts. Labor was free."

"I imagine it was. You think you could find yourself a nice home-security expert next, Trish? Because I'm going to be updating my security system at the Block by adding cameras."

"It might help if you actually turned your security system on."

"For your information, I'm going to start activating the system every night."

"Good. For *your* information, I date men because I'm attracted to them. Not to get work done."

"Right. Does your Honda have that new sunroof yet?"

"It's actually called a *moon* roof, thank you very much."

"I'm on my way there," I told her. "Can you stay put and keep your eyelids up?"

"Nothing I'd rather be doing than your surveillance," she said.

"That's because you're so gloriously good at it, Trish. See you in twenty minutes."

Since Ox was already driving us back to the Block, I asked if he wanted to take a detour. Like an insurance policy, he was good to have along, just in case. Twice before, I'd asked him to join the Barnes Agency as a partner, and twice he'd graciously declined. He didn't need the money, he said, and besides, who would run the Block? Despite not wanting to officially be on the agency's payroll, he willingly jumped in to help whenever I asked—and sometimes when I didn't.

"Happy to detour," Ox said. "Where we headed?"

"Senator Sigmund Ralls's beach house, where his son Walton lives."

He made a few turns and pointed the Benz in the direction of Wrightsville Beach. "The one who got kicked out of the Citadel and is into computers?" Like Spud, Ox had been kept up to date on the Chesterfield case.

"That's the one. It seems he's had a visit from a couple of women. But oddly, they parked three houses away."

"Two women who didn't want to be seen at the house," Ox thought aloud.

"Not your typical partying teenagers. Who are they?"

"Good question."

"Can't you summon the spirits?"

"They're on break."

I reached Dirk on his mobile phone and he obliged my request for a tag check. The Buick was a rental. Either the women had flown in from out of town, or they were locals who didn't want to be seen in their own vehicle. Which didn't narrow things down at all.

The short drive to Wrightsville Beach was dotted with sleepy residential communities and remnants of farmland that were now overgrown with wild vegetation, and the peaceful afternoon sped past while I sat deep in thought. It had rained the night before and the roadside trees, freshly bathed, glowed a healthy green.

Even the tall, skinny Carolina pines sparkled and seemed to wave as we passed. We were just crossing the Intracoastal Waterway bridge that led to the beach when Trish called again.

"Miss me?" I asked in greeting.

"The women just came out of the house and the blonde is walking like she's wasted. She can barely stand up . . . hang on, let's see what they're doing," Trish said, reporting a live play-by-play. "They're walking to the Buick. The boy isn't with them. You want me to follow them if they leave? Oh, wait. Hang on. The one in the hat just helped the wasted one into the driver's seat and shut the door. But she's not getting in on the other side, she's walking off. Crap, the car is pulling out."

The women hadn't been in the house long enough for one of them to get stumbling drunk, and smoking pot wouldn't make somebody lose that much physical coordination. And why had the mystery women arrived together but left separately?

"Are you in a position to block the car?"

"No, she's already moving."

"Stay with her then, would you?" I asked. "Call the Wrightsville Beach P.D. Tell them you're behind a dangerously drunk driver and see if you can get some blue lights on her. We'll go check out the beach house." Although the Wrightsville Beach Police Department was a small one, an officer could get to any location quickly since the island was only about four miles long.

"Will do," Trish said and hung up.

Minutes later, Ox and I found the beach house empty. We circled several blocks surrounding the senator's summer getaway, and found the sidewalks empty as well. There was no sign of Jared or the mystery woman in the floppy hat. I shot Ox a look of frustration, hoping for a dose of his spiritual intervention, but none was forthcoming. He shrugged his shoulders and said something witty about me having to actually make use of my investigative abilities. I wondered if he somehow already knew the outcome, but didn't want to let me in on it. He caught me studying him and raised an amused eyebrow.

"You think me and my guiding spirits are withholding on you?"

I didn't have a chance to reply because my mobile rang and an out-of-breath Trish was on the other end. I put her on speaker-phone. The Buick had run a stop sign, been clipped by an inter-secting concrete truck, and crashed into a light pole. A cop had pulled in behind the car just in time to witness the accident. Trish stopped along with the cop and was inspecting the scene as she talked. Emergency Medical Services hadn't yet arrived, but Trish was certain the driver no longer had a pulse.

"At least now we have a place to go where we're sure to find a clue," I said, thinking that it might be easier to view a dead person with Ox by my side.

"Clues are good," Ox agreed.

Heading to the accident scene, our thoughts were on Jared. He was running out of time.

TWENTY

Trish, Ox, Soup, and Spud were gathered around my kitchen table sharing a box of early morning Krispy Kreme doughnuts. Oddly, Spud kept glancing at his watch. I wondered what he was masterminding, but had more important things to concern myself with at the moment. The calendar had rolled into a new month and my nerves were taut.

It was July first. SIPA transfers would begin flowing at noon and continue throughout the day. Social Insecurity would awaken on cue and its tentacles would snake out to amass a fortune. In response, Soup's planted code would quietly place the funds back where they belonged. It would all occur in an electronic battle-field, quietly, invisibly, discreetly. But Jared's battle would take place in a more tangible arena. We had to find out where, and do so soon.

There was no need to study the photographs Trish had taken in front of the senator's beach house yesterday because, despite all the blood at the accident scene, I had immediately recognized the dead woman. It was Barb Henley. Jared Chesterfield's surrogate mom. The angry, bitter one who had been blackmailing him for petty change. I was perplexed. What was Barb doing in town, and more importantly, how did she know the Ralls family?

Trish and I had been politely questioned by both the Wrightsville Beach cops and a detective from New Hanover County Sheriff's Department. I refused to say why I'd employed Trish to watch the place, but cooperated in passing along the fact that Barb Henley had been in the senator's beach house just prior to the car accident, and that she'd been there with Walton and another, unidentified woman. Thanks to Trish's meticulous record keeping, I was able to supply the exact times and photographs.

A surge of scandal-fueled curiosity rippled through the police department immediately after it became known that the prominent senator from Georgia, Sigmund Ralls, might be involved in what was presumed to be a lethal party scandal. It made no difference that the senator and his wife were out of town at the time, attending a fund-raiser.

The press had gotten access to supposedly confidential blood-test results, which showed that Barb Henley's body held lethal amounts of cocaine and PCP, more commonly known as angel dust. A speculating morning news reporter surmised that Barb Henley didn't die from crash injuries, but rather drugs obtained at the senator's house. Walton Ralls was wanted for questioning but had seemingly vanished. Nobody, including his shocked parents, knew of his whereabouts.

"Somebody give the dog a bite of doughnut, for crying out loud," Spud said. "He's drooling all over the place."

I pinched off a piece of glazed doughnut and fed it to Cracker, who had shoved his snout into my lap. As I often did when a case had me stumped, I'd called for a brainstorming session with the few people I trusted implicitly. Our small group of assorted genius collectively mulled through the facts and assumptions. Quite a bit had transpired in a two-week time period.

It seemed only days ago that I'd officially retired and was meeting Bill for dinner. He had introduced me to an old college friend, Lolly, who engaged me to find out if Samuel Chesterfield was having an affair. He wasn't, but his firm's computer system was infested with the Social Insecurity virus. His accountant was killed. His son was kidnapped. His assistant died of an overdose. The alleged kidnappers arranged to collect their ransom cash at Fort Fisher tomorrow, a day *after* the SIPA transfers. Barb Henley was dead. And the Feds were still treating the case as a kidnapping.

"This virus is going to fire up in a few hours," I told the assembled group, "and won't finish doing its thing until late today."

"At which point, they will have no more use for Jared Chesterfield, if in fact he was kidnapped and not in on the whole thing from the beginning," Trish said.

"Either way," Ox said, "they won't need him anymore."

Between mouthfuls of sugary doughnuts and coffee, we considered all angles and made zero headway with the original conundrum I'd been working on since Chesterfield handed me a retainer check: where was Jared Chesterfield?

Dirk appeared at the door and rapped his knuckles against it twice before letting himself in. "Spud, you've got to be more careful about where you and your poker pals park the Chrysler."

A veil of red appeared beneath Spud's tanned face and his jaw froze in mid-bite of a lemon-filled.

"Lucky for you I was dropping by to see Jersey, and came the back way, through the alley," Dirk continued. "I just caught somebody trying to steal your car! He looked suspicious, so I questioned him. He said he's a friend of yours, but I didn't recognize him so I ran his name." Dirk reached for a jelly-filled. "Turns out he has a prior for auto theft."

Veins pulsed in Spud's forehead and his ears glowed a bright shade of red. His lips moved for several seconds before words came out. "Damn it!" A string of curses spewed forth, entwined in an unintelligible, rambling sentence that ended with, "Oh, for crying the hell out loud!"

Expecting a much different response—a thank-you perhaps—Dirk raised his eyebrows at Spud.

Trying not to laugh, Ox spewed some coffee. At first, it was a grin that displayed even, white teeth beneath olive skin. Then it turned into a deep chuckle that became a full-blown laugh erupting from his midsection as the weight of his body tilted the kitchen chair to rest on its rear legs. It was unusual to hear Ox laugh uncontrollably and Trish couldn't resist joining him. Soup sat back and Cracker sat up to watch the developing scene unfold.

I glared at Spud with disbelief. "What have you done now?"

"Rainbow said this guy would know what he was doing! I paid him three hundred bucks! And gave him my spare key so his thief wouldn't waste time trying to hot-wire the dad-blasted thing."

"You know Rainbow?" I asked.

"Paid who three hundred bucks?" Dirk asked.

Already having figured it out, Ox and Trish doubled up laughing and got Soup going, too.

Spud stood and waved his arms around like a maniac. "Of course I know Rainbow! Everybody knows Rainbow!"

It was news to me. I thought only gamblers knew Rainbow.

Losing his balance, Spud sat back down to keep from falling over. "I paid him three hundred bucks to have this guy steal that piece-of-crap sedan of mine. He said it would be taken to one of them chop shops where they cut it up for parts. So I could be rid of the thing and get my insurance money!"

"I'm not hearing this," Dirk said, polishing off his doughnut. Cracker sidled up next to Dirk, gave him a pitiful starving look, and was rewarded with a pinch of sugary treat.

"Do you realize how much money this car has cost me?!" Spud yelled at nobody. "A lot! It's the car from hell! From hell, I tell you!"

Dirk cleaned his sticky fingers with a napkin. "I take it you're still trying to sell your car, Spud?"

"How can I sell it when nobody wants it?"

"Let me get this straight," I said to my father. "You paid Rainbow to have a thief steal your car."

"When I put it out there for the hoodlums to steal, they took it for a joyride and returned it. You need a job done right, you hire a professional."

"I'm still not hearing this," Dirk said, using his napkin to wipe Cracker's drooling mouth. "Any coffee left?"

"Then you had to go and mess it all up!" Spud threw the accusation at Dirk. "Can't you just leave well enough alone and let a man earn a living?"

"Sorry Spud," Dirk soothed, "but I earn my living by stopping the bad guys—oh, like car thieves, for example—from earning their living."

Ox's guffaws had simmered down to a wide grin, but Trish had the giggles. Spud turned his angry glare, full force, on her.

She smiled sweetly at him. "Spud, why don't you find a cute sugar momma to take care of you? Keep the Chrysler so she can cart you around in it?"

The color in his face toned down a few notches as Trish's suggestion sunk in and his mouth moved from side to side in contemplation.

"Our car thief is cuffed and resting comfortably in the backseat of my unmarked. Thanks for the breakfast, but guess I'd better go check on him. By the way, Spud, what is your official position? Is he a friend of yours? You did give him a key in a roundabout way, through the bookie."

"I don't even know the guy! And what kind of an idiot would steal a car in broad daylight, anyways?" Spud said.

"The kind of guy that doesn't plan on getting caught," Dirk answered. "He paid a fine and did community service for the prior. Picking up a car for a friend so he can wash and wax it isn't doing anything illegal," Dirk said offhandedly. "On the other hand, insurance fraud is *very* illegal."

It took a few seconds for Spud to clue in.

"Yeah, yeah, for crying out loud," Spud said. "I know the guy, er—"

"Michael Lowes," Dirk supplied.

"Michael, right," Spud continued. "Yeah, Mike's a good kid—"

"He's sixty-two," Dirk interjected.

Spud forced a laugh. "At my age, I call everybody kid. So I guess you'd better let my good friend, ah . . ."

"Mike."

"Right, Mike. You'd better let Mike out of your police car so he can go wash and wax the Chrysler."

"I'll make sure he drops it back here and leaves the key at the Block," Dirk said.

"Ask him to vacuum out the trunk, would you?" Spud said, always one to push his luck. "And put that shiny stuff on the wheels."

"Thank you," I told Dirk, since Spud hadn't. "What were you stopping by for when you happened upon the car thief?"

"I almost forgot," Dirk said, turning at the top of the stairs with a Columbo move. "The beautiful Mrs. Sigmund Ralls and her son appeared at the Wrightsville Beach police station this morning. The kid maintains that Barb Henley and a friend were in town and dropped by to talk with his mother, thinking she might be at the summer house. They stayed for fifteen minutes. He swears they didn't do any drugs. Supposedly, the Henley woman met the senator's wife at some social function. Hanna Lane Ralls says that Henley was probably trying to solicit support for a new environmental charity."

I tried to digest this new information, but it disagreed with me. Barb Henley wasn't the type to donate her time or energies to a charitable cause.

"Who's the supposed friend?"

"Walton said he didn't know her. For that matter, he said he didn't know Barb, other than he met her once at a political thing. What's interesting, though, is that when we were questioning the kid, he tripped up and called them sisters. Then, he said that he meant friends—not sisters—and reiterated that he'd never met the woman in the hat before." Dirk relayed the information to five sets of skeptical ears. Anticipating my next question, he continued, "Walton says the women arrived together and left together. He has no idea why Barb drove off and the friend walked away."

"What did they talk about?"

"The senator's political rally. The weather. The annual king-mackerel fishing tournament."

"Is anybody actually buying their story?" Trish asked.

"Of course not. But the senator has some powerful lawyers, who by the way, convinced a judge that the search of the beach house was illegal. Since their rights were so abhorrently violated, they're threatening to sue the Wrightsville department."

"Our judicial system at its finest," Ox said.

"So as of now, no charges are pending against Walton Ralls and mommy has indicated that all future correspondence and/or questioning will be coordinated through daddy's lawyers."

"Walton is living back at the beach house, then?" I asked.

"That's the address they gave as a current residence for the kid, but I doubt he's really staying there."

After Dirk left, our assembled group mulled over the situation. We mulled and talked and mulled some more. When the coffee ran out, Ox went downstairs to prep the Block for the lunch crowd. Soup headed back to his apartment to do some genealogical research on Barb Henley in search of a possible sister, but only after reminding me that my tab was approaching the size of a Royal Caribbean cruise rather than a mere week on my boat with Captain Pete. Trish agreed to monitor both Walton's and Chesterfield's mobile phones. Spud called Bobby and Hal to see if they'd drive him to Tippy's, where he was going to ask Rainbow for a refund of his three hundred dollars. And I put on a tank top and my favorite ratty pair of sweats. I thought about hitting the salon for a half-hour massage but decided to go for a run instead.

TWENTY-ONE

The familiar network of sidewalks and streets in the historic district that paralleled the river glided by as I fell into a comfortable rhythm. I paced myself with medium strides that would take me three or four miles before I'd slow my gait to a brisk walk. I concentrated on breathing, filling my lungs to capacity with the balmy Wilmington air while I tried to think about nothing except breaths going in and out. Annoyingly, my thoughts strayed to Bill. We hadn't spent much time together lately and I missed his company. But at the same time, I couldn't fathom growing old together. I had no desire to hold his hand after our joints had turned knobby and arthritic. I didn't even like the thought of shopping together for new furniture or sharing a bank account. On the other hand, he adored me. After a few blocks of this internal struggle, as if I'd conjured him up by magic, my mobile rang and it was Bill on the other end of the tower. I'd taken the time to strap the Sig to my ankle and the phone to my elastic waistband. Whenever I saw someone sitting atop a Lifecycle at the gym chatting merrily on their phone, I thought it looked ridiculous. I wondered if right now, a bystander might think I looked ridiculous, jogging and talking.

"Hey, what's up?" I said, a bit breathless.

"Calling to say hello, Jersey. I miss you."

"Just think, we'll be on *Incognito* soon," I said, daydreaming about our upcoming excursion. Calming water, sunshine, booze, food, Bill in a bathing suit, and no worries. Except for the concern that he might start talking marriage again. I approached an intersection and jogged in place a few seconds to let a horse-drawn carriage pass.

"You're breathing really loud, Jersey. Is this going to be an obscene phone call? Because if it is, you should probably tell me what you're wearing."

"I'm out jogging, to clear my head. But I'm all for getting obscene with you soon."

"Looking forward to it," he purred. "Until then, anything I can do to help?"

"Just be ready for my postponed retirement celebration."

I stepped off the curb to cross a cobblestone street when I heard a compact explosion, a whistling hiss, and the jarring sound of a bullet hitting metal, seemingly all at once. I dove and tucked into a roll, protecting my head with my arms. Landing on my feet, I zigzagged to the other side of the street where I took cover behind an illegally parked car. From my crouched position, I retrieved the Sig and scanned the streets, adrenaline pumping, senses on maximum alert. Screaming tires caught my attention, but all I could make out was the tail end of a white compact vehicle turning the corner. I couldn't see the plate number or the driver and wasn't positive about the make of the car. Thoughts of chasing it on foot were immediately quelled by the realization that it would be a futile effort.

Gripping the Sig, I unfolded my body and stood, realizing that I still held the mobile phone in my other hand. I was really getting tired of being shot at. The mix of tourists and locals passing by curiously checked out their surroundings for evidence of a disruption. Finding none, they carried on with their day, assuming the sound they'd heard was a car backfiring or perhaps a mischievous teen playing with firecrackers. Drive-by shootings just didn't happen in Wilmington. I put the phone to my ear.

Bill remained on the other end. "Jersey? What's going on?"

"Nothing. I tripped and fell, but I'm fine. I'm heading back to the Block, so I'll catch you later."

"Okay," he said. "Love you."

I flipped the phone shut without answering and returned to the other side of the street where I found a damaged black-and-white ONE WAY street sign. The bullet had punched a hole through the center of the arrow shape and lodged itself in the bark of an aged oak tree just beyond. Using a stone, I pried the bullet out and pocketed what appeared to be a flattened chunk of lead that might have traveled from a .38 Special. I gave the majestic tree a pat of apology for enduring a nasty assault and jogged back toward the Block. I took several unnecessary turns and scrutinized each approaching vehicle. When I got closer to home, I dialed Ox and, after explaining what had happened, asked him to take a look around the Block for anyone idling in a white car.

"Retirement doesn't seem to agree with you, Jersey," he said before hanging up.

The remainder of my run was without incident and my home telephone was ringing as I climbed the stairs to my residence above the Block. Plopping down at the kitchen table to remove my running shoes and ankle holster, I answered it.

"Barb Henley's sister is Lisa Wentworth," Soup said in greeting. "Same father, same mother. You want the full story?"

"Soup, you are amazingly good at what you do. I'll take the dime version." I drank Gatorade from a liter bottle and listened.

"Barb is two years older than her sister. They were born and raised in Long Island. Father shot himself in an apparent suicide when they were teenagers. The newspaper blurb didn't say why he shot himself, but apparently Lisa witnessed it. The mother reverted to her maiden name, Brown. Lisa kept her dead father's name, Wentworth. And Barb changed her name to Henley after the man her mother remarried, even though the mother kept using Brown. The mother got herself arrested twice for driving under the influence. After crippling another driver in a wreck, she went to a judge-ordered alcohol rehab. She divorced a year after that, and it appears that both girls left home and went separate ways. Barb was seventeen, Lisa only fifteen."

"What might Lisa be doing now?"

"Oh, that's the best part," Soup said after a slurp of something, mentally calculating my tab, which was growing by the minute. "It's going to cost you more than a dime."

"Give me the quarter version."

"Lisa hooked up with an elderly boyfriend who took her in, made her finish high school, and then put her through college, according to a disapproving neighbor. I found the street address through DMV records for learner's permits, and then rounded up the neighbor who, luckily, still lives in the house next door. The benevolent boyfriend has since died. Anyway, Lisa passed Sugar Daddy one-o-one with flying colors, and got pretty decent grades in school, too. Grew into a beautiful, leggy, natural blonde. Became a successful model, but never quite made it to the supermodel category. Ringing any bells yet?"

"Good God." When Bill had first introduced me to Lolly, he'd mentioned her real name was Lisa.

"You got it. Lisa is Lolly. She had her first name legally changed to Lolly, I guess for a modeling stage name. I ran a basic background on Lolly and Samuel Chesterfield the first go-around and you already saw those results. They revealed prior employers and no criminal activity. I didn't dig further."

"Well, I didn't see a need to," I said to us both, the implications seeping in.

"There's more if you want it, but nothing crucial. You've got the meat."

"I'm not upping the ante to fifty cents." I thanked Soup for what seemed like the umpteenth time in the past few weeks and disconnected with a promise to add a bottle of Corazon tequila to the supplies for his upcoming week on my boat.

Cracker materialized and nudged my hand with a wet nose, then chest-butted my chair, his way of demanding attention from his humans. I scratched him between the eyes, right on top of his snout. It was one of his favorite places to be rubbed and he angled his head so I could have a better reach.

"You and the Sig have a nice run?" Spud asked, ambling into the kitchen. My discarded running shoes were on the floor and backup weapon was on the table.

"Just being careful, like you said," I told him. He clicked his teeth a few times and made a sound that ended in "harrumph."

"You know, kid, I been thinking . . ." he began and I knew by his tone of voice that a revelation was forthcoming. "Since the LHS has been all cleaned up and waxed and has that shiny stuff on the wheels, it's a pretty nice-looking ride. I might just keep it to have something for my girlie babes to carry me around in, like Trish suggested. Plus, Bobby can drive it pretty good." He watched for my reaction over an upturned chocolate Yoo-hoo bottle.

"That's a fine idea, Spud. Just keep your insurance policy up to date."

"You think so? Even though I can't legally drive it?"

"Sure," I told him, not much caring either way. His ongoing love-hate relationship with his car was the last thing I cared to ponder at the moment. "You can always sink it or blow it up later, if you decide you don't want it anymore."

"You're right," he said. "I'll keep it for a while and see how things go."

"Barb Henley's sister is Lolly Chesterfield," I told him.

"Holy friggin' cow!" Spud responded. "You think she's in on the missing kid? Her own stepson?"

"Odder things have happened."

"That's reminds me. Samuel Chesterfield wants you to call him at home, and it's urgent. Said you didn't answer your mobile."

I phoned Chesterfield and learned three things.

One, after a call from one of the agents, he'd rushed home to find a ransom note in place of his wife. It appeared to be the same paper and same typestyle as Jared's ransom note. Lolly was additional insurance to ensure the ransom money was delivered, it said. The Feebie who was stationed at the penthouse had gone down to the lobby to accept a food delivery. When he returned, a lamp was overturned, a torn magazine was on the floor, and Lolly was gone. None of her belongings were missing. I asked Chesterfield if his wife had been on birth control and he said, yes, pills. I asked him to check and see if her birth control pills were there. He returned to the phone shortly, telling me that they were not in their usual place in the top bathroom drawer. Which meant she probably hadn't been abducted, even though somebody wanted it to look like she had. Clothing and cosmetics could be easily purchased, but prescription drugs would be more of a hassle to replace.

Two, Melinda Hertz's lawyer called offering some information in exchange for dropped charges. The theft and drug dealing were all done by her husband Gary, she maintained, and he had been the actual property manager. Chesterfield agreed that if her information directly led to finding Jared alive, he'd drop the charges against her. If not, no deal. The other condition was that she had to provide the information immediately. Melinda Hertz claimed that the day she and Gary had skipped out of their apartment, she was in the Bellington Complex lobby getting a newspaper and overheard a young man calling Jared on the courtesy phone. The conversation led her to believe the visitor was an old friend and that he and Jared were getting together. And no, the courtesy phone wasn't viewed by a security camera. But *after* he hung the phone up, Melinda distinctly heard the kid mutter to himself, "You'll enjoy Piney Place, Jared. You'll blend right in with the trailer trash." The kid was white, tall, and lanky with longish hair and jeans. After the jail time cleared her head of a drug-induced haze and she'd had some time to contemplate things, Melinda remembered the incident and it dawned on her that it occurred right before Jared disappeared.

Three, Chesterfield was reaching a breaking point. Controlled and together though he was, I wasn't sure how much more he could take and I didn't want to give him any more bad news to contemplate—at least not until I had his son safely back home. I hadn't told him what I'd learned about Lolly.

I called Trish for an update and found that she'd finally had some luck with the tracker in Walton's mobile phone. He'd made a call from it just minutes earlier and she managed to catch a few snippets of conversation. From what she surmised, Walton was planning to get on a plane tomorrow and wherever he was going, he was going with someone. Even better, Trish got a reading on the GPS location of the phone. Walton was still in the Wilmington area, and my handheld GPS device could pinpoint his location—at least the location he'd been when he placed the call on his mobile phone—to within twenty feet. Bits of the puzzle were plummeting into place and a rush of charged energy filled my body and stimulated my mind. It was the same feeling I always experienced when getting close to solving a case and I thrived on it. In a flash-forward instant, I felt a sense of loss. Something I was going to miss in retirement.

After studying a map and comparing the GPS coordinates with the Piney Place neighborhood, I discovered the two overlapped. Definitely a clue.

Steaming hot jets of water pounded the back of my shoulders and, despite the fact that it was the day of reckoning, I stood beneath the shower much longer than necessary as I visualized the various scenarios that could happen and what my response to each would be. A calming type of mental preparation I'd learned working for the government, it had become habit.

I dressed in what Ox dubbed my combat duds: black hiking boots, stretch jeans that were popular with the teen crowd and had enough assorted pockets to carry a few tools including my backup piece, and a custom designed bullet-resistant vest that molded nicely around my size Ds. The vest was covered by a plain T-shirt, and a lightweight black jacket concealed both the vest and the Glock. I'd requested Ox's company and when we met downstairs at the bar, he grinned, even though he didn't know my outfit also concealed a pair of sexy striped Victoria's Secret briefs and lace-lined cami. Or, considering his mysterious powers of observation, maybe he did know.

"Planning on some action, Barnes?" He was dressed no differently than usual, although I knew he'd strapped on his carry weapon of choice, a Kimber .45 automatic. He had several weapons, if you counted the two knives that he was never without and the two hands that could kill as easily as they could comfort.

We ordered food more as a necessity for body fuel than a social pleasantry. While we ate boiled shrimp and hush puppies, I brought him up to date and told him that there had better be some action soon, or else Chesterfield had hired the wrong woman. Ox agreed that Piney Place was where we needed to be.

I touched his arm. "Put on your vest before we go, okay?"

"Worried about me?"

"I don't want anything to happen to you."

"Ditto, Jersey Barnes."

TWENTY-TWO

When we climbed into my car and went in search of Jared, the evening was growing dusky and would soon go dark. In the electronic dimension, SIPA transfers to Chesterfield Financial's system were drawing to a close.

"Thanks for coming along, Ox."

"You're welcome," he said simply.

Piney Place turned out to be a rental community of single and double-wide mobile homes. Just on the other side of the bridge—the one leading south on Highway 17—the area was heavily wooded, giving the illusion of privacy between the postage-stamp lots. Most yards were landscaped with layers of pine straw in lieu of grass. As we canvassed the neighborhood, there was little activity other than some teenagers gathered in one backyard passing a cigarette between them, and the occasional bluish, flickering glow of a television through a window. With the exception of a man taking his poodle for a walk from behind the wheel of a golf cart, the streets were empty.

We spied Walton's white Mustang convertible parked in the dirt drive of a nondescript double-wide with rotting white lattice boards covering the crawl space where vinyl skirting otherwise would be. A real estate sign, indicating the home had been for rent, rested against a tree. We parked in the street.

Communicating with our eyes and hands, we agreed that I'd take the front door. Ox vanished into the backyard. In the distance, a small dog yapped but other than pulsing, tinny music emanating from a cheap radio, there were no sounds coming from the trailer. Heading in with my weapon drawn, I found the front door unlocked, noiselessly entered, and crouched against a wall. A stale cloud assaulted my nose. It reeked of cigarette smoke and the odor of someone who hadn't bathed in a long time. The front door opened into the living room and Walton sat on the sofa, facing me. His half-nude body was leisurely stretched out, face aimed at the ceiling, eyes closed. A female knelt on the floor in front of him and her head of short blond curls methodically moved up and down between his legs. Nobody else was in sight.

Trying to ignore the distraction of two people having sex twelve feet away, I studied what I could see of the rental. Aside from empty beer cans and wadded-up remnants of fast-food meals, the place was tidy. To my left was a small dining area that led to a kitchen. To the right was a hallway with three doors. One was open and revealed a bathroom. The remaining two were closed and I assumed them to be bedrooms. I also had to assume who the bobbing head belonged to, even though I could only see the back of it. I may have found the mystery woman.

Seconds later, Walton's eyes flew open and revealed a mixture of bewilderment and pleasure as he registered my presence at the same time an orgasm overtook him. When the woman turned to see what Walton looked at with such wide eyes, I discovered that the head of white-blond curls did in fact belong to Lolly.

Keeping my back to the wall, I stood and aimed the gun at her but kept my peripheral vision on Walton, just in case he was a cold-blooded killer, too. "Stand up, Lolly."

Looking almost comic, Walton got up and scrambled to get back into the pants that were discarded on the floor. Resembling a veteran prostitute, Lolly slowly wiped her mouth with the back of a slender hand and stood to face me with a slow smile. She was fully clothed in a solid black pantsuit and sandals and made sure that she kept herself behind the kid. She knew I wouldn't shoot her if there was a risk of killing Walton in the process. For that matter, she knew a person with morals wouldn't shoot an unarmed woman.

"Why, hello, Jersey," she said. "You've found our little love nest. I do hope you won't tell Samuel. It'd just break his heart." The voice was no longer pouty and sweet. Instead, it was deep, the words perfectly enunciated. The eyes were darker than I remembered, more intelligent, more calculating. To give Ox time to do whatever it was that he was doing, I played her game. I was in no particular hurry.

"Lolly, Lolly, Lolly. To think you were worried about your husband cheating on you," I said sadly.

She brushed the hair from her face and casually reached for her purse that rested on an end table.

"Hold it!" I said. "That's a no-no."

Sighing, she retrieved a tube of lipstick from atop a rickety end table and taking her time in twisting up the stick of color, applied a layer of cherry red to her lips without the aid of a mirror. "I had to know if he was, Jersey, because I want a divorce and could have used that as cause." She fluttered her lashes demurely at a stunned,

254 / T. LYNN OCEAN

motionless Walton. "Nothing compares to the endurance of a twenty-one-year-old."

"Why'd you marry him to begin with?"

"Oh, it's something I've wanted to do for a long, long time," she said flippantly and when she moved to replace the lipstick on the table, she grabbed Walton into a bear hug against the front of her body, turning him into an even better shield.

"Don't worry, darling. She won't shoot you," she cooed into his ear as she reached into the handbag on the sofa behind her and removed a revolver that was pointed at me. The heeled sandals made her nearly a head taller than Walton and I felt certain that I could immobilize her with a shot to the shoulder before she got a round off at me. Or kill her with a shot to the head. Knowing Lolly, though, she'd have just enough psychotic energy to shoot either me or the kid on her way down. I went the safer route by waiting to see how things played out, but didn't drop my armed stance. It was a standoff.

"What are you doing with a pistol, Lolly?" Walton sputtered. "Are you crazy? You said nobody would get hurt!"

We both ignored him.

"I'm curious, *Lisa,*" I said, emphasizing her real name, "why did you really employ me to begin with? You knew Samuel wasn't having an affair."

"Oh, I see you've caught on to me. Well, that was just a distraction. When Bill told me he was dating a detective-type, I figured that the cheating-husband front would confuse things a bit. Make a more interesting story for the cops after I disappeared. You just happened to be convenient."

"Convenient *and* free," I mused. "Huh. So where are you headed from here?"

"To a beautiful tropical place. To live happily ever after with my gorgeous man." She let out a long laugh that finished like an ugly snort and I wondered who she was referring to as gorgeous. Surely not Walton.

"And kidnapping Jared?"

"Another distraction," she said, momentarily releasing her grip on Walton to place the strap of her handbag over a bare shoulder. The other hand, the one gripping the revolver, remained steady. Ignorantly, Walton remained in place in front of her. "Besides, I've been kidnapped now, too. I wonder if Samuel has told my mother?" Her head tilted slightly with the question.

"You're going to let your own parents think you've been kidnapped?"

Her eyes narrowed and squinted with instant anger. Her thumb slid across the top of the hammer, cocking it. I readied myself to fire and zeroed in on her facial expressions. I'd only have a fraction of a second to beat her to the pull of the trigger, when and if she chose to pull hers. Most likely, when.

"I said *mother*, you moron. Not mother and father. I don't have a father. Samuel Chesterfield took my daddy away and left us with nothing. Nothing!" Her voice rose to a screech. "He thinks he can just screw people over and destroy families? Go on his moneymaking merry way, living in luxury—while I'm living in a roach-infested apartment? Sharing a pullout sofa with my sister? Watching my mother drink a bottle of vodka a day after Daddy killed himself?"

For a split second, her body shook with rage and just as suddenly, she calmed. Enjoying the moment, she wasn't yet ready to fire the gun.

"What about Darlene? Was her overdose your handiwork, too?"

"That was just to irritate Samuel. He relied on her to keep his schedule straight." Lolly smiled, shrugged. "Besides, she never treated me with the respect I deserved."

I kept my sights on Lolly but threw a question at the senator's son. "You're in on all this, Walton? I figured you to be smarter than that."

"Despite his miserable attempt at a higher education," Lolly said, "Walt is really quite the genius. I discovered that when we met at one of his daddy's boring fund-raisers. The rack of lamb was delicious, but the conversation on the verandah with Walt was even better."

The gun, a Smith & Wesson .38 revolver, remained pointed at my chest from her stance behind Walton and it occurred to me that Lolly was the driver who'd shot at me while I was jogging. She was also the disguised person who tried to shoot me through the car window as I sat on the side of the road, taking notes from Soup. I was close enough to see the rounds snuggled in the gun's cylinder, but I wasn't close enough to disarm her before she had time to react by shooting me. I wanted to keep her talking and luckily, she wanted to talk. She was enjoying bragging.

I inched closer, figuring it would be better to disarm her than exchange fire. "Was that before or after you married Samuel Chesterfield?"

"Oh, long before," she answered, then nodded her head toward Walton. "Is your little bug still in place, darling?"

"Bug?" I asked, sounding perplexed. "What bug?"

"Nothing that concerns you, Jersey. It's one of those computer things you wouldn't understand," she said to me but looked at Walton, awaiting an answer.

"Y-y-yes. I checked it earlier. It was doing its thing, just like I told you it would," he reported, like a child seeking approval from his teacher.

Her face displayed something near ecstasy when she turned back to me. "Yes, that was long before I married the son of a bitch. I was actually introduced to Samuel at the same party where I met

Walt and discovered his daddy was on the finance committee. But I'd been learning all about Samuel for many, many years, even before Barb went to work at his office. Can you believe my idiot sister ruined her body to have the bastard's child? That wasn't part of the plan. She was only supposed to get inside Chesterfield Financial to learn what she could," Lolly said, shaking her head left to right once.

I remained silent, waiting for more, and took another miniscule step toward her. "So you met Samuel and Walton at a party?" I prompted, keeping the Glock up.

When she nodded, her gun dipped slightly. I was almost close enough to take it away from her. "Samuel was telling me all about the SIPAs and how his firm would soon be on the approved list. And later Walt mentioned how unstable the whole system was because it was happening in cyberspace. He said the government's security wasn't worth a damn and that Chesterfield Financial's probably wasn't much better. Then I found out that his Citadel roommate was Samuel's son, the gay little golden child that Barb gave birth to. Can you *believe* the coincidence? That's when it hit me! There had been a reason for all the things that happened, after all. It was fate. Fate! I decided right then and there that I would marry Samuel and live well until I could destroy him like he destroyed my daddy. I'd destroy his family and his business. The more I talked to Walton, the more the plan came together, like it was meant to be. All the years of watching and waiting for the right opportunity finally paid off," she said proudly. "It only took four months to get an engagement ring and two months after that, I was Mrs. Chesterfield. It's amazing what a good blowjob can accomplish."

Walton turned his head to look over his shoulder and Lolly realized her mistake. "It's different with you, darling," she crooned into his ear, and seeing Walton grin stupidly, I realized that he was as stoned as he was gullible. "Go get in the car, sweetheart," she said, and as Walton did so, she positioned herself to keep Walton between us, her revolver steadied on me. The Glock remained fixed on her as I moved to block their exit.

"Not another step or I'll shoot," Lolly threatened. As they side-stepped a wide arc around me to the door, I caught a whiff of marijuana smoke clinging to Walton's crumpled clothes.

"What does cyberspace and the SIPAs have to do with anything?" I said, playing dumb to keep her talking.

"Oh, you'll find out eventually. If you live that long."

"And Eddie Flowers?" I persisted.

Lolly paused, like an actress delivering a grand exit. "Samuel's accountant? I overheard Samuel talking on the phone and knew he was flying to town. He could have been dangerous, so I shot him. He was such a nice man, too. Jared never should have told him about giving Walton that memory stick."

"Memory stick?" I said.

Gesturing at me with the gun, she sighed. "I'm growing bored with your questions. I think I'll shoot you now."

Like a striking snake, Ox appeared from behind the sofa and punched Lolly's extended arm toward the ceiling. The gun fired, discharging a round into the air before Ox took it away from her. Bits of wood and plaster plunked down on them. With one large hand, he held both of her wrists behind her back. She struggled briefly, but stilled with a screeching yelp when he tightened his grip.

"Jared's in the bedroom," Ox told me. "Unconscious, but he's got a pulse. And track marks. They had him tied to the bed and they've been keeping him drugged. Apologies for keeping you waiting—they had the back door bolted and chained shut." Even entering noiselessly, he'd gotten inside within minutes. And I knew he'd cut Jared loose from the bed.

While Ox kept an eye on Lolly, I ran outside to collect Walton and found him in the Mustang. When he saw it was me instead of his lover, his eyes grew wild. He'd heard the shot and assumed wrongly. "You shot her! Did you kill her? I loved her!"

"I didn't shoot her, Walton," I said, yanking him out of his car and losing patience. "Stand up and shut up."

Neighbors peeked at us from behind curtained windows. Someone had probably dialed 911 to report a disturbance and possible gunshot. I hauled Walton back inside the trailer, where Ox restrained a venomous Lolly.

"She just kicked me in the shin, twice," he said. "She does it again, I'm going to get irritated."

A glass bottle sailed through the window. It was stuffed with a burning rag and shattered when it met the floor, throwing gasoline and instant flames throughout the living room. Trying not to breathe the caustic smoke, we cuffed Lolly and Walton together, and while I went for Jared, Ox guided the pair of lovebirds outside with one hand and held his Kimber .45 in the other.

I dashed to the rear of the mobile home, where Jared opened his eyes briefly but they were unseeing. The wrist was raw and bloody and the fingers were a bluish white. There were dark circles beneath his eyes, his hair was damp, and his body stank with stale sweat. But he was alive.

Fed by synthetic carpeting and curtains, darting flames crept into the bedroom and bellowed pungent smoke. I ripped a set of mini blinds away from the room's single window, unlocked and opened it, and kicked out the screen. Jared felt light when I lifted him from the bed and, carrying him in front of me, stuffed us both through the window feet first and jumped the four or five feet to the ground. We fell into the dirt when we hit and I immediately rolled beneath some scrappy bushes to survey the yard. Somebody had thrown the bottle so Lolly had at least one other cohort. Sensing nobody in the immediate vicinity, I slung Jared over my shoulder and tried not to grunt with the effort as I stood and cautiously made my way to the road, one arm holding his un-resisting body in place and the opposite hand holding the Glock.

I made my way along the side of the trailer and stopped short when I came into the small front yard. Ox stood next to Lolly and Walton, leaning against the Benz and a man stood eight or ten feet from them holding some major firepower that was aimed at Ox. Taking a second look at the weapon, I recognized it as an Uzi and taking a closer look at the man, I realized it was Bill. For a split second, my brain would not process what my eyes saw and in the next instant, betrayal slammed into my chest like a sledge-hammer. For a flash of a second, the night went darker than it al-ready was and I thought I might pass out. Partially hidden by shadows and Jared's limp hanging arms, I slid the Glock into the waistband of my pants at the small of my back.

"Get up here and unlock their cuffs," Bill demanded of me.

"I have to put the kid down first," I said. No longer the easy-going boyfriend I'd come to know, he nodded once with a precise movement and he held the Uzi one-armed like he knew what he was doing. Dismay churned in the pit of my stomach as I looked into the stranger's eyes.

Keeping one hand in the air and moving slowly, Ox opened the back door of my car. As I placed Jared's limp body in the rear seat, keeping my weapon out of Bill's line of sight, I glimpsed Ox's gun on the ground. My ex-boyfriend was smart enough not to risk bending down to pick up the weapon. He'd also managed to get the upper hand when Ox had come out of the trailer. Had Ox not been holding two struggling people, it would have been a differ-ent situation.

I shut the car door and faced Bill, reminding myself to stay in the moment. There would be plenty of time to absorb the situation later, but right now, my goal was survival and I couldn't be distracted. I drew a calming breath to steady my nerves and shoved all emotion aside but my heart continued to pound ferociously, like the bass drum in a rock band. After a second controlled inhale and exhale of air, the beat slowed to a rapid thud.

"I'm absolutely blown away, Bill. You were in on this scheme all along?"

"No, not when we first started dating. I really did like you, for what it's worth. But Lolly approached me with an offer that was too good to turn down." He dipped the gun, pointing. "Let me see your hands."

I spread my fingers and showed him my palms. "So the whole marriage thing was a scam, too?" I asked, thinking that I'd stressed over his proposals for no good reason.

"In actuality, I would have loved to marry you. But Lolly offered me a much more attractive net worth. A guy can't earn a decent living from modeling gigs." His eyes narrowed. "Take your gun out—two fingers only," he said. "Don't test me. I'm quick."

I lifted my arm so he could see the empty shoulder holster. "Don't have one."

His mouth spread into a tight grin. "Sure you don't. I'll give you one more chance before I open fire on your half-breed bartender."

"Actually, Bill, he is a full-blooded Lumbee Indian," I said, showing my back as I removed my gun with two fingers as instructed and dropped it into the grass. "If you're going for insults, at least get your facts straight."

"You always did have a smart-ass attitude," he said, shifting the Uzi from one arm to the other in a lighting-quick move that placed Lolly and Walton between himself and me. It was the type of action that was typically acquired through military training.

"Where did you learn—"

"How to handle a weapon? From the arms consultant they brought in to train the actors for *Vengeful Vandals*." Months earlier, Bill had proudly shown me the independent film in which he scored a minor role. It hadn't been very good.

I thought about going for the Sig, which was beneath the flap of a pocket in my cargo pants. My draw time would be slow, making the move risky, not to mention that Bill was using Walton as a human shield. Ox was quick enough to drop Bill with a thrown knife, if he could get a clear line of sight.

Something crashed inside the trailer and spirals of fire began to dart through a hole in the roof. Sirens sounded in the distance.

"Wh-wh-who *are* you?" Walton asked Bill. "Who is he, Lolly?"

"He's our chauffeur, darling," Lolly answered through a sinister smile.

"He's going with us?" a naïve Walton asked Lolly. Everyone ignored him.

"I said, uncuff them, Jersey. Do it now!" Bill demanded.

I patted my pockets and threw a sincere look his way. "I can't, I don't have the key. I think I dropped it when I was getting Jared out of the bedroom . . . the fire and all . . ."

Hissing flames completely engulfed the trailer and the resonance of multiple sirens drew closer. Clumps of neighbors gathered to watch the show and their silhouettes were highlighted by the fire's glow. I spotted Bill's silver pickup truck parked behind Walton's Mustang.

Bill snorted with disgust as he made a decision. "Get in the truck, Lolly. I've got bolt cutters; we'll get you apart once we get out of here. Hurry up, doll." He kept his weapon aimed loosely at a spot between me and Ox.

Cuffed together, Lolly and Walton ran awkwardly toward the

truck. Lolly almost fell when Walton stopped suddenly to turn. "My luggage!" he yelled.

"Forget your luggage!" Bill said.

"I need my laptop!"

"I've already got your laptop," Bill yelled. "Shut up and get in the truck!"

Before tossing the firebomb, Bill had taken time to get Walton's computer out of the Mustang, but not Walton's luggage? And he'd referred to Lolly as "doll"? He was obviously Lolly's lover and the pair of them had no intention of taking Walton anywhere. The virus had activated, they had his computer, and Lolly would have made sure she knew how to access the account on the receiving end of the stolen Social Security transfers.

Bill's pickup truck started rolling as soon as the three of them were inside it. Ox and I threw ourselves at the ground when a barrel appeared through the truck's rear window. An explosive burst of bullets pinged off the front of the armored Benz. Bits of gravel stung my face as a few rounds spattered off the pavement by my head. With a squeal of tires, the shooting ceased and the truck roared into the darkness.

"You hit?" Ox called.

"No, you?"

"No."

We pulled ourselves off the ground and checked for injuries. "He's not worth the risk of losing focus," Ox said, knowing the recesses of my mind were harboring what could be an incapacitating dose of realized deceit. "Don't think about it right now."

"Trust me, I'm not."

"Good."

Bill hadn't bothered to take our weapons and Ox recovered them while I checked out my car. Miraculously, the tires hadn't

264 / T. LYNN OCEAN

been hit. I made a mental note to buy a set of run flat tires, even if they were ridiculously expensive. I didn't want to take such a chance again. On the other hand, a retiree shouldn't need to worry about her tires being shot out. Especially by an ex-boyfriend.

A piece of the Mercedes' star hood ornament, dangling gracelessly over the front grille, caught my eye. The rest of it had been blasted off. "Oh, *man*! This really bites."

"What?" Ox said.

"He shot off my hood ornament."

"Add it to Chesterfield's tab."

A fire truck and an ambulance slid to a stop. The cops would arrive shortly after and I didn't want to get held up with questions. Reading my mind, Ox retrieved Jared's nearly lifeless body from the backseat, slung him over a shoulder, and we ran to the ambulance. Paramedics had a stretcher out in preparation, and Ox deposited the kid on it before running back to the Benz and slipping behind the wheel.

"The kid needs a hospital, quick," I told the paramedics. "He's had a drug overdose."

"Which drug? Who is he?"

I told them I didn't know the answer to either question. Ox pulled up in my car with the passenger door already open.

"Anybody in the house?" a firefighter called.

"No, it's all clear!" I yelled and jumped in. We peeled out, leaving a burning trailer, a growing assortment of flashing lights, and much general confusion behind.

Ox passed over my Glock.

"Thanks," I said.

"My pleasure."

Bill's first mistake was in not realizing that Lolly was a psychopath who could kill him just as easily as she'd murdered Flowers and Chesterfield's secretary, not to mention her own sister. His second mistake was in not realizing my car was armored. He thought he had disabled it when he peppered the front end with bullets as the pickup truck sped away.

I removed the CAR-16 from its compartment in the backseat and readied it, just in case. "We are retired, right?"

Even though we moved at nearly one hundred miles an hour, my Benz hugged the road and Ox handled it like a pro. "That's a matter of perspective."

"True," I agreed.

One of the best parts about doing what I do is delivering the good news. I called Chesterfield with a condensed version of events that didn't include Lolly or Bill. When he realized his son was alive and safe, Samuel Chesterfield was speechless with gratitude.

Two cop cars flew by us in the opposite direction as we headed away from Piney Place in search of the silver pickup truck. We figured Lolly and Bill wanted to get out of town as quickly as possible and decided the airport was a logical place to look. Although they'd gotten a good head start, we caught up with the pickup truck in less than five minutes. We weren't sure if they were on their way to the airport or if we'd just gotten lucky but either way, we wouldn't lose them a second time.

Ox positioned the Benz inches from their bumper. Bill did a double take in his rearview mirror. He changed lanes erratically a couple of times, just to be sure it was us. We ensured him that it was. A middle window in the rear of the truck slid open and the Uzi appeared. Lolly, still attached to Walton and twisted awkwardly, was behind the trigger. A spray of metal showered us and deposited a row of quarter-size spiderwebs in the bulletproof windshield.

"How much more use do you think they have for the kid?" I asked, rolling down my window enough to get my arm and the Glock through it.

"Not much. Walton is spare baggage to them at this point."

"That's what I was thinking. They'll kill him as soon as it's safe enough to stop and uncuff Lolly from him."

Another explosion of bullets came our way and Ox reflexively angled the sedan to keep my open window away from them. I rested the Glock's barrel between the door and the side mirror, aimed, and shot once. The right rear tire blew and the truck fishtailed as Bill struggled to keep it under control.

"Nice shot, Barnes."

In soldier mode, Ox always called me by my last name. I liked it. "Thanks," I said.

The crippled truck careened into a twenty-four-hour convenience store parking lot and, after clipping a gas pump and ripping it from its base, bounced to a stop at an adjacent pump. We stopped twenty feet behind it. The brightly lit parking lot was deserted. Lolly fired at us a third time while Bill fished around behind the seat, most likely in search of his bolt cutters. We didn't have a clean shot to return fire without the risk of hitting Walton, and could only watch events unfold. Bullets continued to bounce off my car and I knew the damage would be extensive.

An instant of stillness was immediately followed by another spray of bullets as Lolly covered Bill while he jumped from the truck, pulled a fuel nozzle from the overturned pump, locked the handle in an open position, and threw it on the ground.

"Oh, hell," I heard myself saying.

"This thing fireproof, too?" Ox said.

"I don't know."

"I'm guessing you want to save the kid?" he asked.

"The senator would appreciate it."

As a glassy pool of gasoline spread into the parking lot, Bill sprinted to the passenger's side of the truck, going the long way around to use the vehicle as cover. He threw three lightning-quick punches into Walton's face before cutting the cuffs in half, freeing

Lolly. She passed the Uzi to him and, clutching her purse and Walton's computer, positioned herself so that the truck was between us. We still didn't have a clean shot to take either of them out, and thoughts of chasing on foot were quelled by the rapidly growing puddle of gasoline and the danger it presented to Walton.

The last thing we saw before Bill lit an emergency road flare and threw it into the growing puddle of fuel was the two of them running away, him possessively gripping her upper arm. A barrier of hungry flames instantaneously appeared and licked at the gas pumps and the abandoned pickup truck. We didn't have much time.

Ox threw the vehicle into low gear and, driving straight into the wall of fire, slammed into the rear of the pickup and kept his foot on the gas pedal until we had pushed it forty or fifty feet beyond the flames. I jumped out before we'd come to a good stop, retrieved a bloody and half-conscious Walton, and dragged him into the backseat while the Benz was still rolling. The explosion came in the same instant we sped away, the force of it lifting our rear wheels off the ground.

"You're going to have to start doing background checks on your boyfriends," was all Ox said as the car regained stability and we accelerated into the night.

TWENTY-THREE

Although it was well after midnight and the Block was officially closed, the booze flowed freely. The self-serve decree was in effect and Cracker must have sensed my good mood because, breaking a rule, he helped himself to some dry-roasted peanuts from a wooden bowl that sat on a table. Lying on his belly and using his front paws, he delicately shelled the peanuts with his front teeth before gobbling the encapsulated morsels.

The Block's cook had put out baskets of chicken fingers and french fries and everyone was snacking. An assortment of law-enforcement folks, mostly off-duty, roamed and chatted, congratulated each other, and gossiped. Preferring to keep a low profile, Ox and I deflected all attention away from ourselves.

Bobby and Spud were in a heated discussion about the best way to attract a sugar momma babe and Soup rummaged behind the counter, apparently in search of something to eat other than chicken. Trish, with Steroid in tow, was making the rounds to see everyone. She smiled cheerfully when I asked how the moonroof on her car was working out, and if she'd talked her new boyfriend out of a phone tracker yet.

A day had passed since we'd recovered Jared. Lolly and Bill had not been found, but carjackers fitting their description stole a Cadillac half a mile from the gas station. The car was found an hour later at a small landing strip just outside of Wilmington. For all I knew, Bill was a private pilot and the two of them were long gone. I tried not to beat myself up over how trusting I'd been where Bill was concerned and vowed that it would never happen again. Jersey Barnes would not be fooled twice.

After melding all the puzzle pieces into one large picture of Lolly's life, Ox and I learned that her father was a known gambler who bet not only on sports and cards, but also on stocks. He traded on margin, using Chesterfield Financial's brokerage services, and went so far into debt that he was being hounded by legitimate collection agencies and not-so-legitimate loan sharks. The story that Lolly's mother told everyone, including her daughters, was that their father lost the family savings and home by taking bad investment advice from Samuel Chesterfield. The seemingly innocuous lie was a fertile seed, which took root in their young and moral-less minds and grew into a layered path of cancerous revenge and greed. Based on his cell phone records, Bill had only entered Lolly's picture two months earlier, when Chesterfield first made plans to move his family to Wilmington. I surmised that the pair dated during college and just recently sparked up an old relationship. Whatever their situation was, I didn't care.

Walton survived the beating to his face with only a broken nose and had been taken into police custody. He told interrogators that he and Lolly were going to collect the ransom money and run away together, and that he knew nothing about Bill. Lolly had gotten them fake driver's licenses and passports and had bought tickets to Aruba, where they were supposed to start a new life together, because they were in love.

Before he was questioned, I told Walton that we knew about Social Insecurity all along and that the virus had been thwarted. Wisely, he didn't mention anything to the police about his hacking skills. I don't think investigators believed that a woman who was married to Chesterfield would run away with a stoned Citadel dropout, but mysteries were what kept them in business. Aside from Ox, Spud, Soup, and Trish, only Chesterfield knew the real story that began with a single gunshot to the head of a distraught gambler. And of course Walton, who'd confirmed my guess that he opened an overseas bank account to receive the stolen money. Chesterfield's face had gone pale when I explained Social Insecurity, and it went white when he learned how close his brokerage firm had come to hosting the theft of tens of millions of dollars.

Jared had a near brush with death and lost vital signs for nearly two minutes in the ambulance before paramedics restored his heartbeat. Doctors had stabilized him and given him something to counteract all of the dope in his system. He was going to be fine.

"Damn, I'd like to have seen the look on her face when she realized there was no money in the overseas account," Chesterfield said quietly to Ox and me. The three of us were seated at a table and Chesterfield sipped a shot of Dewars on ice.

"Is there anything we can do for you?" I asked him.

"No. I think I'm still in shock. I thought I was a pretty good judge of character, but Lolly sure had me snowed. They both did. Barb, way back then when she worked for the company. And, Lolly right up until two days ago."

"It could happen to anybody," I said, speaking from firsthand experience.

Chesterfield poured some more Dewars from a bottle that sat on our table. "Jared kept apologizing to me in the hospital," he told us, needing to talk to someone. "Apologizing about giving Walton the SIPA information, even though he got the flash drive back. Apologizing about giving Barb money all these years. He told me he's gay, and apologized for that. He told me everything and apologized some more."

"He's a good kid," Ox said.

"Yes," Chesterfield agreed. "He's going to do very well in the business. Now that he no longer has anything to hide, there's no telling how far he'll go."

He started laughing suddenly and I wondered if he was about to lose it from all the stress. But the laugh faded to calm as he shook his head in wonder. He gave my hand a squeeze. "I've got to get back to the hospital. Earlier tonight, they told me Jared will sleep for a long time, but I want to be there when he wakes up."

"Be good for Jared to see you first, when he comes to with a clear mind," Ox said.

Chesterfield stood. "Jersey, Ox, thank you. Thank you from the bottom of my heart for saving my boy. They were going to set the place on fire, whether you'd showed up or not. They wanted him dead. Him and Sigmund's son, too."

"Do you want Lolly found?" I asked, standing to see him out.

Chesterfield thought for a few seconds before replying. "Yes. But for her, being on the run with no money might be a worse punishment than jail ever could be."

He was right. Living on the run in fear of being caught—without the advantage of wealth—would be a life sentence in itself.

"Before you go," I said to Chesterfield, "may I borrow your cell phone for a moment?"

Without bothering to hide my actions, I opened the battery compartment and removed the tracker that Trish had installed. Chesterfield looked from me to Trish, who sat at the bar engaged in conversation with a Wilmington detective.

"I thought she looked familiar," he said through a smile. "She's the one that bumped into me outside my office and asked to use my phone? She works for you?"

"Yes, at times," I admitted as a new thought occurred to me. "You know what I was just thinking? If Jared hadn't felt bad about being blackmailed into giving that USB flash drive to Walton and decided to get it back, I'd never have found it in the gym bag and Soup never would have uncovered Social Insecurity. The flash drive Jared stole from Walton was an altered version of the original database. That's what put everything in motion. If it hadn't been for Jared's conscience, we never would have stopped Social Insecurity."

We all thought about that for a moment and drank some more.

"He put it in a gym bag? Where was the gym bag?" Chesterfield thought to ask, still standing.

I realized my mistake, but figured Chesterfield wouldn't much care. "In your hall closet."

"I paid you to break into my own home?" he asked without expecting an answer. "Those bugs the agents found in my condo? Yours?"

"Yes, and yes." Ox and I stood to see him out.

"Do you have anything else planted anywhere on me? In the heel of my shoe maybe? On one of my cars perhaps?"

I assured him that I didn't. He shook my hand before leaning in to bear hug me. He did the same with Ox.

"Tell Soup that I'll look forward to seeing him in the office next week, would you? I'd tell him myself, but I think he's back there cooking and I've got to run," he said and disappeared to the parking lot.

"Tell Soup what?" I said, although my hearing was fine.

"Chesterfield paid Soup an excessive amount of money to retain his services for the next year. Soup's going to overhaul the entire Chesterfield Financial e-commerce security system," Ox informed me.

"No kidding?"

"No kidding. But he said that doesn't mean you're off the hook for the tab you owe him. I think he wants your boat."

"Yeah, I promised it to him for a week."

"No, forever," Ox said, as we sat back down. "He wants you to *give* him your boat."

Looking around, I didn't see Soup. He was probably whipping up a tasty beef bouillon. He had every right to be cocky. The SIPA transfers had gone smoothly. Chesterfield Financial's reputation was intact. From a financial standpoint, nobody was hurt and from a public-scare standpoint, nobody was the wiser. Yes, he had a right to be cocky. But not *that* cocky.

"Speaking of the boat, I was going to have my retirement celebration tonight, with Bill."

"I know."

"I'd much rather celebrate with—"

Ox's fingertips brushed across my mouth, halting the flow of words. "I know," he said, the two syllables emerging like rich, decadent, pure understanding. Stunned, I looked at Ox and my body flushed and relaxed simultaneously. He returned my gaze with hungry eyes when an agitated voice snagged our attention, breaking the spell.

"But Dirk told me your car was for sale," a cop was saying to Spud. "My wife's getting into real estate and I thought I'd buy it for her. It would be perfect for driving prospects around to look at houses!"

"Nah," Spud told him. "The car is not for sale. I'm gonna hang on to her."

"You sure? I can pay cash."

"Of course I'm sure! She's a great car. I'd be crazy to get rid of her, for crying out loud." Spud's voice carried, his walking cane rising into the air for emphasis.

Without warning, Ox pulled me off my chair. "Everybody get down! Get down now!" he shouted, reaching for the holstered Kimber.

The noise level dropped as all the cops in the bar reached for their service weapons and scanned the bar for the threat that put Ox on alert. Trusting his instincts, I drew my Glock and remained in a prone position.

A split second later, Spud's Chrysler LHS ripped through one of the industrial garage doors, propelled by a garbage truck's front-end forklift. It was the type of collection truck that serviced Dumpsters at restaurants and construction sites, and emptied them by turning the Dumpsters upside down over the bed of the truck. The long forked rods had impaled the Chrysler's two side windows and the momentum of the two vehicles sounded like a train wreck as they impacted the Block. Twisted sheet metal from the garage door squealed and wood tables and chairs splintered as the trash compactor kept coming. People scrambled to get out of the way. When Spud's car and the giant truck plowed to a halt in the heart of the bar, an enraged Lolly jumped from the cab's driver's seat and threw a laptop computer at me. It sailed over my head and shattered a row of liquor bottles.

"What did you do with my money?"

Apparently she'd checked her overseas account balance, only to find it sitting on zero. No fewer than twenty guns were sighted on her, so I didn't see a need to point my own. Bill was nowhere in sight, though he could have been hiding in the truck. More likely was the probability that Lolly had killed him, realizing that he was no longer of use to her.

Unfolding from a crouched position, I holstered the Glock, wishing I hadn't already taken off my vest. "I don't know what you mean, Lolly," I said. "What money?"

"Don't play coy with me, bitch. Where's the money?"

"Well." I paused to stare at the ceiling, wrinkling my nose at the stench of rotting trash that emanated from the truck. "There's about two hundred dollars in the cash register. You're welcome to take that, since you're in a pinch. Pay it back whenever you can."

Red face contorted with rage, Lolly reached into the cab and produced the Uzi. Every cop in the place opened fire on her as she ducked to take cover behind the front end of Spud's Chrysler, which was suspended a foot off the ground. I hit the cement with a tuck and roll as she blindly opened fire in my direction and kept the trigger engaged. Glass shattered and things popped as she fired the submachine gun in a sweeping arc from a squatting position behind the Chrysler. Bursts of rapidly placed single shots fired back at her and the majority of them pinged off Spud's car. Lolly took a hit in the lower leg and another one or two in her arms but continued firing the Uzi until her magazine ran out. Still crouching, she threw the worthless weapon over the hood of the car, in the same general direction she'd thrown the laptop. The shooting stopped and, ears ringing, I inhaled the smell of spent gunpowder and stood.

"It's over, Lolly. You can't win this game." I didn't see Ox and couldn't tell if anybody had been hit besides Lolly, but we needed ambulances. With the noise we'd just made, the cavalry was surely already on the way.

"I'll kill your boyfriend if you don't tell me what you did with my money." Her voice sounded strong, despite the blood pooling around her.

I studied a broken fingernail. "Really? I thought he was your boyfriend."

"Two-bit detective bitch," she spat, emerging from the cover of the Chrysler, holding a revolver. In the same instant, Bill ran through the ripped-open garage door, directly behind Lolly, and everyone momentarily held their fire as she spun to face him. Nobody wanted to be the one who accidentally shot my ex.

"Lolly, put the gun down!" Bill screamed at her. "No more killing!"

I caught a glimpse of Ox moving in behind Bill. Lolly got off a single shot that ripped through Bill's midsection in the same instant Ox threw a knife that landed squarely in her chest. Ox dove for cover as Lolly fired twice more during the seconds it took her to quietly crumple, her body getting peppered with incoming bullets on the way down.

In the echoing aftermath, Ox and I gravitated to each other. His hands found mine and we automatically checked each other's body for signs of damage before making the rounds to check on our guests. Spud had been grazed in the upper thigh, a federal agent had taken a single round in the forearm, and Soup had a deep gash in his back from flying glass, but miraculously, nobody was seriously injured.

With limited first-aid supplies, a group of us tended to Spud and Soup and the wounded agent. Soon, paramedics filtered in as everyone shook themselves off and regrouped to survey the damage to the Block. It was extensive, but nothing that couldn't be fixed. Strangely, I wasn't even panicked by the two dead bodies. Lolly would not be destroying any more lives. And Bill had simply made a bad choice by getting caught in the crossfire of her flawed

278 / T. LYNN OCEAN

scheme. Neither one of them scared me, even though I had a phobia about being around dead people.

"It's over," Ox said behind me, spinning me into a tight hug.

"Yes," I agreed.

As they wheeled him out on a stretcher, Spud was livid. "Would you look at my car? It's demolished! Completely demolished! You'd think the deranged woman would have at least picked a garage door that didn't have a car parked in front of it, for crying out loud!"

Arms crossed over his chest, Dirk leaned back on his heels to study the broken car. "Tires still look nice from that shiny stuff, though."

Cracker ambled up to the heap, sniffed a rear wheel, cocked a leg, and let a stream of pee flow.

Ox's rich laughter danced in my ears as we went outside to breathe fresh air and look at the stars. There were plenty of them, glittering from their orbits millions of miles above the Wilmington night.

"Guess I really am done working now," I mused. "Better learn how to play shuffleboard."

He looked from the sky to my face and grinned. "Plenty more adventures to come in your life."

"Even in retirement?"

"Especially in retirement," he said, and moved in to kiss me.